D0925700

MIRROR
of the MOON

PHILIP THATCHER

Volume II
The Raven Trilogy

For Ryan —
May these words
be good ones for
your journey —
Philip Thatcher
August, 2003

CORONA
PRESS

Copyright © 2003 Philip Thatcher

For performance rights to the plays in this volume,
please contact the author at
Corona Press
1605 Kilmer Road
North Vancouver, B.C.
V7K 1R6
Canada

National Library of Canada Cataloguing in Publication Data

Thatcher, Philip, 1939-
　Mirror of the moon / Philip Thatcher.
(The raven trilogy; 2)

ISBN 0-9686687-1-2

　I. Title. II. Series: Thatcher, Philip, 1939- Raven trilogy; 2.
PS8589.H356M47 2003　　c813'.54　　C2002-906045-
PR9199.4.T43M47 2003

Cover painting: "Mirror of the Moon" (2003), by Aiona Anderson

Corona Press logo by Daniel Koppersmith
Author photograph by Frank Doll
Layout and Design by The Vancouver Desktop Publishing Centre
Printed in Canada by Ray Hignell Services

In memory of Stephen Edelglas
and for Seis^^lom

On this side of the light
I listen as hard as I can.

—*David Zieroth*

And when you have lost
The face you know so well,
When it has become
Just another part
Of this lake of mirrors . . .
Look still further.

—*Kirsten Savitri Bergh*

I

The moon clothes Lance with cool light. Jet black, his hair streams down to the small of his back; the beadwork of the sun eagle hanging from his neck captures the moonlight. That and the moccasins on his feet are the only articles of clothing he wears. Strange, that a tall man should have small, beautiful feet. But Lance is a beautiful man.

I had never thought of a man as beautiful until I met Lance . . .

Toward the end of August, I step into a Native gift shop tucked away in Vancouver's Gastown, and the young Native woman behind the counter greets me.

"May I help you?"

"Not really. I just wanted to look around." Then I notice her staring at me.

"You're Solomon's brother-in-law, right?"

"Yes, I am. Cameron McLean. And you are—?"

"Juliet White. Solomon and I were in high school together."

"Of course. I should have recognized you."

She smiles. "That's okay. It's been six long years since we graduated. How is Solomon doing?"

"I don't know. He left us suddenly three years ago, during the last days of the Oka crisis. He was pretty upset about it all."

She nods. "We met up the day the police raided the Pines. It was as if he suddenly woke up to being Indian. But then it was something like that for all of us." Pausing, she takes me in. "And you haven't heard from him since then?"

"No. Have any of your classmates heard anything?"

"Nothing. We've all been wondering where he's gone."

"And how are the rest of you?"

"Good enough, most of us. Except for Anwar. He was killed in Iraq during the Gulf War, when the Americans bombed Baghdad."

Her face shows little emotion, but I can see the pain in her eyes.

"I'm so sorry. He seemed to be a likeable person."

"Yes, he was. We all loved him."

"And what about Anika? The girl Solomon seemed to be close to?"

She straightens a wooden carving hanging on the wall beside her. "We haven't seen much of her for a few years. She dropped out of sight about the time Solomon left."

I glance about the shop, looking for a reason to stay. "Are you looking for anything in particular?" she asks, as if sensing a need in me I can't yet speak.

"No, I don't think so." Then, my hand about to open the door on my way out, I know what it is I want. "Do you know anything about sweat lodges?"

"Well, we don't do them here in the shop," she says with a laugh. "But, yes, I do know something about the sweat lodge."

"Have you been inside one?"

"Yes."

"What is it like, doing a sweat?"

She takes her time answering, as if she wants to peel the question down to its essentials. "A sweat can mean many things, depending on what you bring to it and what you want to find."

"Do you know where I could do a sweat?"

She studies me, a question in her eyes. "Yes, I know someone who could help you do that."

H e had driven north from Vancouver on the Sea to Sky Highway. Just beyond Squamish he turned northeast on a gravel road and found the bridge over a creek where he was to pull off the road.

As he was locking his car, he saw a man leaning against the bridge. "Are you Cameron?"

"Yes."

The man stepped away from the bridge. The sun blazed forth from the sun eagle that lay against his turquoise shirt, and his moccasined feet barely touched the earth. Cameron caught his breath as he put out his hand. The man looked at the outstretched hand, smiled, then closed his fingers across the back of it. Their palms pressed together, he lifted their joined hands toward the sun. "I'm Lance Thunderchild. Follow me."

Lance led the way up the bank beside the creek, then along the creek bed, following a faint animal trail. The sun at their backs had slipped past noon, and the light fell in patches through branches of fir and cedar. Already the air was drier than it had been at the coast, though there was still moss on the north side of the trees. His lungs drinking in the scent of fir, Cameron kept stealing glances at the man in front of him.

At the crest of a hill the trail leveled out, leading into a large clearing beside the creek. Beyond the clearing the land rose sharply once again as the creek became a falls that dropped into a shallow pool at its bottom.

An older man crossed the clearing and took Cameron by the arm, as if Cameron were a child about to step onto an uncertain log across a river. "I'm Alfred. We've been waiting for you. Change into your shorts and don't walk across the space between the lodge and the fire."

Cameron changed under the trees at the back of the lodge. Then he walked around to the north side of the lodge, facing the creek, as Alfred had told him to do. The door to the lodge faced the east. Just beyond it, the fire licked at wood stacked upon a large pile of river stones. There was a mound of earth between the lodge and the fire, with two eagle feathers sticking up from it, surrounded by pouches of tobacco, and a long-stemmed pipe resting against it.

Cameron took the package of tobacco Juliet had told him to bring and handed it to Alfred. Alfred cradled it in both hands, as if holding something waiting to be born. "What do you seek here, my brother?"

What do I seek? Funny, how he says it, like an old priest to whom I once confessed.

"I'm looking for a doorway."

"A doorway to where?"

Where?

"To where I can live. And where my face won't get in my way."

Alfred closed his hands about the tobacco. He gazed at the creek, at the sun's light hard upon the falls. "Maybe the sweat lodge will be the doorway you seek. We'll see."

Alfred placed sage and cedar leaves upon a flat stone, brought a coal from the fire to it, and began the smudge. Cameron, along with five other men, including Lance, stood in turn before Alfred. Each cleansed himself with the smoke—the hands, eyes, ears, mouth, across the forehead and down the back of the head, the shoulders, arms, heart, stomach, loins, and down the legs to the feet. Cameron turned around. Eagle feather in hand, Alfred brushed the smoke against and along his back. Closing his eyes, Cameron tried to release himself from thoughts that wanted to hold onto him.

Each of them entered the lodge on his hands and knees from the left of the doorway around to the right, until they were all seated on the cedar boughs that covered the lodge floor. One by one, Lance brought in on a shovel the stones from the fire—the grandfathers—at first, one for each of the four directions, then others. Sitting just inside the doorway, Lance pulled down the tarp and blankets that covered the lodge. The light vanished and the lodge was swathed in darkness, except for the sparks that flashed up from the red glow of the stones as Alfred dropped sage and cedar down upon them.

Out of the silence that descended upon them, Alfred began to speak. Cameron listened as the speaking became more than words, became the stones that burned in the pit before him and the darkness that closed in about him as if wanting to take him back to the moment of his birth . . .

In the beginning . . . What? Warmth wrapped in darkness? And then the first touch of daylight . . . if daylight had to be . . .

Alfred continued to speak. This, the first of four rounds, was for the brothers and sisters lost on the streets, in the jails, in the grip of addiction . . . the addicted and the lost and the wounded. *For those who cannot lie or stand or sit.* These last words rose up from within Cameron, though he could not say how they had come to be there. Solomon? Maybe he had heard them from Solomon . . .

Alfred dipped a fir bough into the bucket of water beside him and began to splash water upon the grandfathers, once, twice, a third time, then a fourth, for each of the four directions. Alfred went on splashing until the heat that was now fire and water bore down upon Cameron. Sweat poured from his flesh.

Gently, yet with great power, a drum began to sound. As the stick in Alfred's hand touched upon the heart of the drum, the drum became the beating of the heart. Is this where it all began, and begins? Where I can begin again, in the sounding of the heart and the pulsing of the blood that beats the heart?

Now Alfred's voice lifted itself into the heat and darkness, chanting the first words of creation, fire becoming light, then water, then flesh, yet ever longing to return to fire.

O, that this too too solid flesh would melt—

Now the sweat dripped from Cameron's skin and his skin went to water, until it seemed that flesh and water and fire could become one.

Thaw, and resolve itself into a dew!

The drum stopped and Alfred's voice fell silent. One by one, other voices began to speak. Each in turn spoke into the darkness of his struggles and pain and hope. Then out of the heat and the scent of sage and cedar lingering in the heat, a hand placed an eagle feather into Cameron's hand. It was his turn to speak, but Cameron's words were few and muted. He passed the feather on to the hand at his left.

Lance lifted the tarp across the doorway onto the sweat lodge roof. As daylight flooded into the lodge and the first round ended, a feeling of loss overwhelmed Cameron. Crawling out with the others, he circled to the right around the back of the lodge, around the fire, then again around the lodge, before taking a pinch of tobacco from the mound and offering it to the fire.

He hesitated for a moment at the bank of the creek, then plunged in. The numbing water took the sweat from him, along with something like sludge from within himself that had come out with the sweat, and carried both away. Yet as he rose up from the water, Cameron realized that the shock of the water had also restored his flesh to its solid state.

Lance handed Cameron's towel to him, the sunlight golden upon the darkness of his skin.

"How are you doing?"

Once again Cameron caught his breath and nodded in reply. Lance smiled, then led Cameron back to the sweat lodge for the start of the second round.

Toward the close of the third round, Cameron started to cry as the feather came to him. Let the tears come if they want to do that, Alfred had counseled him when the second round ended. Yet Cameron could not let the tears flow freely from him. There were also words he wanted to speak, about skin and the binding of skin, but he could not say them. He held the feather for a moment, then passed it on.

It was between the third and final rounds that he saw Lance standing in the falls. Even as the water flowed down and away from Lance's body, the texture of his skin drank the sun in.

Lance came forth from the water and sat beside Cameron, his back against an aging fir. It was a moment or two before Lance spoke. "You're choked up with junk, and you don't want to cry it out. Tears are good, Cameron. They're the sweat of the heart. That's the way my AA sponsor, Wesley, said it the first time I cried at a sweat."

"When was that?"

"After my first month of sobriety. In the foothills of the Rockies, not far from where Wesley lives. And not far from where my people live. Where do your people live, Cameron?"

My people? Who are my people?

"I was born in Nova Scotia, but moved when I was young. I've lived in many places."

"Many places and no people." Lance smiled gently, as he cupped his hand about a fly that had landed on his thigh. "You were looking at me, when I was standing under the falls."

"Yes, I was," Cameron admitted.

"And what did you see?"

"A beautiful man." Shaken by the candor he had not intended, Cameron waited for Lance to reply.

"You're a beautiful man, too, Cameron, in spite of the shit you wallow in. Have you ever tried to wash that shit away before now?"

Moved by the question, Cameron let himself go back, then back some more. "Yes, once. I was a boy. My parents and I were at a beach along the east coast of New Brunswick. I went into the Atlantic, probably because my father didn't think I would."

"And?"

"The water was clear and clean and alive. My skin was alive when I came out onto the beach." Cameron watched the sun's light dance at the lip of the falls.

"And you were glad to have your skin back, all cleaned up?"

"Yes. At the time."

"And now?"

Cameron let himself gaze directly at Lance. Unlike most of the other men there, Lance did not avert his eyes from a direct gaze but met Cameron's eyes straight on.

"Now I'm not so sure I want it back," Cameron said.

"That's not such a good thing, Cameron," Lance mused. "How can skin touch skin if there is no skin to touch?"

Cameron looked away, his tongue numb with confusion. He glanced in the direction of the sweat lodge where Alfred knelt beside the mound, filling the pipe with tobacco. Alfred, in turn, was looking at Lance and at him.

The fourth round began. Now the sweat lodge itself seemed to be melting into the waterlogged blast of heat that rose from the fire pit as Alfred splashed water onto a pile that held all the heated stones, save one. Breathing in the sage, cedar, sweat and heat, Cameron gave his body over to the sweat in which it swam.

Close . . . so close to melting down, melting through, melting away . . . this too too solid flesh—

"All my relations." And then the round was over.

Outside the lodge, the men stood in a circle as Alfred lit the tobacco in the pipe. He took the pipe, in turn, to each person in the circle. The sacred pipe links us to the creator and to the earth and to all living things, Alfred said.

After Cameron had dressed, Alfred appeared at his side and took him by the arm. "You have made a start today, my brother. But it is only a start. You have much work to do."

Cameron looked around for Lance, but Lance had already left. Both relieved and disappointed, Cameron walked back along the trail, thinking about Alfred's last words to him as he went. He came down the last hill to the road and saw Lance leaning against his car.

"I'm trying to figure out how I'll get back to Squamish," Lance said.

"I'll take you," said Cameron.

And it was that simple.

"What do you mean, simple?" Alan asks.

"Just what I said," I reply, with a glance at Cyril. "Is it that simple?"

"Cameron, please," Cyril says, balancing cup and saucer on his knee. "A meeting of minds may be possible. Now then, Alan, let me recall how you said it. The Christian way of transformation is a journey into darkness and death, into a rock-lined chamber sealed off from the world by a round stone rolled across the entrance. A very specific and convincing description, by the way."

"I've been to the Holy Land and I've seen the tombs," Alan says.

"So you told us," Cyril continues. "And then you said we journey into that passage in fear and trembling yet in faith, in the hope that the chamber is not a dead end. From within the chamber we wait for the risen Christ to roll the stone aside for each of us, as he rolled it aside that first Easter for all of humanity. From within the chamber itself. You stressed that point several times. Do I have the gist of it?"

"Yes. What do you find simple about it?"

"Cyril, mind the cup!" Mavis Elspeth interjects.

"I'm minding it, my dear. I said nothing about it being simple, Alan. That was Cameron's word. In fact, as a metaphor for those moments when each of us feels trapped within this bemusing world or our not so bemusing selves, I find your words quite apt. And then, enigmatically, the stone rolls aside and there is a way out. Whether or not we come out into anything other than simply another tomb, albeit one larger and more gracious than the one we have just left, is another question again. But setting that question aside, I find the resurrection of Christ the most convincing of all metaphors for the moment of release in itself."

"And that's all it is for you, a metaphor?" Alan asks, disturbed but trying not to appear disturbed.

"Alan, for a teacher and lover of literature, a metaphor is everything. The metaphor of tomb and a stone being rolled away from the mouth of a tomb is as close to disclosing the reality in which we live as we will ever get."

"Cyril doesn't go near the garden," Mavis says, "or he would know a stone of any size is more than a metaphor. But Alan, why an Easter sermon on Thanksgiving Sunday?"

"Why not?" he answers, crossing his legs. "Every Sunday is an Easter day. And autumn is a time when nature dies all around us. Did you find my sermon inappropriate, Margaret?"

The question is directed to my wife, and Alan waits for her answer. He is about thirty, Margaret's age, and St. Cyprian's is his parish as of this past June. Alan is a traditional prayer book priest, young enough but no longer green, and wise enough not to ask us to call him Father Eliot, even though he would like us to call him Father Eliot. Except for Margaret. I observe the way he looks at my wife and know he would not want her to call him Father Eliot.

"Your sermon was just fine with me, Alan," Margaret says. Something leaps in his eyes as she speaks and as he looks at her.

"Why so, Margaret?" Mavis asks.

"My grandmother died recently. In the last week of September."

"I'm so sorry, Margaret. Did you go back to your village—how do you say its name?"

"Duxsowlas."

"Thank you. Did you go back for the funeral?"

"No, I didn't."

Mavis looks over at me, a question in her eyes that she can't quite put into words. However, I know what the question is. "I've never met Margaret's grandmother," I say.

In the silence that ensues, I wait for Alan to offer a moment of pastoral consolation to Margaret, but perhaps they have already engaged themselves in pastoral conversation. Feeling detached from them both, I smile to myself.

"Mavis, what have you been reading all this time?" Cyril asks, to nudge the silence aside.

"A poem, called 'Death Is a Lie,' from this book, *The World Is as Sharp as a Knife*. It seemed to find its peculiar place in the fabric of our conversation. Whoever wrote this says something about receiving a message sent by himself from another life, then goes on:

And if the message says
(as it does say)
"Time is the question and Death is the answer,"

then I know
that the message I have sent my self
must be a lie . . .

Time is the lie.
Death is the lie.

Mavis looks up at me. "It sounds like your kind of book, Cameron, and your kind of poem. Who wrote it?"

"Wilson Duff. He was a professor of anthropology at UBC. He died in August of 1976. The book you're holding is a tribute to him."

"How did he die?" Alan asks.

"He shot himself. In his office."

Mavis closes the book and sets it down on the coffee table. "Oh my!" she says.

I step away from the window, where I have been standing with my back to the quiet world of the street outside, sit in the chair opposite Alan and resume our conversation.

"However, now that Mavis has brought Wilson Duff into our midst, let's go back to my main thread. I agree with you, Alan. The tomb is much more than a metaphor. It is the reality in which we seem to live. But is it the reality in which every people lives? Does all of mankind have to go into the tomb you speak of to enact a genuine transformation of self?"

"What are you suggesting, Cameron?" Alan asks.

"Is it possible that your path of transformation is not as universal as you might want to think? That there may be those who don't live in the tomb of Western humanity and for whom the death of self of which you speak is unnecessary and therefore a lie?"

"As your poet, Wilson Duff, suggests? And whom do you have in mind?"

"Native peoples, for instance. Many of their transformation stories don't involve death, or at least, death as we're speaking about it. In Northwest Coast stories, animals transform into humans, then back into animals. Yes, they shed their skins from time to time, but that's not the same as dying. I think these stories are not just speaking about animals, but about those who told them, as well. Time and space are not impermeable barriers that require death in order to pass beyond them. This may be a world in which the tomb of your sermon has little meaning."

Alan thinks about what I have said. "I see. In some corner of fallen humanity there is a remnant that has not fallen. Is that what you're suggesting?"

"Or not fallen as we have. Yes, that might be a way of putting it."

He sighs. "An ancient wish that never seems to go away."

Cyril shakes his head and laughs. "You do have your own whimsical take on the world, Cameron. That's why your students like you. In fact, one of them even married you. Well now, Margaret, what do you think about your husband's thesis?"

"Yes, Margaret, what do you think?" I ask.

"Cameron, please don't." And that is all she will say, but her eyes flash up from the chair where she sits: *You son of a bitch! Don't you do that to me.*

I gaze into her anger and do not blink. Once I would have cared what she thought or refused to say, and the words of refusal would have gone like a splinter into my heart. But right now, I could care less.

"You said people and animals shed their skins?" says Alan. "That's what those stories say?"

"Yes."

"And do these people and animals ever die?"

"Yes, but—"

"Forgive me, Cameron, but it all sounds like dying into the tomb to me. I don't know the stories of the people of this coast the way you seem to know them, but I do know I have never met a people or any person who has escaped the Fall. There may be an aboriginal innocent wandering about, somewhere, but I have never met him and don't expect to meet him. Until I do, I'll stand by what I said this morning."

Now he looks straight at me, his eyes filled with conviction, perhaps because he now suspects that Margaret does not support my view. But then he might have stood his ground even if she had done so. I have to respect him for that.

"Do you have any news of your brother?" Mavis asks.

Margaret draws her gaze away from me before she responds. "Yes. He wrote me at the end of the summer."

"He certainly took his time in doing that," Mavis says. "It's been three years, hasn't it? Where did he write from?"

"Wales."

"Wales?" says Cyril. "What was he doing there?"

"Preparing to go to Ireland, he said. And getting on with his life, I guess," says Margaret, making it clear she will say no more.

"Time to go, Cyril." Mavis stands and straightens her skirt. "Thank you, Margaret. It was a lovely Thanksgiving dinner."

Margaret sees them to the door. Alan leaves last and lingers a moment with her on the porch.

In the meantime, I start to gather up the cups and wait for her to tell me what she thinks about what I just did to her. However, she comes back into the living room, sits, and says nothing about that. Instead, she takes up the book with the poems by Wilson Duff and says, "Cameron, please put this away. It scares me, you having it out on the table as often as you do. It really and truly scares me."

Then her eyes meet mine.

Yes, Margaret, you are scared. Indeed, you are.

"Dr. McLean?"

I stand at my office window, overlooking the quadrangle at Simon Fraser University, and she stands in the doorway. Sometimes I don't recognize my students, but I recognize her. Third row, five seats from the aisle, in my Modern History class: From whenever to whatever; three credits; two papers and one test; three hours a week.

"Dr. McLean, is something wrong?"

"No, nothing at all. Please sit down."

"I want to ask you about the paper due Monday, and about the test."

The test. They always worry about the test. Fifteen minutes later, she is gone. Still seated at my desk, I stare at the empty doorframe.

Dr. McLean?

It was eleven years ago, just about now in the Fall semester. She stood in the doorway and I recognized her at once, a second year student in one of my survey courses. She never sat in any one place, but just before the beginning of each lecture, I had found myself noting where she was sitting that day. A young Native woman. Beautiful.

May I come in, please?

Yes, of course.

I'm Margaret Jacob. I want to ask you about your lecture today.

Yet as she sat and our eyes met, I knew: *That's not really why you came, is it?*

"Cameron?"

Cyril Elspeth stands in the doorway, wearing the tweed coat he has taught in ever since we have known one another.

"Are you in, Cameron?"

"No, Cyril, I'm on the moon."

"That's about what it looked like, because you didn't seem to be here, wherever you had gone."

"I'm in, Cyril. Sit down."

"Thank you. I shall do that."

And he does. I watch as he takes his pipe from the inside coat pocket and fills it from a worn tobacco pouch. He always smoked his pipe whenever he decided to mentor me and still fills the bowl for such an occasion, even though he can no longer light up inside our academic sanctuary. Cyril decided I needed a mentor when, at age twenty-six, I arrived on campus twelve years ago. Did I need a mentor? I had wondered. However, he was determined to mentor me and has been doing that ever since. I sit back in my chair and wait for him to begin.

"You were a bit hard on Alan on Sunday."

"Was I?"

"Yes, you were. Go easy on him, Cameron. Alan has the makings of a good priest, despite that lingering aroma of Anglo-Catholicism. And I think he knows himself better than your first estimate of him might suggest."

I gaze out the window beside my desk into a quadrangle empty of people. Simon Fraser is a big university, but no one is crossing the quadrangle at the moment. There are only manicured patches of green earth surrounded by concrete and glass. Already on its way to the horizon in the west, the sun flashes back at itself from the glass surfaces.

Coming back to Cyril, I realize I don't care enough about Alan Eliot one way or another to expend energy being hard on him. Except, perhaps, for the way he kept looking at Margaret. But no, not even for that.

"All right, Cyril. If you think he's that fragile, I'll let him up from the mat sooner next time."

"Thank you, Cameron." His eyes move to the wall that runs from the doorway to the window. "Those prints are new, aren't they?"

"Not all that new, but new enough."

"I know the Picasso, of course."

"*Guernica*."

"Yes, I know."

"A Basque town in the north of Spain. German planes flew over the hills round about it on April 26, 1937, and bombed it to pieces. Bombed everything to pieces."

He stares at me, pipe in hand. "I do know about Guernica, Cameron. And what is the other print?"

"It's called *The Box*—four sides of a box, in fact, placed side by side. The Haida artist Albert Edenshaw made the box itself sometime in the last century, or so Wilson Duff thought."

"The man who took his life?"

"The same. He referred to the box as the final exam in Northwest Coast art. Bill Reid redrew the sides of the box into a continuous print."

Cyril studies both prints, then places his pipe in his lap and folds his hands.

"So then. *Guernica*. Broken, fractured human and animal bodies scattered about a room."

"Yes. Bits and pieces in a closed room."

"I see that. Everything is broken or contorted, or both. And there's a light bulb against the ceiling, shooting light into the room."

"A hard, frozen light that goes nowhere and illuminates nothing."

"But there is a head and hand coming into the room, over there, from somewhere else. And the hand holds a lamp."

"Yes, but the lamp is dead. And the head and hand are just as trapped inside the room as everything else."

"And this reflects . . . ?"

The gesture of my hand takes in the room in which we sit, then the world beyond it. Cyril nods and takes up his pipe. "And the Bill Reid print? A similar commentary on the human condition?"

"Perhaps. And perhaps not."

"Ah! Tell me more, Cameron."

"Look again at the print, Cyril. What do you see?"

"What do I see? A limb of some creature or maybe two limbs compacted together, and a head above them. Then more heads, limbs, lines and forms—bits and pieces, with no relation to one another that I can make out. What was I supposed to see, Cameron? Something different in kind from the Picasso?"

I lean back in my chair. "Picasso puts his bits and pieces together in a way that compels us to see them as just that, bits and pieces blown apart from any wholeness they might have ever had. But this other artist, whoever he was, invites us into the secret of a closed box, from the outside in. The one who can see through what seems like bits and pieces will see inside the box. Look again, Cyril. The bits and pieces are related to one another. Each of the eyes sees the others."

Cyril begins to smile. "I see now. So, we've returned to the theme of fragmented Western humanity versus not-so-fragmented aboriginal humanity. Am I correct?" He brushes his hair back from his forehead. With his white hair and rosy cheeks, Cyril could pass for jolly old St. Nick.

"Yes. Does that strike you as an unreasonable thought?"

"As a wish, no. But as a thought?" Cyril sighs. "The trouble with you, Cameron, is that you're an historian. As with most historians, you search through the rubble of events and players and motives and causes like a child turning over stones on a beach, thinking he can bring the stones together into some kind of motif or pattern that will make life less cowardly and stupid and more glorious and sensible. Who wouldn't wish for that, especially at the closing of this dreadful century we may yet survive?"

I look out my window once again. A lone figure is walking across the quadrangle. Her steps slow until she stops at a line where sun and shadow meet. Hesitating at the edge of light and shadow, her head bared, she seems frozen somewhere within herself as if she has suddenly been struck to stone by a terrible truth she has kept at bay the whole of her young life. I want to get up, walk through the walls of concrete and out into the quadrangle where she stands, and hold her until she is able to move on.

Instead, I turn back to Cyril. "And you? What does a teacher of literature wish for as he gathers together the rubble of humanity?"

He considers my question. "Each story, poem, novel you read, I tell my students, is not what it pretends to be, a fragment of reality caught in the writer's snare. It is, instead, a mirror image of life, a metaphor, yet that metaphor is a reality we can know and trust. It is not what it is, yet is what it is not—a lie, but not a lie, and as close as we ever come to flashes of recognition that life itself will never give you."

"Will not give, or cannot?"

"Both, perhaps. It comes to the same thing in the end. Treasure the flashes of recognition, I tell them, for they are like water becoming wine, and wine becoming the blood of Christ, and do not ask for more expansive patterns of meaning. Take what the metaphor gives you, for that can become the bread of life."

"And that's the whole of it? Flashes of recognition in metaphors?"

"In essence, yes. Connect them as you wish, but just know that the connections begin and end with you. Don't imagine that you, the historian, can come closer to the truth of the stabbing of Julius Caesar than did Shakespeare the playwright."

"And what was the truth for Shakespeare?"

"Ambition. They killed Caesar because of his ambition."

"Ah, yes. And Shakespeare was an honourable man."

Cyril returns my smile.

"And what about Jesus? Is he a metaphor, too?"

"Of course. The ultimate metaphor."

I laugh. "Mirror of mirror. Metaphor of metaphor. Very mirror of very metaphor. I see."

I return my gaze to the figure I had left standing at the threshold of shadow and light, but she is gone. The late afternoon sun is closing in upon the western horizon and its light rebounds from the windows around the quadrangle.

Once a bird flew down into the quadrangle from the depth of sky that arched over the campus. I sat at my desk and watched it dart from building to building, waiting for it to soar upward, back to the heavens from which it had come. But the bird flew from window to window, flew toward the images of sky mirrored in each and every window. Becoming more and more frantic, the bird hurled itself against one window, then another, until it fell to the concrete below and died.

I turn back to Cyril. "Solomon took a course from you, the spring before he left. On Yeats and Eliot."

"Yes, I remember him well in that course," Cyril says. "Why do you bring it up?"

"We had lunch in the Pub, on his twenty-first birthday. He had just come out of a class with you and was full of a poem by Yeats, called 'The Two Trees.' He even read me lines from it:

Gaze no more in the bitter glass
The demons, with their subtle guile,
Lift up before us when they pass,
Or only gaze a little while;
For there a fatal image grows . . ."

"I know the poem, Cameron."

"Of course you do, Cyril, and I too made a point of knowing it after my conversation with Solomon. Yeats suggests to me that not every metaphor may prove to be the bread of life. Tell me, what did Solomon think of your view on metaphors and mirrors?"

"Yes, Solomon. He did have his own ideas about things. In fact, he submitted a final paper for the course that I found intriguing. As I remember it, he said: Maybe a metaphor is more an eclipse than a mirror. It shuts out the world as we usually see it and lets something we don't usually see shine through. It was a remarkable—"

"Flash of recognition."

"Yes, it was. I think I gave him an A. Why did he leave so suddenly, Cameron?"

"Margaret and he had a fight. At least, that's what she told me."

"And the letter to her this past summer was the first word from him in all the time he's been gone?"

"Yes."

Cyril stands. "It's a pity he left. I was looking forward to having him in a fourth year class. How are things between you and Margaret?"

The question comes unexpectedly and I wonder why he is asking it. Then I remember that Cyril was my best man at our wedding. As well, he observes people closely and isn't stupid.

"We're doing all right."

"Forgive me, Cameron, if my question has offended you, but I do care for both of you."

I shrug and smile. "Well, there are days when we seem to be two metaphors in search of a flash of recognition, but we'll be fine."

"You've hoisted me on my own petard, Cameron," he says, "so I'll take my leave now. But to go back to where all of this began, please—"

"Yes, I know. Be kind to Alan. I'll try, Cyril."

Now I am alone in my office, looking through the window into the quadrangle. The only human presence I see is an image of myself stuck in the glass through which I look as the lines from Yeats sound within me:

For all things turn to barrenness
In the dim glass the demons hold,
The glass of utter weariness,

Made when God slept in times of old.
There, through the broken branches, go
The ravens of unresting thought;
Flying, crying, to and fro—

I turn the words aside. Pieces of paper lie on my desk and I look at them, hoping to find something that will claim my attention. Then a remembered presence draws my gaze back to the open doorway.

May I come in, Cameron?

Margaret stood before me. It was no longer fall but spring, and she was no longer just another of my students.

She sat in the chair, a smile playing about her lovely mouth.

Is it about the paper, Margaret?

No, Cameron. It's about me. About you and me. I think I'm in love with you.

Yes, Margaret, you were.

He stood on the front porch of his house, a cup of tea in hand, on a Tuesday in November. It had rained all night, but now he heard only the dripping of water from the eaves of the house and from the branches of the trees along the street.

His family had moved to Vancouver from Nova Scotia at this time of year, and he had hated the rain. Eight years old, Cameron was torn away from the world that had cradled him. For years he lived for the summers when his parents and he would return to Nova Scotia to see the aunts, uncles and cousins that waited eagerly for their annual visit. His father's parents had died before Cameron was born, and his mother's mother, shortly afterward. There was, however, the grandfather who lived in Newfoundland and who always came to see them in Nova Scotia, because Cameron's father was unwilling to make the trip across that last length of water that separated Newfoundland from the rest of Canada. Cameron, however, was the only child of his parents, and his grandfather would have crossed any stretch of water to spend a few weeks with his grandson.

This was the grandfather who had stood with his father on the beach in New Brunswick the summer Cameron was nine and watched Cameron plunge into the Atlantic, the moment of cleansing he had told Lance about. Summer after summer, Cameron would hurl himself into the breakers that seemed to come from a magical world far out at sea to lick, caress, tease at the sand on which he stood and at the skin that he suddenly found himself wanting to shed so that he could give himself fully to the sea that was becoming his friend.

The summer he was twelve, however, this friend nearly took Cameron's life. His family had gone to Peggy's Cove, on Nova Scotia's south shore. His grandfather had come, too, and they all stayed in the house of a fisherman who was away either fishing or engaged in a smuggling operation of some sort, as his grandfather had intimated.

Cameron stood that long afternoon at the lip of a slab of granite, flanked by more slabs and by boulders like the heads of giants, peering into a surge of water that foamed up from some kingdom of the sea hidden away in the depths below. He stood, as well, at the edge of adolescence, startled by and shy of all that had begun to surge up within him. He woke many nights with erections he didn't want and didn't know what to do with, though he had already found a way of momentary relief. But he sensed that the deeper urging forward could not be relieved in that way. What was this awakening, so concentrated in one part of himself, and what did it want from him? Where would it take him, and to whom? And did he really want it, the bewildering pleasure it brought, along with its enigmatic counterpart: the face in the mirror and the intense awareness of self reflected in it. Suddenly, his world seemed to be closing in on him at one pole even as it yearned to expand at another, and it was all too much for him.

So he fell forward into the surging water. Looking back at the moment, Cameron often asked himself what he had intended to do. Bring his life to an end? And if not that, then what? But he had never been able to penetrate that act of will itself, despite intimations of motives that became nothing more than intimations. All he knew then, and all he could remember now, was his body falling forward and then the waves covering him over. As the currents drew him deeper down, he could feel his body start to fall away from him. His eyes rolled upward to the light that played upon the skin of water overhead. Then the light was no longer overhead, but glowing from a depth of water far below him . . .

He released his breath, to let go of his body and let the sea take him fully—

In that instant, his grandfather's hand found him and yanked him free of the water. How his grandfather's hand had found him, how his grandfather had gotten himself across the rocks and into the sea to free his grandson, Cameron never learned. He only knew he was jerked back into the air and the light, jolted back into himself as his body slipped from his grandfather's grasp and landed on the face of a rock.

He started to cry, his parents standing over him. His mother also cried, while his father's mouth spewed out words to his grandfather and to anyone who might be listening, fearful and angry words Cameron could not even remember. Then his grandfather sent them both away, taking charge of that moment in Cameron's life as he had never done before or was ever to do again.

Wrapping Cameron in his own great flannel shirt, his grandfather propped him up against the side of a rock, vanished for a few moments, and then returned with a double armload of driftwood. Soon a fire blazed up from a slab of rock.

His grandfather sat, folded his arms about Cameron and held him, as the sun let the afternoon go and the afternoon deepened into a smoky blue evening. The last light of day faded from the skin of the water as his grandfather began to tell the story of Sinann.

It was an Irish story, his grandfather said, about the naming of the Shannon River. The well of Connla lay beneath the sea and six streams of wisdom flowed from it, only to return bringing the five salmon that would eat of the nuts of knowledge that the nine hazels dropped into the well. The druids wanted to protect the knowledge and hold it back from those not ready for it. Eat of the salmon that eat the nuts, they said, and that will be wisdom enough for anyone. But Sinann wanted to find the nuts themselves and eat of their juice. She leapt into the water and the druids retaliated. As she drowned, they transformed Sinann into the seventh stream that flowed from the well, the Shannon River.

Warm in his grandfather's arms, Cameron had drunk in the story and pictured a welling up of light in that depth of the sea where the nuts of knowledge could be found.

As if reading Cameron's thoughts, his grandfather ended the story by saying, "The river took Sinann out to sea, but the well of the heart was what she was truly seeking."

So, where would his heart lead him, now that he had been pulled away from whatever the depths of the sea might have given him?

Thrust back into the dawning of his adolescent years, Cameron began to steal glances at the girls who shimmered at the horizon of his expanding awareness of the world and himself. Now and then the girls glanced back, but with glances so transient that they promised nothing that might answer the intensity drawing itself together somewhere between his solar plexus and his loins.

Only the slender boy who sat by the window in grade eight, who stood silently on the playground and watched the games in progress—only this boy had eyes ready to meet the question in Cameron's eyes.

The eyes of the slender boy were sea gray. His hair was the colour of the sand that waited for the sea to kiss it. The slender boy gazed across the playground at Cameron as if he knew a secret locked within

Cameron that Cameron could only suspect. Gazing into the withheld secret, the slender boy waited for Cameron to cross the playground and come to him. But Cameron did not cross. And then the slender boy vanished from Cameron's class and from Cameron's life, just as a few of the girls seemed ready to seek out Cameron's eyes with questions of their own.

Uncertainly, yet unable to imagine that it could be any other way, Cameron turned to the girls. Then Margaret inserted herself into his life, knowing that she wanted him, and everything seemed to fall into its proper place.

Yet on this Tuesday morning in November, Cameron gazed once again into the eyes of the slender boy and into the secret those eyes had withheld all these years.

It began to rain again. He closed the front door, went into the kitchen, and began to clear up the breakfast dishes. Hot water poured from the tap into the sink, turning the detergent into bubbles. Solomon had also come close to death by drowning. Nathan, as his brother-in-law was known then, had fallen at the age of two into a pit of oolichan oil at Duxsowlas. His mother had rescued him just in time. No one knew how he had fallen in, except a girl his age who had seen it happen, and all she said was, "Raven."

Margaret had told him the story early on in their marriage, when she was still willing to tell him about such things.

The dishes washed, Cameron made himself another cup of tea. He had no classes that day and all the time he wanted to drink his tea and think about his life.

Taking his tea into the living room, Cameron removed two books from a chair and sat. He wrapped his hands around the warmth of the cup and closed his eyes. Opening them he took in the prints that hung on the walls of the room: Bill Reid, Robert Davidson, Art Thompson, Danny Dennis, and others. He had started collecting them in the early 1970's, at the end of his teen years, before collecting Northwest Coast art had become a fashionable thing to do. The Bill Reid print *Children of the Raven* had looked out at him from the wall of a small shop, no longer there, on Robson Street. Gazing into the face that gazed out at him from within Raven's eye, he had realized: The man who did this knows something I want to know.

What is it I want to know?

Perhaps it was the art that had kept him in Vancouver when his father died and his mother moved back to Newfoundland. He had brought the prints with him to his marriage with Margaret, and was taken aback when she made it clear they were of no interest to her.

Cameron sipped at his tea and looked at the top of a shelf of books facing him, where their wedding photograph stood. Margaret had been young, only twenty, yet mature well beyond her years. Eight years older, he had not felt young at the time.

So, what were you interested in, Margaret, when we exchanged those vows, and what did I want from you?

And if I had crossed the playground and plunged myself into the eyes of the slender boy, would I have ever wanted anything from you?

Cameron had done a second sweat at the end of September, then another late in October. On the first occasion Alfred asked him to pick Lance up in Squamish, on the way to Alfred's sweat lodge by the creek. Lance and Cameron talked about many things and about nothing much—different ways of doing sweat lodge ceremonies, Lance's intention to become someone who could conduct ceremonies of his own, but little about Lance's tribal origins.

"Which tribe do you come from?" Cameron asked.

"I don't know anything about tribes, Cameron."

"I mean, who are your people?" Cameron realized his face was flushed, as he tried to rephrase his question.

"Native people are my people. And maybe you are my people, Cameron."

Cameron nodded, as if he understood. "And where do you live now? On a reserve?"

"On a rez? Not likely, Cameron. I live wherever I can lay my head."

On the way back to Squamish, Cameron did most of the talking, about Nova Scotia and about his teaching at sfu, while Lance just listened and smiled now and then.

"And what about your wife, Cameron?" Lance said suddenly.

"What about her?"

"You haven't talked about her."

Cameron took his time in responding, waiting until he had passed a car that was slowing him down.

"She's Native," Cameron said, "from a village up the coast."

"So she's Native. And that's important to you?"

"It was important."

"But not now?"

"Not so much," Cameron replied. "Why do you ask?"

"Because being Native was the first thing you told me about her. Does she have a name?"

"Yes. Margaret."

Lance got out at a stoplight in Squamish. "Alfred is doing another sweat in October," he said, and handed Cameron a scrap of paper. "Give me a call and I'll let you know when. You can pick me up on the way and tell me more about Margaret. And about what you really want for that skin of yours, besides a good cleansing."

Cameron watched him as he crossed the Sea to Sky Highway and felt the knot in his loins.

In October, Alfred led Cameron through his third sweat lodge ceremony, then took him aside when it was over. "We need to speak, my brother," Alfred said.

Cameron finished buttoning his shirt and waited for Alfred to continue.

"I don't think the sweat lodge is your path," Alfred said.

Cameron's jacket fell from his hand. "I don't understand," he said.

"No," said Alfred, "you don't understand. That is why you need to walk another path."

"Have I done something wrong?"

Alfred's eyes searched his. "On the outside, no. Not yet. But your heart is not clear."

Cameron stared back at him.

"Your heart is not clear," Alfred insisted. "Search your heart, my brother, and ask what your heart truly wants."

"Are you saying I can't do any more sweats with you?" Cameron asked after a moment.

"The sweat lodge is not your path," Alfred said, his voice very firm. He turned and went back to the fire.

"What did Alfred say to you?" Lance asked on the way back to Squamish.

So Cameron told him. Lance said nothing until Cameron stopped the car to let him out. Then Lance turned to Cameron and placed his hand on the back of Cameron's.

"If you want to do another sweat, call me."

The print called *Transformation #3*, by Eric Gray, hung on the wall beside Cameron. Drinking down the last of his tea, he looked up at the human figure trying to step free of the form of Raven that held it fast, its head buried in Raven's head, in Raven's seeing of the light he had stolen and released into the world. Caught and lost in the head of Raven, the ravens of unresting thought . . .

The print was stained with tea. "Where did that come from?" he had asked Margaret.

"Solomon and I had a fight," she said, "and I threw a cup of tea at him."

"A fight? About what?"

"About Oka. It seems we have differing takes on the troubles in the Pines, the virtues of Mohawk warriors, and the injustice of it all. He thinks I don't care, and I don't think he cares in the way he wants to think he cares. He's gone out somewhere to bandage his ego. He'll be back."

But Solomon had not come back, and they heard nothing from him for three years. Then the letter to Margaret arrived, the day he had done the sweat with Lance. The letter Margaret had told him about, but had not let him read.

After another long look at the wedding photograph, Cameron took a scrap of paper from his wallet and went to the phone.

The rain dies down to a drizzle as we leave the parked car and walk down to the bank of the river. Lance leads the way, a blanket wrapped around his drum, and I follow him along the riverbank.

Our way crosses over smooth, wet stones that gleam up at me in the gray afternoon light. The bed of stones widens, then narrows again until we can barely squeeze ourselves past the dripping branches that slap at or caress our bodies as we pass.

December twenty-eighth—the murder of the holy innocents. It's been nothing but a murder of innocence, for hundreds of long, gray years.

Why then am I doing this? Like a leper of old, I long for fire and water to cleanse my flesh, to dissolve bone and skin and sinew to primal innocence. Indeed, cleansing alone is not enough, nor even baptism. Nothing but dissolution will release me from the knotted fist within that impels me along this riverbed.

Stones crunch beneath my feet as if in protest. The river gnaws at the stones and at my feet. The river wants to seduce me into its faster, deeper currents that whisper barely audible secrets into my ear. Long ago my grandfather's hand lifted me free of the sea's seductive currents, yet the river still whispers to me.

Out on the river's ever-changing face, ribbons of light touch down, lengthen, then die away.

Lance climbs the bank and I follow, over several large stones and between the trunks of two massive cottonwoods. The bank opens into a clearing where a sweat lodge stands, covered with a dark blue tarp.

"I started building it last summer," Lance says, "but have never done a sweat in it. So today will be a first. Let's gather the grand-fathers and get the fire going."

Once the stones are in place, Lance removes the tarp from a stack of wood at the edge of the clearing. "This should be enough for a good, hot fire," he says, as we stack pieces of dry alder, fir and cedar against the grandfathers.

It's dark by the time the stones are red-hot. Overhead, clouds draw apart from one another and the sky begins to clear. Water drips to the drenched earth from the bare and evergreen branches that close the clearing in. To the east a full moon lifts itself free of the mountains and begins to rise into a sky filling itself with stars.

Lance stands, eagle feather in hand, and looks upward.

"It's good to see the stars haven't gone away. In the city, it's easy to think otherwise."

He places the tobacco I have brought on the mound between the lodge and the fire, along with a pipe and an eagle feather that he sticks into the rise of earth. We strip to our underwear, smudge ourselves and with a shovel bring the first of the stones to the fire pit inside the lodge. Although the inside of the lodge is damp and cold, the roasting stones soon turn the dampness into a liquid heat.

As Lance draws the tarp down across the doorway, the darkness within the lodge eclipses the darkness of the night outside.

Splashing the first drops of water upon the grandfathers, Lance says, "This round is for opening us up, Cameron, and for all who need opening up."

The heat builds, enfolds me, and sweat begins to drip from my skin, as Lance drums and sings. Closing my eyes, I swim in water and fire as in a warm womb that should never be abandoned. I wait for the darkness and warmth to take me back to the moment of my birth and beyond that moment, into the darkness before any light and the pain of living in the light . . .

I am close now, closer than I have ever been . . .

Then the lodge door flies open and the night air rushes in.

Fighting a sense of loss, I pick my way over the sodden earth and leaves, then stones, to the river. The river grasps me as I plunge myself into its current, and kneads my flesh back to its solid state. I lift my body away from its hold and stand in the moon's light, as water drips from my skin.

Lance stands a few feet away from me. We do not speak.

The door to the sweat lodge closes once again and the second round begins.

"This round is for you, Cameron."

The grandfathers hiss, then whisper, as Lance brings the water-laden pine branch to them. As the darkness around us breathes against it, my skin wants to glow like the skins of the grandfathers and be swallowed into the smouldering darkness, into whatever is beyond it.

Lance places the eagle feather in my hand.

What do you want, Cameron?

The heat drives me toward the earth. My mouth opens, but the words stay locked in my throat.

Speak to me, Cameron!

Then my throat breaks open and the breaking open becomes a high wail that will not be held back.

My voice fills the lodge—no longer my voice alone, but that of ancestors long removed from me. The keening of ruined men and women sounds forth from my mouth like the current of the river just beyond the lodge—yet not the current of a river but the currents of seas that kiss and batter the coasts where I came into this world.

The voices of my ancestors rise, crest above the steaming grandfathers, then fall back upon the waves that brought them, brimful of their crushed lives, to this beautiful and terrifying land.

And then it is one voice alone, almost mine, but not my voice here or now or at anytime of my life in this flesh. Heartbroken, she moans forth from me. I know who she is, though there is no name I can give to her. Nor can I place her in the land where she lived and died, to wait for her time to come round again.

Yet she cries out from within me as she plunges down into an unfathomable depth of water seeking fire and light to be found in no other way . . .

And now the weeping is mine alone. Lance takes hold of me, leads me from the lodge and into the creek, into the cold, crushing water.

Back on the riverbank, I stumble toward the fire, his arm around me. He lowers me to the ground, then holds me as my nostrils drink in the sage and cedar aura his skin radiates. Locked together, our bodies warm one another.

His mouth at my ear, Lance murmurs, "This next round is for us, Cameron. For us."

The moon clothes Lance with cool light. Jet black, his hair streams down to the small of his back; the beadwork of the sun eagle hanging from his neck captures the moonlight. That and the moccasins on his feet are the only articles of clothing he wears. Strange, that a tall man should have small, beautiful feet. But Lance is a beautiful man.

I have never thought of a man as beautiful until I met Lance. Solomon is also beautiful, now that I let myself think of him in that way. And even the slender boy was beautiful, now that I let myself remember in that way. But not like Lance.

Lance stands at the window in a pool of moonlight, as he stood in the sunlight that afternoon I first met him. The falling water polished his skin; the light from the sun stripped him naked, only I had not seen then or wanted to see what the sun was revealing as the water pressed his hair against his back and shoulders.

"Come back to bed, Lance."

My words hang in the darkness between us. Then his hands, long-boned and delicate, lift his hair from his shoulders, to let it fall and ripple along the dark of his skin. Slipping into bed, he reaches for me. My arms take hold of him and our bodies come alive together.

Then, awash in the undertow of our lovemaking, I hear Lance's voice at my ear: "A Haida guy came to my AA meeting in Calgary and told a story about a child floating on wide-open water, because it couldn't find a foothold on what little land there was. Up pops a grebe and says, 'Your powerful grandfather at the bottom of the sea asks you in, so he can give you what you need to make solid ground for yourself.'

"That Haida guy said that for years he had dived to the bottom of the bottle, hoping to find a powerful grandfather who would give him what he needed to live on this earth. I listened to him and knew that was what I had been trying to do when I was drinking—dive to the bottom of a bottle, not to ground my skin, but to get rid of it. My dad and mother died of booze, both my brothers were in jail, and my sisters were trying to drink themselves free of marriages they hated. And me? I couldn't love the way everyone else did and was scared to love the way I wanted to. I didn't want the skin the Creator had given me for loving.

"Then one morning I came up from the bottom of the bottle, my head battered from smashing itself against it, and knew there was no powerful grandfather down there that would free me from my skin. I had to live in it. So I started to sober up, started to live and love in my way, and took back my skin."

Lance tightens his arms around me. "I know where you're at,

Cameron, and what you think you want from the sweat lodge. Only with you, it's not a matter of drowning your skin, but burning it up. We're going to take another road, though, you and me, and along that road, I'm going to give you back your skin."

Yet the ebb and flow of his words barely settle into my ear before they are swept away into the undertow of our lovemaking.

Cameron felt Cyril standing in the doorway of his office but did not look up.

"May I come in, Cameron?"

"If you wish."

"Would you rather I didn't?"

"Suit yourself, Cyril."

"Then I shall come in, for a moment or two."

Cyril sat in the other chair in Cameron's office, took out his pipe, and began to stuff it.

"Are you going to light that thing, Cyril?"

Cyril started. A baffled look creased itself into the lines of his face. "No, given the current state of regulations on this campus."

"Then stop playing with it, please."

The baffled look dissolved into a laugh. "My, my! You are testy today. What are you working on so diligently?"

"My new course, starting Tuesday."

"Ah, your new course. Yes, you were telling me about it just before we all disbanded for the holiday season. And you're calling it—"

"Whatever I'll decide to call it." Cameron turned over the paper on which he had been making notes and went on writing.

"Whatever I'll decide to call it," Cyril repeated. "A challenging title, in itself. But surely, Cameron, your course, title and all, is recorded on a sheet of paper somewhere, to be made available to students who might wish to take it?"

"Then go and find that sheet of paper if knowing the title matters that much to you."

"It doesn't matter to me one iota, Cameron. I'm simply interested in what you're up to in this course of yours."

Cameron wrote a few lines more, then set his pen down. Cyril sat in the chair, his half-stuffed pipe in his lap, and waited.

"And I'm not interested in a critique of my course, Cyril," Cameron said. "Not when I'm just putting the pieces together."

"Who said anything about a critique? But just what pieces are you putting together?"

"Whatever telling pieces I can find."

"And what do you expect the pieces you find to tell you, and your students?"

"Whatever might light up when we bring them together."

"Ah so! Like your Picasso, and your Bill Reid, only there isn't a trace of light in the Picasso, as I remember."

"Let it go, Cyril!"

The force of his words took Cameron by surprise, but Cyril simply raised his hands, palms outward, and smiled.

"Consider it gone, Cameron. In fact, my visit has nothing to do with your course."

"Then what is your visit about?"

"These." Cyril drew forth some newspaper clippings from his coat pocket and placed them on Cameron's desk. "Abuse in residential schools. Here are some recent articles I have clipped for you."

"Why would I want to know about abuse in residential schools?"

"Because it's a piece of nasty history about to catch up with us, and you are an historian. As well, these may throw some light on your relationship with your wife."

Cameron picked up his pen and turned it over, once, then again. "What about my relationship with Margaret?"

"There seem to be times—how shall I put this?—times when your respective worlds don't mesh or, more to the point, are at odds with one another. Or perhaps it's that Margaret is reluctant to let you into a world you know little about. These articles may help you know more."

"Why do you think abuse in residential schools has anything to do with Margaret?" Cameron asked. "She went to a public high school in Port Hardy."

Cyril shrugged. "Call it a hunch. Take the articles, Cameron, so that the time spent in clipping them won't prove to have been futile."

Cameron considered him. "No, you take them, Cyril, and give them to someone who has more time to read them than I do."

"As you wish," Cyril said, taking up the clippings. "However, you surprise me, Cameron. I didn't think Alan and you would have in common such an aversion to telling current events."

"How does Alan come into this matter?"

"Because I offered a similar set of clippings to him and he too refused them—not so surprisingly, given that the church is one of the culprits in residential school abuse. However, he relented in the end."

"You mean he took the clippings?"

"Yes, he did." Cyril stood and made as if to return the clippings to his coat pocket. Cameron leaned back in his chair, looked down at the notes on his desk, then back at Cyril.

"Leave them, Cyril. I'll glance at them when I can."

"Ah, another change of mind. Well then, here they are, when you're ready. Now I must be off. Mavis insisted I be home early today. Good luck to you with your course, Cameron."

"Thank you."

Cameron returned to his notes, then looked up again. Cyril stood in the doorway, his hand on the doorjamb.

"By the way, who was that Native man who stopped by here yesterday?"

Cameron's pen lifted from the paper and stayed poised in midair. "His name is Lance. I do sweat lodge ceremonies with him. Why do you ask?"

"It's just that I saw him standing right here, when I was on my way to bring these clippings to you." Cyril paused, his eyes intent upon Cameron. "He's a striking man, Cameron. One could even say beautiful."

"Yes, Lance is a striking man. Good night, Cyril."

Cameron did not look up again until he knew Cyril was no longer standing in his doorway. Then, his hand shaking, he set the pen down on the desk and shivered. His office was suddenly cold, and he wondered why.

In the dead of night Cameron stood in the upstairs room of his house, the room that had been Solomon's. He sat at the desk that had been Solomon's and turned on the desk lamp.

On the wall above the bed was the carving Solomon had done for his grade twelve project: a circular slab of yellow cedar with a crescent moon in relief along the bottom. The two heads of Sisiutl, the double-headed sea serpent of the Kwakiutl, extended up from the tips of the crescent on either side, their tongues joining to become the upper curve of the moon. Unlike those of the Sisiutl print hanging above his desk downstairs, the two heads faced toward one another.

The head of the Raven emerged from the plane of the circle above the crescent. The rest of the Raven's body was carved in relief in that circle, while the suggestion of a central face of Sisiutl appeared in the crescent below. Solomon had worked unceasingly on the piece during the few weeks just before the project presentations, and then had almost forgotten to show it when he had finished giving his talk.

Cameron had looked at the carving many times since, trying to puzzle out fully what Solomon had attempted to reveal through it. At times he thought he knew. Solomon, however, had been reluctant to speak directly about that part of his project, even when Cameron prompted him to do so. Now Cameron wondered if Solomon himself had truly understood his creation.

Everything in the room was as Solomon had left it, except for the eagle feather that had hung from a nail on the wall at the head of his bed, just below the carving.

Opening one of the bottom desk drawers, Cameron thumbed through a pile of main lesson books from Solomon's years at the Chinook Park Waldorf School until he found a bound copy of the written part of Solomon's project, *From Raven to Newton: The Art of Bill Reid*. Cameron opened the book and turned to the page where Solomon described his first visit to the Museum of Anthropology at UBC, to study Bill Reid's carving of *The Raven and the First Men.*

The words were now very familiar, for Cameron had read these pages a number of times. Yet he still wondered at Solomon's powers of observation as Solomon had walked once, then again, around the carving, first taking in the gestures of the six figures emerging from the clamshell, coming finally to the last of them: dying, dying into the light. Then on the second walk about, he had taken in the expressions on the Raven's face: contemplation from afar, becoming doubt, defiance, sadness, that "gotcha" grin, then disinterest . . .

Solomon's words tried to bring it all together:

Bill Reid's telling of the Raven's stealing the light stressed the inky darkness covering everything before the Raven let the light into the world. And where did the Raven find the light? He found it in a box, inside a box, inside another box.

Now it's the other way around. The Raven perches on the clamshell in the light he has released. My dad told me that Raven's feathers turned black from stealing the light, but in Bill Reid's carving, the Raven is drenched in light—trapped in the light, maybe. And where has the darkness gone? Back into the little box in which the light had been kept? And what is that darkness hiding from, and hiding away in itself?

So then, we have Mr. Raven caught in a world in which the darkness has gone into hiding, the world Mr. Raven created. A long time later, a man named Newton would also think up a world in which light would push the darkness aside and into hiding. Newton may have thought it was his idea, but Raven set him up to think that. Newton inherited the Raven's world, and so did Bill Reid when he started carving his way back into the art of his people, the Haida . . .

Cameron looked up from the page at the wall. He pictured Lance standing before him, his body brilliant in the light that both disclosed and sheathed it. At one time he would have pictured Margaret standing in that light, undressing slowly so he could take her in as she undressed and know that she was about to give herself to him. Know that he was about to go into her—

To find what? *What do you seek here?* Light, hidden away in darkness. Was that what making love was? A seeking for the light in the darkness of the other . . .

Alan had once given a sermon on love. Love, Alan had said, was the giving of life to the other. Not, Alan stressed, the act of taking or seeking, but of giving. It had been a good enough sermon, and Alan had waited around after the service for the members of his congregation to tell him so.

But what did Alan know about loving, and needing to find light before you could give it? Perhaps Margaret and Alan had become lovers. Margaret could teach Alan something, no doubt.

Now Cameron found himself at the page where Solomon described his walk from Bill Reid's carving back into the great hall of the museum:

Now I could see on the poles what I hadn't seen when I walked through here on my way to visit the Raven. All around me were faces, paws, teeth, hands, joints, ears, eyes of animals and humans. All these figures were pressing forward against their skins of wood, trying to come out from somewhere, yet being stopped short and frozen fast by the very light that revealed them to one another and to themselves. It was as if they all, each one, had caught a glimpse of themselves in some great mirror and were paralyzed by what they saw.

Then I thought, the light itself is the skin that holds these figures fast. The light is the skin of the world, the daylight skin that holds the world in place. Maybe that skin was what the Haida called the Xhaaidla—the skin that holds two worlds apart even as it holds them together . . .

Cameron had told Solomon about the Xhaaidla, and in a footnote at the bottom of the page, Solomon thanked him for that. Cameron turned the page and went on reading:

For Bill Reid, a "deeply carved" work of art means something well made. Yet when I look at his work and the work of other carvers, I see "deep carving" meaning something more than that. I used to watch my dad carve and wonder, why is he taking so much time on that one line? Then he and I began to work together on a pole and I found my hands wanting to take the blade through the line of Raven's beak, in one instance, to some secret place buried deep within the wood, to a meaning hidden beneath the gleaming grain of it. So, what was I trying to do?

Now I look at the work of those old carvers, at Bill Reid's work, and I think, maybe they're trying to cut through that skin of light that holds the Bear or Raven or Killer Whale fixed in the wood, to let the inside of them out, to let the dark heart of the wood shine through . . .

Cameron closed the book. He pictured Solomon that night, standing in that hall filled with parents and fellow students, fielding questions about his project—especially the one from the man who had listened between the lines: "If Raven's stealing of the light leads to Newton's world sealed tight by daylight, then Bill Reid had to start from the world of Newton and find a way back to Raven's world, and perhaps to a world before Raven. Do I have it right?"

Solomon, hands in his pockets, had grinned and said, "That sounds pretty good to me."

"Then," the man continued, "is Newton's world, and Raven's, a dead end or can one move on from there?"

Solomon, in turn, simply acknowledged that it was a good question and let it go at that.

A way back into the world before the Raven . . . Was that what he had been seeking in the sweat lodge, as he waited for the heat and darkness to dissolve his skin and release him into—

Into Lance's arms. That was where Cameron had gone in the end, to be released from himself in that explosion of self.

"Does your wife know?"

Cameron's head rolled away from him and he stared up from his pillow. "What made you ask that?"

"Because wives usually do. Even before they know that they know."

Cameron shrugged against the press of Lance's hand. "I don't know what she knows."

"And it sounds like you don't care that much. What did you tell her about being gone tonight?"

"Just that I'd be away."

"And that was enough for her?"

"It was enough for me."

Lance fell silent beside him, his eyes also staring up at the stars beyond the ceiling.

"Does it bother you, Lance?"

"Does what bother me?"

"That I'm cheating on my wife."

Lance thought about it for a moment. "No. Does it bother you?"

"No."

Lance turned on his side and slid his hand across Cameron's chest. "I think it does. I think it bothers you." The tip of Lance's finger moved from the hollow of Cameron's neck, along the ridge of his chest, into the valley of his navel. "Where are we going to take this, Cameron?"

The question had startled Cameron, although he would have expected a woman to ask it, sooner or later.

"I don't know? What are you asking of me?"

"Just what I asked. You love me. I love you. Where are we going to take this?"

Love? Is that what this is about?

The question had numbed Cameron's mouth even as it gnawed at his heart. His body suddenly tense, he waited for Lance to push him for an answer. But Lance chose not to push. Instead he shook his head, smiled and rolled onto his back.

Yet the question went on gnawing at Cameron's heart long after Lance had fallen asleep beside him.

Cameron returned Solomon's project to its place in the desk drawer. Getting up, he went to the window that overlooked Burrard Inlet. The water was coal black from the clouds overhead.

There will be a new moon tomorrow. The mirror of the moon at rest . . .

Then he walked into the bathroom next to Solomon's room. When he stepped up to the sink to wash his hands, his eyes met the pair of eyes in that other mirror.

What deep carving can reach into that face and set it free?

To be or not to be—

The prison of me.

I turn the leaflet over and look at it again. "Where did this come from?" I ask Margaret.

She takes it from me. "The Christmas Fair at the Chinook Park Waldorf School. It was at the end of November."

"Why didn't you tell me about it?"

"You weren't here to tell." She gets up from the kitchen table and takes her bowl to the sink. "As I remember it, you were off visiting your new Native friend and preparing for another of your sweats. In any event, belated greetings from Paul Kane. He says he has a book waiting for you."

"What book?"

"One he offered you the day Solomon graduated."

And then I remember. "Thank you. I may take him up on the offer."

"I'd better get going or I'll miss my bus. I hope your day goes well."

She stands at the counter, checking her purse, and suddenly I want to ask her about the residential schools. Then she turns abruptly and gazes at me.

"What is it, Cameron?"

"Nothing, I suppose. Just something I thought about asking you."

"Funny, because there's something I've been wanting to ask you, about your new friend."

We stare at one another. "Another time, maybe," she says, closing her purse.

"Yes, Margaret, another time."

And then she is gone.

The sun warms my back, on a sunny Sunday at the end of January. I ring the bell again and wait for him to come to the door.

"Hello, Cameron. Please come in."

Paul Kane holds the door open, then closes it behind me. "I have an office down the hall. This way."

I sit in the chair he offers me, decline his offer of tea or coffee, and wonder what it is that I truly want to speak about with him.

He sits and I take him in: Solomon's one time class guardian, a tall man with hair still very red, though now marked with streaks of gray. A fire extinguisher hangs on the wall behind his desk, given to him by Solomon and his classmates at their graduation along with a play name in the Native tradition: He-Thinks-So-Hard, His-Head-Is-On-Fire.

"I saw Margaret at this past Christmas Fair," Paul says as he settles into his chair. "She said she had heard from Solomon a few months earlier."

I nod. "From Wales, I gather, on his way to Ireland. It was the first news we had had from him since he left Vancouver."

"And he's home now, in his village?"

"That's what Margaret has told me."

"And how are things for you?"

So, the preliminaries are over. "For me? I'm not so sure. Unclear. Uncertain."

"How so?"

I glance over at the fire extinguisher. Everyone in the hall had laughed when Juliet and Solomon gave him that gift. Margaret had laughed. I had laughed. When was the last time I laughed like that?

"How so? Because that's just the way it is right now. Do you remember speaking to me at Solomon's graduation about a book?"

"Yes, I do."

"You said you had been thinking about lending it to me ever since Margaret's outburst to me at the Christmas Fair that school year, when she informed me that she was my wife and not a tour guide into Aboriginal reality."

"Yes, I remember her saying that. However, it was more something in what I heard you saying that prompted me to speak with you."

"And what did you hear?"

"A sense of loss. A loss of communion—the words you used—with the world around you. And in that sense of loss a touch of despair, perhaps with a question not yet swamped by despair."

I look away for a few seconds. Then I bring my eyes back to his and to the concern that now fills them. "You have a good memory."

"I was moved by what you said. And you're not alone in feeling the way you do."

I cross my legs and fold my hands in my lap. "I wasn't ready for that book when you offered it. I think I might be now."

He stands, goes to a bookshelf, and brings the book back to his desk. I take it from his hand as he sits, a small book with a light pink cover: *The Philosophy of Spiritual Activity.*

"Rudolf Steiner. The man who started the Waldorf schools," I say as I open the cover and find the title page.

"Yes. He wrote the book in 1894, when he was thirty-three years old. How old are you, Cameron, if you don't mind my asking?"

"Thirty-eight. Why do you ask?"

"That time of life can be a rough passage. Things often fall apart."

"Did they fall apart for you?"

"Yes. I had to deal with a glass house or two that I'd been living in."

"Glass houses. That sounds familiar. Did Steiner ever live in a glass house?"

"Yes. In fact, he discovered that we all do. It's the condition of our age. His quest was to understand why that was so, and find a way through the glass without simply shattering it."

"Without shattering it. And that's possible?"

"Steiner thought so. It's like a Zen koan: Getting the goose out of the bottle without breaking the bottle. Steiner had a Zen quality about him."

"And how did he go about getting the goose out?"

"By asking a Zen kind of question: Who put the goose in the bottle in the first place?"

"And that's what this book is about?"

"Yes, in essence."

He observes me as I scan the table of contents: The Fundamental Desire for Knowledge . . . The Activity of Knowing the World . . . Are There Limits to Knowledge?

"I'll take this book, Paul, if you're still willing to loan it to me. It might even help me in a course I'm teaching at the present time."

"And what course is that, Cameron?"

"I'm calling it "The Inside of History." It's the first time I've taught it and I'm taking a risk in doing so."

"What kind of a risk?"

"The risk of discovering that history has no inside. So then, may I take this book with me?"

I look at him directly as I ask, and see the concern in his eyes deepen into a question, like a question in the eyes of a doctor who has handed his patient a medicine that could either cure or kill him.

What's the matter, Paul? Are you afraid I won't understand Steiner's words? I flash him my best easy-going smile.

"I'll read the directions on the label carefully, Paul. I promise."

He laughs and relaxes. "No doubt you will, Cameron. Take your time with the book and bring it back when you're done with it. You might want to start with Chapter Two."

I close the book and look about his office. A picture of Solomon's class hangs on the wall beside the door. "Do you stay in touch with Solomon's classmates?"

"Yes, a number of them, as well as I can."

"Anwar, the boy standing in the last row of that photograph, was killed in the Gulf War. Or so I heard."

"Yes, he was. His family went back to Iraq a year after he graduated. His mother wrote me about his death."

"Those were good years," I say after a moment. "I miss having those young people around."

Paul sees me to the door. As we shake hands, I can still see the concern and question in his eyes.

I arrive home in the late afternoon to find that Margaret is not there.

Where is she? And then I remember. Alan is starting Sunday evening services. And why is Alan starting Sunday evening services? Perhaps he just can't wait for Lent to begin.

Lent. The season you spend on your knees, repenting. Lent, the season of the Litany.

From all evil and mischief . . .
Good Lord, deliver us.

From all blindness of heart . . .
Good Lord, deliver us.

. . . from all the deceits of the world, the flesh, and the devil,
Good Lord, deliver us.

From long nights with Lance,
Good Lord, deliver us.

From the glass houses that hold us fast,
Good Lord, deliver us.

I shut the voice down, make a pot of tea, and let the tea stew until the liquid is nearly black. Then I pour myself a mugful, and take the mug and the book into my study.

From the wall above my desk, the print of Sisiutl stares down at me. The two heads extend outward from the central face in opposite directions, as if each wants to distance itself from the other as far as possible, and from the grimacing centre that would hold them together. No meeting of faces around the moon's curve here, in contrast to Solomon's carving upstairs.

I open *The Philosophy of Spiritual Activity* to the chapter Paul had recommended, The Fundamental Desire for Knowledge, and begin to read. When the chapter ends, I look up at Sisiutl for a long moment, and then read through the chapter again, more slowly, pausing at the sentences with the telling verbs.

Then I close the book, go to the window and open it. The day's end breathes itself into my study. Balancing on a telephone wire, two crows insult one another. To the west the sun is ready to let go of the day.

We separate ourselves from the world as soon as consciousness lights up within us . . .

As soon as the light is let loose from Raven's beak—

Is it, then, the light itself that does the separating, as well as becoming the skin of separation? But if not, what or who does the separating? Uses the light to enact the separation? The Raven? No, not the Raven, unless . . . unless the Raven and I are one.

I have estranged myself . . . I have torn myself away—

Who put the goose in the bottle? Who placed a pane of glass between the world and myself, then fixed my face in it?

And if I have done it to myself, is it then possible that I can dissolve the pane of glass? Release the goose from the bottle? Live here and now in a skin that no longer holds two worlds apart?

Is it possible? If so, do I really want to know that it's possible?

My question startles me. And then I see clearly the question in Paul Kane's eyes. Not, will you understand this book, Cameron? Not that, but, once you do understand, what will you do then?

Cameron stands at a lectern to the left of downstage centre, facing the audience, as if he is addressing a lecture hall filled with students. Behind him, upstage centre, is a dresser with a mirror attached, beside which Margaret stands. Between the dresser and the lectern stand two chairs facing one another.

At stage left, Cyril sits in an armchair. At stage right, Lance sits beside a campfire. A tent is pitched behind the fire.

A light comes up on Cameron at the start of the play, while the rest of the stage is dimly lit. Light comes up on the other areas of the stage whenever the character there addresses Cameron or when Cameron leaves the lectern to move to that area, and dims down again when the action leaves that area. The light on the lectern dims down whenever Cameron steps away from it.

Cameron: *(As if lecturing.)* This may have the appearance of a survey course, because we will explore a diversity of historical phenomena. Phenomena: that's what we call events, situations, whatever, when we haven't a clue what each has do with any of the others.

So then, we will cover a lot of ground in . . .

No, forget I said that about covering ground. We're not going to cover anything. What I want to do with you is to uncover, if we can, the interconnections between historical phenomena. Uncovering—that's what we'll be about, penetrating the surfaces, going beneath, behind, under, around those reflections of ourselves that we call historical events, to glimpse something more . . . if we can, if we are permitted. Yes, permitted. Though you may ask, who gives us that permission? Or withholds it?

(He pauses to think about his question, then continues.) In any event, we will attempt to do what I have just indicated. There will be papers to write, as always, and there will be an exam when the dust of our efforts finally settles. As always. There's always an exam of some kind to be reckoned with, isn't there?

The light on Cyril brightens. Cameron goes on, as if speaking to someone in the audience.

What? What will be on the exam? I can't say, because the truth is, I don't know what will be on the exam. We'll have to see, won't we? As we go . . .

Cyril laughs softly. Cameron turns to him.

Cameron: And what are you laughing at?

Cyril: Oh, I don't know, Cameron. At you, I suppose, for being so in earnest. And at them, for being in earnest about one thing and one thing only: the exam. We want to pass this course, so just give us the exam and the final mark, and the credits. And the diploma, so we can get on with life, whatever the lives might be we are so intent in getting on with. Spare us all those wisdoms you want to sandwich in between what really matters and just hand us the exam.

It took me long years of teaching to hear that, but the message has finally gotten through.

Cameron: *(Gesturing toward the audience.)* And that's it? You really think that's all it means to them?

Cyril: *(With a comparable gesture.)* Does it matter what I think? Or even what they think, when they think? *(He takes out a pipe and tobacco pouch, and begins to stuff his pipe.)* So, Cameron, tell me more about this new course of yours. What did you finally decide to call it?

Cameron: The Inside of History.

Cyril: The Inside of History? A rather pretentious title, don't you think?

Cameron: Cyril—

Cyril: I know, I know. Your everlasting quest to get inside the inside of it all, to suss out the reality behind the mirror image. Well, go to it, if you must. But why impose your quest upon your unsuspecting students?

Cameron: Because they might be interested. Because they might find they have questions of their own they have never dared to ask. Because they just might want to know—

Cyril: The exam, Cameron. That's what they want to know about. And the course mark, and the credits, and the diploma.

           The light begins to brighten on Lance and to fade from Cyril.

Cameron: I heard you the first time, Cyril.

Cyril: But you don't listen, Cameron—

Cameron: I heard you! *(He turns away from Cyril, gripping the lectern.)*

Lance: Don't shout at me, Cameron.

Cameron: I'm not shouting at you.

Lance: Then who are you shouting at?

Cameron: At him. *(He crosses over to the fire, squats down to warm his hands at the flame, then sits.)* At Cyril.

Lance: Cyril. Your professor friend. The one with the chalk up his ass.

Cameron: Did I say that about him?

Lance: Yes, you did.

Cameron: I don't remember saying that about him.

Lance: You said it in a moment of passion, Cameron. Passion and memory don't always mix.

Cameron: Then I guess I said it. *(Pause.)* It chills me sometimes, talking with him.

Lance: *(Smiling.)* That's the difference between him and me.

Cameron: *(Also smiling.)* A big difference. There's nothing chilling about you.

Lance: *(Opening his arms to Cameron.)* Come here.

Cameron settles into Lance's embrace as Lance enfolds him from behind. His head comes to rest upon Lance's shoulder.

That's better, eh?

Cameron: *(Softly.)* Yes, that's good. It's always good.

Lance: *(His arms tightening about Cameron.)* It'll get even better when we close those tent flaps for the night. *(Cameron presses closer to Lance, then falls silent.)*

Lance: What are you thinking about now?

Cameron: Am I thinking?

Lance: You're always thinking, about something, or nothing. It goes with your turf.

Cameron: I was thinking how good it would be to put it all down. Let it all go.

Lance: Then do it. Let it all go. Soar to the sun, like the Eagle.

Cameron: Like the Eagle?

Lance: Like the Eagle. He doesn't need all that bullshit down below. He wouldn't come down at all if he didn't have to eat. Of all beings made by the Creator, the Eagle flies closest to the sun and the sun gives him its rays as feathers. Let it go, Cameron, and lift off like the Eagle.

Cameron: *(Dreamily.)* Yes, I'd like to do that.

Lance: Then let's do it. Let's go away, together.

Cameron: Go away? Where?

Lance: Not to the rez, that's for sure. You'd never survive there. If the broken toilets didn't get to you, the politics would. That's what kept me drinking.

Cameron: Then where would we go?

Lance: A cabin, somewhere in the Rockies. I can even think of one or two waiting to be occupied. A cabin just big enough for the two of us.

Cameron: Sounds like paradise.

Lance: It's not paradise, Cameron. Neither of us are innocents. But it would be close enough. What about it?

Cameron: *(Pause.)* I'm married, Lance, and I have a job. I have students to teach.

Lance: *(Laughs.)* Married? Is that what you call it? I bet you don't even remember when you last made love to her.

Cameron: *(Evading him.)* And what about you? You're training to be a spiritual healer, remember?

Lance: That'll come, in its own time. Besides, Wesley likes to take his time in leading a person into that kind of work.

Cameron: Wesley? He's your teacher, right?

Lance: Yes. I met him in AA.

Cameron: I thought I'd have to go to AA a while back. Then I quit on my own.

Lance: If you quit on your own, you weren't in that much trouble yet. I couldn't have quit on my own.

Cameron: *(After a few seconds' silence.)* Does Wesley know about us?

Lance: *(Now evading him.)* I don't know. I've never told him.

Cameron: Would that matter?

Lance: Matter to what?

Cameron: To your training with him. If he knew about you and me.

Lance: Why should it matter? Stop thinking, Professor, and let's go to bed.

Cameron: *(Standing up.)* In a minute.

Lance: Where are you off to?

Cameron: To take a good long piss. Before we go to bed.

He crosses the stage, toward the lectern, as the light comes up on Margaret.

Margaret: Cameron—

Cameron stops at the sound of her voice and looks at her as if seeing someone once known but long ago forgotten. Then he steps up to the dresser, looks in the mirror, and adjusts his tie.

Cameron: Yes, Margaret?

Margaret: Where are you going? This is the third night this week you've gone out.

Cameron: I have an evening class, Margaret. You once took an evening class of mine. Remember?

Margaret: How could I forget? *(She watches him.)* What are you doing?

Cameron: Straightening my tie. I have to look good for all those eager minds.

Margaret: Did you do that when you taught me? When you knew I'd be sitting there, looking at you? Drinking your words in?

Cameron: *(Flashing her a smile.)* Of course, I did. I always straightened my tie for you, Margaret. *(He turns to leave.)*

Margaret: I bet you did. Where are you going when you finish your class?

He pauses at her words but does not reply. He goes to the lectern and straightens his notes.

Cameron: Where to turn next? Herodotus may be as good a candidate as any. Herodotus, the Greek historian who wrote about the Persian Wars, yet who was as interested in the Persians as he was in the Greeks. In fact, Herodotus was interested in just about everything—places, names, myths, traditions, bits and pieces of that conflict few others would even have noticed. And why this interest? Because Herodotus was convinced that there are reasons for what happened and why, and that he could bring the bits and pieces together in a way that revealed the grounds for human action . . . if only he could think it all together.

Yes? *(He pauses, looking in the direction of the audience.)* Will that be on the exam? Well, I suppose if anyone deserves to be on an exam, Herodotus would certainly qualify. Does that answer your question? Sort of, you say. What do I mean by thinking it all together? Well, I might get around to that if you'd stop worrying about an exam that doesn't yet exist—

Lights up on Cyril, who is laughing and shaking his head as he listens to Cameron.

Cameron: *(Turning on him.)* All right, Cyril. What's your problem now?

Cyril: You, Cameron. And Herodotus. "Think it all together!" Give them a break. Please.

Cameron: And what's wrong with Herodotus?

Cyril: Herodotus was a child. Myth, legend and history so sloshed together, like a bad English pudding, that he hardly knew where one ended and the other began. And what did he turn up in the end?

All the pre-Socratics were children, Cameron. Daring children, beautiful children, I grant you, but they walked on air presuming they could know what held the world together, that there was a golden thread running through all things to all things. It was a hunch, Cameron, and nothing more.

Cameron: All right, it was a hunch. Isn't that where we all start from, a hunch? A hunch that if we take one more step into the dark, something true will light up—

Cyril: Until you discover that the light is but a reflection on the wall of a cave, even though that reflection may take the form of a scientific or artistic triumph worth a lifetime of examination for its own sake.

Cameron: Don't do this to me, Cyril!

Cyril: It's just that we've had this conversation before, Cameron.

Cameron: We have had conversations before. We have not had this conversation before, in the middle of this course. Don't box me in, Cyril—

Cyril: I wouldn't dream of boxing you in. It's this thinking-it-all-together box you're building that worries me.

Cameron: It's not a box, Cyril. It's a way into and out of the box. A way of getting the goose out of the bottle, and placing both the goose and the bottle into a single, coherent picture—

Cyril: And you think all this has something to do with Herodotus?

Cameron: Yes, I do. He was out to paint a big picture, into which everything could fit together: myth, historical fact, gossip—

Cyril: An illusion, Cameron. A tragic illusion, which Socrates shattered, thank God!

Light up on Lance, who is listening in. The light on Cyril begins to fade.

Cameron: That's just my point! Socrates shattered the picture, and perhaps he had to do that. Perhaps the shattering was necessary there and then. But he did it, Cyril, just as we still do it. We do the shattering, not some errant divinity or nameless fate. Which means that we can put the pieces together again. Can't you see that? If I think the world apart, then I can think it back together. Herodotus—

Lance: Who the hell is Herodotus?

Cameron: *(Staring blankly out into the audience.)* Who is Herodotus?

Lance: Over here, Cameron.

Cameron looks over at him, then crosses the stage to the fire.

Lance: *(As Cameron sits beside him.)* I've heard of Socrates, but who is Herodotus?

Cameron: Herodotus was a person who kept track of the history of his people.

Lance: Like a winter count.

Cameron: In a way . . . yes, you could say that.

Lance: Where did he live?

Cameron: In Greece.

Lance: Then he must have used a sheepskin to keep track of all that history.

Cameron: He used the pages of a book. But perhaps it comes down to the same thing. He also tried to understand what he was setting down.

Lance: It sounds like he was some kind of elder.

Cameron: Yes, in a way.

Lance: Did he think about things as much as you do?

Cameron: He thought about many things.

Lance: Then maybe that's how it got started.

Cameron: How what got started?

Lance: The way you people think about things. Maybe it started with your elder, Herodotus.

Cameron: *(A few seconds' pause.)* You think we think too much?

Lance: Maybe. Or it could be the way you go at it. You worry things with your thinking until they come apart. Then you don't know what to do with the pieces.

Cameron: You put that well. I should say it that way to my students.

Lance: Why? Do they want to know that?

Cameron: I once thought they did. Now I'm not sure. Perhaps I'm the only one who wants to know.

He leans into Lance, and Lance puts his arm about him.

Lance: Christ, you're chilled to the bone! Every time I take hold of you I have to warm you up. Maybe it's the work you do, Cameron. It could be time for you to do something else.

Cameron: Yes. I should change everything around. Or put it all behind me.

Lance: Sounds good to me. We might be getting closer to my
            cabin in the mountains.

            Cameron does not respond. A brief silence.

Cameron: When can we do another sweat?

Lance: In the tent, tonight. We always work up a good sweat in
            there.

Cameron: That's not what I had in mind.

Lance: *(He loosens his arm from Cameron, then rests himself on one
            elbow and pokes at the fire with a stick.)* Why are you so hot to
            do another sweat?

Cameron: Because I've been looking for the sweat lodge all my life. I
            can still remember that first time the door dropped down.
            The light was erased. Darkness wrapped itself around me,
            darkness and the glowing of the stones, the glow of the world
            at its first creation, or even before that. And the cradling heat,
            blessing me, releasing me . . . from me. And then . . .

Lance: And then?

Cameron: The door opened and daylight flooded back in. I went out,
            made my offering to the fire, plunged into the creek—

Lance: And we met.

Cameron: Yes.

Lance: After the cold water brought you back to yourself.

Cameron: Yes, back to myself . . .

Lance: It's supposed to do that. Take the sweat and everything
            you've sweated out of you away, and bring you back to
            yourself.

            Lance pauses, but Cameron is silent.

            But that's not enough for you, is it? You'd like to stay in
            the lodge with the flap down forever, close to paradise.

Cameron: You're the one who spoke about living close to paradise.
            About letting everything go and lifting off for the sun, like
            your friend, the Eagle.

Lance: So I did. Maybe it wasn't so smart of me to say that. *(Pauses.)* You say you've been looking for the sweat lodge all your life. You also told me you'd been looking for me all your life. Am I enough for you? What are you looking for, Cameron, really? Me? The sweat lodge? Or a doorway to some world other than this one?

Cameron stands and walks to the lectern. He straightens his tie, then his notes.

Cameron: That last, tragic voyage of Henry Hudson is a case in point. Hudson sailed late in the summer of 1610 through what was later to be called Hudson Strait into the bay that now bears his name. Perhaps his voyage was fated from the outset. *(He pauses.)* Yes, fate—a concept we've considered in other contexts, as well.

However, I am more inclined to weigh some poor choices into the balance, such as a dubious crew ill-disposed toward Hudson from early on in the voyage.

Yet for all that, consider the shock this man must have suffered when he came to himself at the bottom of James Bay and knew, knew beyond a doubt, that he had not sailed through the Northwest Passage into the Pacific Ocean, but had penetrated a massive womb—

(He stops short, realizing what he has just said. Then continues.) Yes . . . yes, that is an apt image. A metaphor, a colleague of mine would call it. Hudson had penetrated a great, watery womb, to find . . . to find there was no way through.

(Light up on Margaret, as Cameron glances out into the audience.) Yes? You don't like that image? Ah, I see. You don't care about the image in itself. You just want to know whether it will be on the exam. Well, why not? Indeed, I'll put it on the exam, just for you.

Margaret has walked from the dresser to one of the two chairs. She stands behind it, her hands upon its back.

Margaret: Cameron—

Cameron: I'm in the middle of a lecture, Margaret. What is it?

Margaret: Don't be late home, please. We're having dinner tonight
            with Mavis and Cyril, and Alan. Remember?

Cameron: A dinner date with Alan, my rector and priest. How could
            I forget?

Margaret: Cameron, please don't! Making friends in the parish has
            been hard for Alan. You know that. He feels comfortable
            with the four of us.

Cameron: Does he? Have I made Alan feel comfortable? Well, I must
            rectify that. After all, a good Christian mustn't feel too
            comfortable in this world of woe, especially if he's a priest
            charged with bringing comfort to his flock.

Margaret: Cameron, please. Just don't be late.

            The light fades from Margaret, as Cameron continues his lecture.

Cameron: I apologize for the interruption. To return to the crisis of
            Henry Hudson, we must also look at the bigger question
            of the search for the Northwest Passage in itself. We
            wanted to force our way through this continent, complete
            the grand circle of our movement westward and return to
            where it all began, our archetypal point of departure, of
            which the East is, perhaps, a metaphor.

            Yes, we wanted to return, but then our Henry gets himself
            stuck in that womb of a bay. Now he knows: there is no
            Northwest Passage. There is nowhere to go from here, but
            here. It was a knowing enough to drive a person crazy,
            and that's what happened to Hudson. He began to crack.
            Then came winter and the blinding sun on the snow and
            ice. The blinding light of winter struck down into that icy
            womb, and all Hudson could see reflecting back at him
            from every shoreline of that bay was his terrible knowing.
            The mirror image of his stark, knowing face.

            Perhaps if Henry had taken a raven on board he might
            have lived. Ravens had led a few Vikings around the
            North Atlantic some centuries earlier. Did you know that?
            (He looks about at the audience.) Well, did you? If not, you
            damn well should know it, and you can bet that will be on
            the exam. A raven can cruise at five thousand feet in

altitude and can see land ninety miles distant. That will be on the exam, too.

Light up on Cyril.

But Hudson had no raven to lead him out of his blinding bay, and when I think of it, why should any raven have bothered? Why should the first bird off the ark care about someone stupid enough to have sailed into that bay in the first place?

Cyril: Going on about ravens, Cameron?

Cameron: *(Turning slowly toward him.)* Was I? Yes, I suppose I was.

Cyril: Do you remember an evening at your house, with Alan? And a conversation that began with "Consider the ravens" and ended with your going after him about abuse in residential schools?

Cameron: Yes. I pushed him hard.

Cyril: I was going to smooth things over with a story about a raven, but my wife cut me off. Remember?

Cameron: No, not really.

Cyril: No matter. I'll give you the story anyway. It may fit into your interesting course. Pliny tells of a raven that lived with a Roman cobbler. The bird journeyed every morning to the platform facing the forum to greet the Emperor Tiberius, and the generals and senators. One day, however, the raven dirtied the cobbler's stock with its droppings one time too many, and the cobbler killed it. The citizens of Rome rose up, drove the cobbler from the district, and gave the raven a grand funeral. They draped the bier with flowers. Two Ethiopians carried it, and wreaths and a flute player preceded it. Amid the praise of its fellow citizens, the raven was buried near the field of Deus Rediculus, the God of the Return Journey.

Cameron: And what does your story have to do with my course?

Cyril: What does it have to do with your course? Well, superficially, the raven died and Hudson died. The cobbler killed the raven and Hudson's mutinous crew killed him. Historical parallels, you might say. Then, in contrast, the raven was buried with pomp and adulation, and Hudson . . . Hudson, for all anyone knows, sank into the obscurity of the bay that now bears his name. But, in fact, my ridiculous little story has nothing at all to do with anything.

Cameron: Then why did you tell it?

Cyril: Because it is a story that has nothing to do with anything other than itself. Anymore than your story of Henry Hudson has anything to do with anything other than itself. Give it up, Cameron. You're looking for meaning where there isn't even a metaphor.

Cameron: You're wrong, Cyril. Hudson is more than a metaphor. He chose to be there, in that icebound bay, staring at himself staring at himself.

Cyril: Of course he chose to go there. Who would dream of contesting that point?

Cameron: Not go there, Cyril. Be there. Hudson chose to be there—

Margaret: *(As the light comes up on her and fades from Cyril.)* Cameron . . .

He turns away from Cyril, slowly, puzzling out where the voice is coming from.

Margaret: Cameron!

Cameron: *(Now wheeling about.)* Do not shout at me, Margaret! *(He walks to the chair facing the one she stands behind and puts his hands on the chair back.)* Now, what do you want?

Margaret: Who is she?

Cameron: I beg your pardon?

Margaret: Who the hell is she, Cameron?

Cameron: I don't know what you are talking about, Margaret.

Margaret: There is another woman in your life, Cameron. I feel her around you every time you walk through that door from wherever you have been with her. I want to know who she is.

He looks long at her, then sits and crosses his legs.

Cameron: There is no other woman in my life.

Margaret: I don't believe you.

Cameron: And I don't give a damn whether or not you believe me. There is no other woman in my life.

She stares back at him. Then she sits.

Margaret: Then what is going on? You're lying, but you're not lying. You're not lying, but you are. God, O God, what is happening to us? What am I seeing? What am I feeling?

Cameron: I don't know, Margaret. I don't know what you think you see, or feel.

Margaret: Then, where do you go when you're not here?

Cameron: I've told you more than once. I go to sweat lodge ceremonies.

Margaret: With this new friend of yours, Lance.

Cameron: Yes, with Lance. Lance Thunderchild, my Native friend.

Margaret: I guess Thunderchild is a Native enough name. But who is he, really, and why haven't I met him?

Cameron: Well now, Margaret, I didn't think you were interested in meeting fellow Indians.

Margaret: That's not fair!

Cameron: It seems fair enough to me, after all these years. As for your first question, Lance is training to be a spiritual leader.

Margaret: A spiritual leader. I see. And who are his people?

Cameron: What do you mean?

Margaret: Who are his people? Is he Cree? Haida? Salish? Iroquois?

Cameron: I don't know who his people are, Margaret. He's never said who his people are.

Margaret: Ah, I do see. A generic Indian spiritual leader. Well, where can I find out more about him? Has he got a business card? A web site? Does he—

Cameron: Stop it, Margaret! Stop pissing on something that has become important to me!

Margaret: And who are you to talk! You piss on things all the time. You piss on Alan whenever you can. You piss on me, just because I won't be who you think you want me to be. Do you realize how often you mock at and piss on things, Cameron? You didn't do that when I married you, because I would never have married you if you had.

She stands, walks to the mirror and gazes into it. Cameron watches her for a few seconds.

Cameron: And what do you see in the mirror, Margaret?

Margaret: I don't know. I don't know what I see, other than a very confused woman. (*She turns to him and leans her back against the dresser.*) You know, if I had thought, just once, that you wanted to know the world from which I came for its own sake—for its own sake, and not just to make use of it for some end of your own—I might have told you more than I have.

Cameron: How could you tell me about a world you've rejected?

Margaret: Maybe I would have told you my reasons for rejecting it, if that's what I've done. Have you ever considered that I might have had reasons? And whether my reasons might give you a picture of my world somewhat different than the one you have made up for yourself?

Cameron: Margaret, I did want to know! I asked; I even begged and pleaded with you—

Margaret: To give you the picture of my world that you wanted to have. Not the world in which I actually lived. You want to live in a world of your own making, Cameron. Maybe we all do. I just wish you would own up to it, that's all.

Cameron: Do I, Margaret? And what do you know of the world in which I wish to live?

Margaret: More than you might think. And it scares me, what I know.

Cameron straightens the seam on his pants, stands and walks over to the fire, as the light comes up on Lance and fades from Margaret. Cameron sits beside Lance as Lance stares into the fire.

Lance: I've been thinking, Cameron.

Cameron: I thought I was the one guilty of thinking.

Lance: Well, I've been thinking, too. And I'm thinking we should call it quits as lovers.

Cameron: *(Stunned.)* Are you serious?

Lance: I'm serious.

Cameron: But why?

Lance: Because I'm no longer sure about you. And because I want to stay sober, which may be harder to do if things start to go wrong between us. *(Laughs.)* Maybe I should get together with your wife and get some advice on how to handle that.

Cameron: I don't think she could help you that much, even if she would.

Lance: You might be surprised, Cameron.

Cameron: So you don't love me anymore?

Lance: Wrong. I do love you. But I don't want loving you to wreck my life, and maybe your loving me, or wanting to, is getting in the way of something you need to do. Something bigger than you or me.

Cameron: *(Pauses.)* Yes, perhaps you're right. Perhaps there is something bigger that I'm putting off.

He stares into the fire as Lance looks at him with concern. Then they both fall silent for a few seconds.

Lance: *(Placing a stick on the fire.)* You wanted to do another sweat. I've arranged for that.

Cameron: *(Not looking at him).* Thank you.

Lance: You'll have to drive into the interior. I'll tell you the way.

Cameron: You'll be there?

            Lance does not reply.

Cameron: *(Softly.)* I want you to be there, Lance.

Lance: *(Pauses.)* Yes, I'll be there.

Cameron: I love you, Lance.

Lance: I hear you, Cameron. I love you.

            Cameron stands and walks to the lectern as the light fades from Lance.

Cameron: The killing at Frog Lake—massacre, if you will—happened on April 2, 1885. It was Maundy Thursday, the day of the Last Supper, and the day after April Fools Day, or Big Lie Day, as the Cree called it. History likes little jokes like that.

            Wandering Spirit, Imasees, and others pushed Big Bear aside and moved in on the whites in the settlement in the early hours of the morning. Wandering Spirit herded them into the church for mass, then intervened and refused to let the priests continue. He and the others forced the whites from the church and ordered them to go to the Cree camp. Thomas Truman Quinn refused to go, so Wandering Spirit shot him dead and the killing began.

            The bare facts, starkly told. *(Cameron sets his notes aside and steps away from the lectern. He begins to pace stage front.)* But when Quinn stopped in his tracks and faced Wandering Spirit, what did each see in the face of the other? Everything hinges on that question. What had the whites seen in the Cree faces all that winter long? And what did the Cree see in those white faces? What image of themselves that they could no longer escape or endure?

            Cameron's pacing becomes more determined. He is no longer speaking only to his students, perhaps hardly at all to his students. Instead, he is feeling out his words for that thread of meaning upon which his life depends.

            And what did the Cree see when they looked out into that

world fast closing in upon them? What did it mirror back to them? You're trapped, just like these white minds that think they can go anywhere, do anything with anyone, and don't know their own glass cages. The Cree said, we don't choose to live in your glass cages, and so they struck out, tried to break out, but couldn't—perhaps because they had begun to live in cages of their own.

(He stops, considers.) Yes, that is a crucial question. Had the Cree and the whites become merely mirror images of one another? Which brings us to Auschwitz—

Cyril: *(As the light come up on him.)* Auschwitz? Come now, Cameron, aren't you stretching history a bit?

Cameron: *(Snapping the reply over his shoulder.)* More than a bit, Cyril. *(He returns to the audience.)* Yes, I know. This is all becoming more difficult than I had anticipated. But we do have to ask, what did the Jews see in the faces of their killers? And the killers in the faces of their victims? When we stand at the doors of the gas chambers, we must ask, what did each see in the face of the other?

Cyril listens intently to Cameron, becoming more and more agitated as he listens.

And what about the gas chambers themselves? Were there mirrors on the walls of the showers? Perhaps that is the final, terrible question we must ask. Did those condemned men, women and children die knowing that each of their faces would be etched forever in those mirrors?

For there are such moments, long before we ever reach the shores of Frog Lake or the gates of Auschwitz—moments when we know the images of ourselves will not vanish from the mirror when we turn away, but become more real than the transient selves that placed them there.

Well then, what about Jesus? *(Pause.)* You look surprised. Why so? Jesus was a historical figure. Let's give him that much. So, we come to Jesus, and to the question, what did they see in the face of Jesus as they were killing him?

Cyril: *(In exasperation.)* Cameron, please! Are you giving a class in history or religion?

Cameron: *(Responding as if the question came from the audience.)* Yes, damn it, this is still a history class! *(Pause.)* It is simply that the crux of our inquiry is here. Right here. What did his killers see in the face of Jesus? Only their fear of him? Their faces full of themselves, did they see him at all? And even more crucial, what did he see as they were killing him?

Is it possible . . . ?

Taken by the very thought he is trying to grasp, Cameron stops pacing.

Is it possible . . . that this one man had the courage to see his killers for who they truly were?

I don't need a cage of glass to protect me and neither do you. Is it possible that Jesus was saying—?

Cyril: Stop it, Cameron!

Cameron: Look at me and behold the man. Behold your true faces. Not mirror images of them, but—

Cyril: Stop it, damn you! Stop it!

Cameron: *(Leaning on the lectern as he turns casually to Cyril.)* Excuse me, Cyril, but do you have a problem with my line of thought?

Cyril: You know not what you do.

Cameron: Ah, I think I do. I know very well—

Cyril: *(Now calm, but with great conviction.)* No, you don't. Do not do this to yourself, Cameron, and *(gesturing toward the audience)* do not do it to them. In the name of God, do not. It's not bloody fair! In fact, what you are doing is downright cruel.

Cameron: *(Leaving the lectern and walking stage left, to the far edge of Cyril's space, where he folds his arms and looks outward.)* I don't understand, Cyril. Please enlighten me.

Cyril takes his pipe from his jacket pocket and, his hands trembling, begins to fill it from his tobacco pouch. Then he stops, cradling his pipe in his hands. His words begin quietly, but with intense concentration.

Cyril:

I was in my third undergraduate year, and I decided to take a philosophy course. Epistemology. Can we know? What can we know? How do we know we can know? That kind of thing. It would be something different, I told myself, from all those required courses in English.

The teacher was a young professor, new to the college, and a good person. Naïve, but good. He liked his students and would ask us to his house for meals, which his pretty, young wife cooked, and the wine was just so. And he would include some of us on walks with his young children. As we walked, he would tell us what he thought he knew and acknowledge what he did not yet know. But, like you, he believed that there need be no panes of glass between whatever reality there is and ourselves. No Kantian limits need stand between us and whatever truth or meaning we seek.

He believed it, Cameron, as you want to believe it. And I believed him. I know now that he simply looked out at the world through his own pane of glass, but neither he nor I saw that at the time.

One of my professor's colleagues, however, did see.

Now Cyril stands and walks to the lectern. Cameron watches him, and then sits in the armchair, continuing to listen.

It happened at an evening lecture, which was open to anyone who wanted to drop in for that one class. And this colleague decided to drop in. My professor was holding forth at a lectern much like this one when this colleague stood up at the back of the classroom, stopped my professor in his tracks, and in fewer sentences than I could have thought possible smashed apart the pane of glass my professor hadn't known he had been holding.

It was horrible enough to watch that glass disintegrate into cruel, cutting pieces that struck my professor everywhere. But then—and this was all the more horrible—this colleague took pieces of glass in hand and finished my professor off. Before our eyes, colleague cut colleague to ribbons, and all we could do was sit and watch it happen.

Cyril walks from the lectern to the far edge of stage left, where Cameron had been standing. He looks out at the audience, though not at the audience, but at the remembered image of that night.

And the most horrible thing of all, Cameron, was that my professor didn't know he had been cut to ribbons. He gathered himself together, thanked his colleague for his contribution, finished the class, and walked out the door, not yet realizing that he was finished as a teacher on that campus.

Cyril pauses. Cameron rises from the chair, goes to the lectern, and looks out at the audience as Cyril continues.

Despite my shock at what my professor's colleague had done, I was grateful for it, because I realized he had done all of us a service, even though he may have done it in a terrible way. I left the lecture hall that night knowing that I want that pane of glass to be there, between myself and whatever reality there is or is not—if for no other reason than to see my image of myself and know that I exist.

Cyril returns to his chair, sits, and continues to stuff his pipe. His final words are matter-of-factly delivered.

If Jesus tried to take the glass away, Cameron, he deserved to die. And if he has forgiven us for killing him, then we can be the more grateful and get on with our lives, as your students want to get on with theirs.

Don't play God, Cameron. Don't seduce them into thinking their world can be other than it is. If you care a damn about them, don't—

The light on Cyril begins to fade with his last words, as the light comes up on Margaret. She stands downstage, in front of the two chairs, gazing outward.

Margaret: There's a full moon tonight, Cameron.

Cameron: Yes, I see it.

Margaret: We used to fish for oolichan in the full moon, when I was a girl. My brother David and I would wade out into the river with our dad and our uncles. Solomon came too, though he was Nathan then. He would wade out as far as he could, and little Frank would follow, trip on a rock in the riverbed, and go splashing facedown. It's hard to believe we netted any fish with all that splashing going on.

Mom would crisp up last summer's half-smoked salmon on the beach, and we all thought that was the best feast ever.

I loved to fish in the moonlight. The moon was softer, kinder than the sun was. The whole of my life was softer, more rounded, then.

Cameron: We made love once, on a beach, under the full moon.

Margaret: I remember. It was glorious, and so good.

Cameron looks down at the lectern, then begins to straighten his notes.

Margaret: It's Holy Week, Cameron. That's the full moon of Easter.

Cameron: I know.

Margaret: And you're going away.

Cameron: Yes. When I've given this last lecture.

Margaret: Don't go, please. Not this time.

Cameron: I have to go, Margaret. Lance has arranged a sweat for me and I have to go.

Margaret: Cameron, please.

Cameron: I have to go, Margaret, and that's it. Now please let me finish this lecture.

Margaret: Cameron—

The light fades from her. Cameron straightens his tie, then begins.

Cameron: So then, we have come to the close of our excursion into the inner riddles of history. Strange, isn't it, where such excursions sometimes take one? Unexpected things turn up and other things don't turn up at all. I confess that I'm no longer sure just where I wanted to take you. If I ever knew. I'll read your evaluations carefully and rethink the course before I offer it again.

Now, to the exam. Well, it's simple, isn't it? You arrive at the right place at the right time and the exam will be there, waiting for you.

He pauses and stares out at them.

But suppose, just suppose, you arrive and there is no exam to be found. What would you do then? You have lived all semester for the moment of the exam, and there is no exam. There is no mirror to tell you you've passed or failed. Even a failing grade would give you some sense of security, wouldn't it? A failing grade tells you that you exist, even if your existence is a failure.

But to discover that there is no exam at all—that there is nothing worth testing, or that can be tested, but only a question you must put to yourself—what would you do then? What in the world would you do then?

Cameron draws his gaze away from the audience. He gathers up his notes as if to take them with him. He looks at them, then drops them back down upon the lectern. He starts to walk toward the fire, and then stops short. Lance is no longer there. The light comes up on Margaret, where she stands behind one of the two chairs.

Margaret: Cameron—

Cameron: *(Going to the other chair and placing his hands on its back.)* Margaret?

He crossed the Port Mann Bridge just as the sun was setting. Turning off the radio, Cameron drove on in silence toward the darkness that was gathering itself together at the eastern end of the Fraser Valley.

It was Wednesday of Holy Week, and he had left Margaret sitting on the couch, looking at *Transformation #3*, at the Raven's human form forever trying to free itself from that other image of himself in which he was caught.

Last night she had turned to him as he got into bed and placed both hands down the front of his pajamas. Her hands were on fire, and then he was on fire. Their lovemaking continued until they came together with a ferocity that took his breath away. Swept into her by the desperate surge of her passion for him, he gave himself to her—until his mind began to wedge itself between them: Who am I loving? And he began to pull away within himself even as he was pouring himself into her.

Then they lay side by side as a moon already on the wane shone down upon them through the window by their bed. Once, he reached out to touch her, to tell her—tell her what? But she knew and did not respond to his touch. Filled with knowing that she had failed to prevent him from going wherever he was about to go, for whatever reason, she stared up into the darkness beyond the moon's light until they both fell asleep.

By the time he reached Chilliwack, the night had closed in around him except for the last slivers of light that gleamed from the current of the Fraser whenever the river came into view. Past Hope, the mountains at the threshold of the Fraser Canyon surrounded him with a density of their own, until the rising moon cast its first light over their peaks and ridges. As his headlights sought out the lines of the highway that threaded its way up the canyon, he began to think about leaving Margaret.

The tunnels came and went. He crossed the bridge at Alexandria, putting the river to the west of him, and tried to picture leaving Margaret. What would they do with the house? Where would he live? How would they sort out what belonged to whom? And when all of that was done, would he simply jettison his career at Simon Fraser University and go to Lance, wherever Lance was?

More tunnels came and went, until he drove through Boston Bar. Now the moon was fully risen and dropped its smooth, pale light down on the roof of the hotel, the roofs of cafés, gas stations and houses, and then, beyond the little town, on the contours of land that sloped westward to the edges of the canyon. At the canyon's bottom, the river gnawed its relentless way to its mouth, sweeping into its currents anything that resisted it.

The Fraser was a deadly river and many had died in its waters from thinking otherwise. Cameron had heard stories of some who had so died, had read of Indians in communities along the canyon who had driven off ferries into the currents. Drunken deaths, sober deaths, and chosen deaths—the Fraser knew them all and accepted them all without discrimination. He too could choose such a death. All he needed to bring it about was to watch for the moment when the canyon's edge kissed the edge of the highway, cross the centre line and drive through the guardrail that could not hold him back once he had made the choice. Then the swallowing water would rip him free of the car and dissolve all remnant of him by the time it emptied itself into the Strait of Georgia.

He turned in abruptly at a gas station along the highway at Lytton. After filling the tank, he bought a coffee, and, hands numb on the wheel, drove back onto the highway, more slowly now, as the Fraser drew away from him to the north and west. Entering the Thompson Canyon at the point where the Thompson River poured its cleaner water into the gray-brown silt of the Fraser, he remembered the provincial park just up the highway. When his headlights picked out the entrance to the park to his left, he turned down into the parking lot, shut off the ignition and got out.

Cameron stood for a moment in the moon's fraying light, then made his way through the shadowed pines that dotted themselves about the patch of park until he came to the chain link fence that overlooked the Thompson Canyon. He peered over the fence and down the sides of the canyon, slashed with darkness and moonlight, to the dark ribbon of the river itself. Turning away from the river, he leaned his back against the fence and gazed into the sky overhead.

The silence about him deepened, broken only by the occasional sound of a passing car up on the highway. A light wind stirred at the pine needles all about him; the pines sighed in response. In the sky to the south, the moon continued its journey toward that moment when it would fade away, then vanish into the sun, into the darkness of that unforgiving light, to be born anew on the other side of it. But was that birth anything more than the moon's dreary repetition of itself?

Just east of the moon, a point of bright light thrust itself into the night: Jupiter, of course, gazing down upon him as if it would speak to him, as if, this very night, it would disclose a secret long held fast within that brightness.

Well then, speak if you can, if you will, if you have anything to disclose. I won't even care if the message doesn't get to me, or if I don't understand it, as long as there *is* a message and a meaning within that shining of yours.

Margaret had said that he mocked the world about him. Yes, perhaps I do that. But if so, why?

Despair—

Despair of what, Cameron?

Of meaning.

He had never doubted God, or Christ, or that Christ was what two thousand years of Christianity had said he was. Never anything of that. But what did it all *mean*? Where was the inside of it all?

I thought I was getting close to the inside of something, teaching that course. Then the inside of it and of everything, including me, fell apart into just another outside.

From the far side of the canyon the sound of a passing train touched into his hearing. Cameron turned to see the headlight of the engine flickering off the canyon walls. It was a long train; the groaning of the engine told him that. Then as the engine drew away from him, the wheels of the freight cars began to sing. Pressed tightly against the steel rails that led them on, the wheels sang their thin metallic song to the night, and to him. Cameron listened intently to the song, listened for what the song might mean, then gave it up and went back to his car.

The Trans Canada Highway climbed to a crest of land above the canyon, then dropped, twisting and turning, to the level of the river. Holding each curve of the road, Cameron glanced at the torrent of water to his left, white in the moon's glare upon it, as the river reached out hungrily and sucked the fragments of the moon down into itself.

He crossed the Thompson River at Spences Bridge. An Indian reserve lay in the shadow of a line of bluffs to the south, along the Nicola River. Once across the bridge, he saw the gas station and the café Lance had told him to look for.

He parked in front of the café and thought about going inside for a coffee. However, he didn't really want to do that and stayed in the car until the lights of the café and gas station eventually went out. A few figures came from the now darkened doorways, made their way to their cars and drove off. Now his was the only car left. He didn't look at his watch but knew it was sometime just after midnight.

Cameron got out of the car. The glassy-eyed moon was now at its height. Standing alone in a moonstruck desert, with sagebrush-covered bluffs at his back, Cameron drew his gaze away from the high benches of land south of the Thompson River and looked at his watch, to assure himself that he was where he was supposed be and when. Park at the café, Lance had said, and I'll meet you there. But Lance was nowhere in sight and Cameron had no idea where to go to find him. Perhaps there was a motel nearby where the two of them were to go for the night. And then perhaps not . . .

Having wanted to believe for the past six months that he could live in two distinct, even contradictory worlds, Cameron suddenly realized the two worlds could not go on co-existing side by side. He had to make a choice. But in this eerie moonscape that some creator had thrown together, what did it matter which lover he chose? Perhaps Cyril had been right all along. We choose whatever metaphors will make our lives bearable, and one lover is as good as another.

Yet Cameron tried to imagine a choice. Margaret was still young. She would be hurt and angry, but the hurt and anger would pass, and one day she might even thank him for freeing her to find someone else. And perhaps he would get a teaching position in Calgary, if he could persuade Lance to live there. Calgary was close enough to the mountains. As for Simon Fraser University, well, one lecture hall was as good as another. His students didn't need him, and he didn't think he needed them.

Cameron looked again at his watch. It was close to four o'clock, and he was still the only person standing in front of the café.

Then he spotted the headlights in the distance, coming along the Nicola Valley Road. They traveled through the reserve, turned east onto the Trans Canada Highway, crossed the bridge and came toward him. The truck pulled into the parking lot next to his car and stopped.

Cameron sank back into himself. Lance did not drive a truck. Yet the door of the truck opened and a man got out, leaving the lights on and the engine running. The man wore a cowboy hat and boots.

"Are you Lance's friend?"

"Yes . . ."

"Then get in." The man turned and walked back to the truck. Cameron hesitated, then locked the doors of his car.

Inside the cab of the truck, Cameron tried to make out the face behind the wheel: Native, and older than his; a lined and tough and knowing face.

The truck pulled away from the café, back down the highway. They crossed the bridge, then turned onto the Nicola Valley Road. "I'm Wesley. Wesley Drum," the man said.

"Where's Lance?"

"Did you bring a name with you?" Wesley asked, ignoring his question.

"Cameron."

"Cameron McLean, right?"

"Yes. How did you know?"

"Lance told me about you."

"Then why did you ask my name?"

"I wanted to find out if you still remembered it." The truck slowed and Wesley made an abrupt left turn. The headlights snatched a narrow dirt road into view. Groaning, the truck rose up on what was left of its springs to take the first of many bumps to come.

"Where's Lance?" Cameron asked again.

"In a detox centre in Calgary. He went on the drunk of a lifetime two days ago, deciding what to do about you. I'm his sponsor, so the centre staff contacted me. When he'd sobered up enough to loosen his jaw, he told me about the good times the two of you have been having."

The road leading up to the benchland above the Nicola grew steeper. Wesley shifted into a lower gear as he swung the truck around another tight bend and continued to climb.

"And then you drove all the way from Alberta to meet me at Spences Bridge," Cameron said, after a moment's silence. "Why?"

"Because Lance is about as messed up as I've ever seen him. Which means you're pretty messed up, too. I decided someone that messed up was worth meeting."

Cameron drew back into himself as Wesley spun the truck into yet another hairpin turn and smiled thinly into the darkness about him.

You're right; I am messed up.

"Lance says you have a wife. Tell me about her."

What was there to tell? "Her name is Margaret, and she's Native."

"Well now, you truly are into cross-cultural relationships. Where is she from?"

"A Kwakiutl village, up the mainland coast."

"Does it have a name?"

"Duxsowlas."

Wesley took the name in, turned it over, then spoke again. "What was Margaret's last name? Before she got mixed up with you."

"Jacob."

"Ahh! And does she have a brother who stayed with you when he was in high school? He'd be about twenty-five now."

"Yes. Solomon. Do you know him?"

"I know him. He's my cousin, and so is your wife, though she and I have never met. Jacob, as he called himself at the time, stayed with Sarah and me for close to three years, putting his life together after running from the two of you and just about everything else."

With a sharp turn of the wheel, the headlights slashed across a slope of sage before finding another steep grade. Wesley shifted right down, and the truck now climbed with a determined growl somewhere in its bowels.

"Where are you taking me?"

"Lance said you were itching to do a sweat, so we're going to do a sweat," Wesley replied, and then gave himself over to the truck and the road as Cameron settled back into a numb silence.

The road began to level out, high above the Nicola and Thompson Valleys. The truck came over a rise of land into a pale blue dawn filling the sky to the east. Sagebrush grew all about them, and here and there a pine rose up above the patches of snow that still gripped the earth. The road dipped down to cross a small creek, then rose again. Wesley turned off westward into the sagebrush beside the creek and stopped the truck.

The sweat lodge stood northwest of the truck and creek, its doorway facing eastward. A fire burned to the east of the lodge, where a young man stood placing more wood against the stack of stones. Between the lodge and the fire lay a mound of earth. A large ceremonial pipe leaned against the mound, with a smaller one beside it. An eagle feather rose from the top of the mound, surrounded by several packages of tobacco.

Cameron winced as he got out of the truck and saw the mound. He had brought a tobacco offering, but it was back in his car.

"Sit down, Cameron," Wesley said, as he sat in a patch of snow.

Cameron hesitated and Wesley laughed. "It's just snow, Cameron. Give your ass a treat, and let it know it's still alive."

Cameron sat. "I left my tobacco in the car," he said.

"So you've decided to give up smoking. That could be a start," Wesley replied. "Now, what do you want from this sweat, Cameron?"

Cameron looked out at the sagebrush and at a pine standing just north of the sweat lodge. What do I want? I don't know anymore.

"You met Lance at a sweat, right?"

"Yes."

"Then try to remember what brought you there, before you got the hots for Lance and forgot everything else."

Cameron stared blankly into a patch of snow and into the chaos his life had become. Then he spoke. "I wanted to melt away. To become fire, and water. To become what I was when it all began. Before it all began."

Wesley turned Cameron's words over in silence, then brushed some snow together and cupped it in his hand, releasing it bit by bit as he spoke.

"That's a powerful thing you're asking for, Cameron. A very powerful thing. It's good that we heated up some extra grandfathers." Wesley stood. "Get undressed and come to the fire. Sundown will smudge you."

Cameron walked back to the truck, took off his jacket, shirt and pants. As he laid them on the seat, he remembered he had also left in the car the pair of shorts he had brought. Stripped down to his briefs, he looked at the patches of snow he had to cross on his way back to the fire and decided to leave his shoes on.

"Did you change those briefs this morning, Cameron?" Wesley asked as Cameron approached the fire. "If not, take them off and your shoes and socks, too."

Cameron balked at that idea. Wesley smiled. "Don't worry. I have a woman back home that I love dearly and I'm not attracted to men's bodies in the way you seem to be. My interest in you is purely professional. Strip down, Cameron. If we're going to melt the flesh away, then let's make it flesh only."

Cameron complied. The rising sun glanced off his skin as he picked his way through the sagebrush to the fire.

"Sundown, this is Jacob's brother-in-law," Wesley said to the young man. "Give him a good smudge."

Sundown looked Cameron over before taking up the flat stone covered with burning sweetgrass and the eagle feather from the mound. Standing before him, Cameron smudged himself the best he could. He turned his back to Sundown and felt the eagle feather brush the smoke along his back.

"You know my brother-in-law?"

"Jacob. Yes, I know him. Ho!" The feather lifted away from Cameron's back. As he turned and the young man's waiting eyes met his, he remembered. "All my relations," he said.

Inside the lodge, Cameron watched as Sundown brought in the red-hot stones, the grandfathers, and placed them into the pit. Then Sundown placed blankets and a tarp across the doorway, leaving Wesley and Cameron in darkness.

Wesley splashed once for each of the four directions, then continued to splash: For the women. For those on the streets. For those in prisons . . .

The heat started to build. As Wesley began to chant and drum, Cameron drew the heat to him until the sweat ran from the pores of his body. Wesley's voice rose and fell as the heat continued to build. Fire rose from the rocks and licked at the sweat in which Cameron's body swam. Licked, savoured, devoured—

Cameron gasped and lowered himself to the earth. Wesley's hand reached for his, to pass the eagle feather to him, but even though Cameron fumbled for it and found it, no words would come. In the beginning was the Word, yet no words would come. Wesley lifted the feather away, and the door of the lodge opened.

Outside the lodge Cameron staggered to his feet, into the biting morning air and a blaze of sun. Stunned by the heat, he swayed as if he were going to faint. Wesley took him by the arm, led him sunwise around the lodge, around the fire, back around the lodge, and then placed some tobacco in his hand. Cameron dropped the tobacco into the fire; then Wesley led him to the creek and pushed him forward into a pool of water.

The shock of cold drove the fire from Cameron's body. Wesley took him by the arm and led him back into the lodge. Sundown brought in more grandfathers, then closed the door.

For the elders. For the young people. For the confused and messed up ones—Wesley splashed for each as he named them and continued to splash. The heat flared up and gripped Cameron until it drove him to the earth.

Wesley splashed the stones, sang, chanted, prayed and splashed some more. Cameron lay with his face to the earth, consumed by this microcosm of fire and water and word, as Wesley continued to chant. Was this then how it had been in the beginning he had yearned for all his life? Before the curse of embodied life in the world was forced upon him?

But you chose it, Cameron. You chose to be here. Remember?

No, I did not choose this. I chose nothing of this . . .

Cameron began to cry. Wesley chanted and Cameron cried. He wanted Lance, and he didn't want Lance. He didn't want Margaret, and he wanted Margaret. He wanted this self he had chosen to be, and he didn't want it—

The door of the lodge opened. Wesley led Cameron to the creek and forced him into the water when Cameron tried to resist. Coming up from the creek bed, Cameron collapsed on a snowbank at the creek's edge.

"It looks like that heat is going to kill you before it melts you down, Cameron. But let's give it one more try. If you can't take it any more, say, All my relations."

The door of the sweat lodge closed. The pit at the centre of the lodge was filled now with burning grandfathers—our oldest relatives, Wesley said, and they've seen it all—as the first splash of water struck the stones.

For those we love. For those we want to love, but can't. For those we no longer love. For those who love us, even when we don't love them. For our own flesh, and the breath in our flesh. For the fire and water in our flesh—

With each splash, the marriage of fire and water consummated itself, consumed itself, until Cameron no longer knew where his flesh began or ended. Let me go through, he prayed. If only I could go through. If the God I have never doubted exists, let this despair end and let me go through—

But however fervently his spirit prayed, he could not take his flesh through.

All my relations . . .

Was that his voice?

All my relations—

The daylight struck him in the face as Wesley pulled him from the lodge, dragged him to the creek and threw him in.

Cameron tried to free himself from the pool, but Wesley threw him in again. Then again. Cameron came up from the water to feel Wesley taking him by the shoulders. Wesley yanked him from the creek into a bank of snow. Wesley rolled Cameron about, scooping snow over him as he did so.

"Damn! That flesh is stubborn. It's not going to melt away, Cameron. So we'll have to go a different path."

Wesley eased himself down beside Cameron and put an arm around his shoulder. "Are you back in the land of the living? That's good, because we need to talk about where things are at with you. Being messed up isn't much fun, but it's not the end of the road, either. Unless you decide it's the end of the road. Jacob was messed up when he came to us, and he too had to make a decision. You know where he made that decision, Cameron? On the back of a horse, staring down into the black bottom of a canyon and getting ready to ride off the canyon's edge. I was a few yards away as he was deciding, and called him back to himself. But that's all I could do for him—call him back to himself. He still had to choose if he would live or die. If he had chosen to die, one good nudge against the flanks of his horse would have done it, and no one could have prevented that from happening. Are you listening, Cameron?"

Cameron nodded.

"Good, because you're also at the edge of some canyon within yourself. And you too have a choice to make. I'll call you back to yourself, if I can. Then it's up to you. Come over to the fire."

As Cameron sat beside the fire, Wesley dropped a blanket about his shoulders. Then Wesley took up the two pipes that had been leaning against the mound, and sat beside Cameron.

"White Buffalo Calf Woman brought the pipe to my people long ago. The bowl is from the mineral world, and the stem, from the plant world. The eagle feather that hangs from the stem comes from the winged ones of the air and from the one who flies closest to the sun. The tobacco in the bowl holds the fire that brings the pipe alive. That fire lives in us as we walk the earth and love it, and everything about it, even the things that have gone wrong. White Buffalo Calf Woman gave us the pipe so that we could walk upon the earth in a good way, praying as we walk and knowing that the pipe can bring earth and the Creator together, for both are part of us. Both, Cameron—the earth, as well the Creator."

Wesley fell silent, remembering. Then he spoke again. "My grandfather died that summer of 1945 when your people exploded the first atomic bomb, way to the south of here. From then on you have been wanting to blow up the whole of creation, the earth and the sun together. Why? Because you have messed everything up so badly you don't see a way forward? It does seem that's what much of your history has been about, messing up the earth, then wanting to bring the earth to an end or to escape from it to somewhere else. But you can't escape,

Cameron. There's no beginning of things to go back to, so no sweat lodge can take you there. You've got to take responsibility for the mess you've made, for the stinking thinking that made the mess, and start turning the thinking and the mess inside out. Are you a Christian?"

"Yes . . ."

"'Well then, doesn't your religion tell of a God who loves the earth? Of a Christ who wasn't shy of human flesh?"

"I guess so."

"You guess so. Then if so, go home and listen again to your religion. Your people have made many mistakes in the name of your religion, but that doesn't mean your religion itself is a mistake. Do you see this big pipe?"

"Yes."

"This would be the time to smoke it, together. But we're not going to light this pipe now, Cameron, not until you decide whether or not you will find a way of walking this earth. Instead, I'm giving you this smaller pipe. It's filled with tobacco, but the mouth of the bowl is sealed. Take it with you and think about your life. When you have decided to live, bring it back to me and we'll do a true sweat together, smoke both pipes, kill the fatted buffalo and have the feast of our lives. If you choose to live."

Wesley stood and left him sitting by the fire, the pipe in his hands.

He reached Hope by early evening, found a restaurant on the main street of town, and ordered a meal he did not finish. Then Cameron continued to sit in the booth beside the large plate glass window looking out onto the street, and drank tea. The waitresses changed shift and Cameron continued to sit.

He knew he would never see Lance again. Wesley had not told him so, but that truth was implicit in what Wesley had left unsaid.

So he was to go home now. To what, and for what? What was there to live for should he choose to live? Wesley's words had stalked him all the way down the Fraser Canyon and had forced the underlying question of his life into the open.

Was he going to live? And what could it mean to live, here and now?

The street outside the café grew dark, and Cameron looked out through the plate glass into the dark street—into the street and into his own face staring back at him from the glass. Was that face mocking his?

I know you well. But where am I?

"Would you like more coffee, sir?"

He looked closely at her. She was a plump, middle-aged woman who had decided to let her hair go gray. And time had been kind to her face, even though the lines were there with their stories for anyone who took the trouble to read them. Standing at the end of the booth, coffee pot in hand, she smiled at him as she would smile at whoever sat in his place, even if the world about her were falling into ruin.

"I've been drinking tea," he said.

"I can bring you a fresh pot of tea."

"Thank you, but I've had enough. I won't be here much longer."

Something flashed up in her eyes as she observed him and listened between the lines. "Stay as long as you like," she said. Her eyes said the rest: I've seen you here before, many times over.

Just before ten he turned back onto the highway. The Fraser Valley towns drifted past him: Chilliwack, Abbotsford, Langley, Surrey, and then he crossed the Port Mann Bridge. The lights of Burnaby flowed together into an extended blur all the way to Hastings Street. He turned left, turned right onto Renfrew, and drove northward until he came to Trinity, his street. He turned onto it, drove two blocks and parked in front of his house.

He sat in the car a long moment before getting out. As he locked the car door, he looked closely at the house. Something wasn't right. The lights were on. It was close to midnight, yet the lights were on.

Margaret—?

Cameron hurried up the steps and opened the front door.

Margaret sat on the couch, where she had been sitting when he had walked out the doorway yesterday evening, still gazing at *Transformation #3*. But something around her had changed. *Transformation #3* hung upon the wall where it had hung since he had placed it there, but everything surrounding it was different. What?

Then, as his eyes swept along the walls, he knew. The walls were empty. His prints were no longer there, the prints by Bill Reid, Robert Davidson, Norval Morrisseau, Art Thompson and others. They were no longer there.

Cameron's eyes moved down the walls. Splinters of wood lay all about the floor; splinters of glass lay all about the floor; shreds of paper, now meaningless, lay on the floor all around him.

Cameron sat on the couch beside Margaret and stared at the fragments of his life.

Daylight finds the two of us picking up the pieces. We go about the task carefully, with no words between us. Together we pick up the pieces as if this is the most important work either of us has ever done.

The whole time, each of us knows exactly where the other is, in which direction the body of the other is about to move, as we place the splinters of glass and wood, with the shreds of paper, into the big buckets I have brought in from the shed at the back of the house. Never before have we been as knowing of each other's bodies as we are during these hours.

Then Margaret makes tea. We sit, without speaking, and drink the tea she has made.

Shortly before noon she leaves for the Good Friday service at St. Cyprian's, and I am left alone in our house.

What does she know? I ask myself as I stand at the sink washing the cups and saucers. But what does it matter what she knows, when the fragments of our life together fill three buckets that stand in the corner of the kitchen beside the door?

April first. Good Friday. The Big Lie Day . . .

Time is the lie. Life is the lie.

I hang the dishtowel on a rack beside the sink and go into the living room. The pipe Wesley has given me lies on the couch. Taking it in hand, I walk into my study, place it on my desk, then sit. The bowl is of reddish brown stone, rising up from its base. The wood of the stem is of a tawny grain, and a single feather dangles from it. An eagle feather, perhaps. The bowl is sealed and is to stay sealed, said Wesley, until I decide to live and to walk the earth in a good way.

Setting the pipe to one side, I take up the book that has been lying on the desk, *The Philosophy of Spiritual Activity*. I have read it through twice, and several parts more than that. Beneath what at times seems to be abstruse philosophic language, the thrust of Steiner's meaning is devastatingly direct and clear.

I, through my thinking, have pulled the world to pieces. I, through my thinking, can bring the pieces together once again, not into a disjointed collage, but into a whole that has meaning—if I choose to think that such thinking is possible.

The print of Sisiutl still hangs on the wall above my desk. You missed this one too, Margaret. I wonder why.

Standing, I place a finger on the glass that covers the print. The two necks and heads of Sisiutl stretch away from either side of the central face and from one another. From the central face of Sisiutl, my face stares out at me, a face strained from trying to hold it all together. A face begging for release.

The tomb is the question and death is the answer . . .

I take *The Philosophy of Spiritual Activity* and place it alongside the pipe, resting a hand upon each.

Will I roll the stone aside and live?

I close my eyes and a picture begins to form. I am twelve and I am standing on the rocks at Peggy's Cove. I look down into the living, tossing water, and see nothing of my own image but only the living water. At my ear my grandfather tells of a well in the depth of the sea where the five salmon wait for the nuts of knowledge to fall from the nine hazel trees.

In the depth of the sea . . . where I once glimpsed a light . . . where the five salmon wait for Sinaan to eat of the nuts of knowledge and for me to go where I can live . . .

Because, I decide, I am no longer willing to live here and now. There is not enough of me left to do that.

I walk into the kitchen and search through a bucket until I find a shard of glass that looks as if it will do the job. Taking it from the bucket, I test its edge.

Where am I going to do this? The upstairs tub. Why not? It's not Peggy's Cove, but it will do.

At the foot of the stairs, I stop. Do I leave a note? What is there to say?

Then I remember the pipe, and the book.

I return to the kitchen and take a scrap of paper that was once part of a Bill Reid print. Back in my study, I write on the back of the paper scrap:

Margaret,

I'm the one who smashed my life to pieces, not you.
The pipe belongs to Wesley Drum. He's your cousin and lives in
Alberta. Solomon can tell you how to find him. The book
belongs to Paul Kane. Please return it to him.

Cameron

Bringing the pipe and the book together, I place the note on top of them.

At the top of the stairs, I gaze for a moment into the room that had once been Solomon's. Going into the bathroom, I undress, drop my clothes to the floor, and run warm water into the tub. I know it has to be warm water.

The water fills the tub, then becomes still. My image looks up at me from its depths.

Your powerful grandfather asks you in . . .

Then I lower my body into the tub, into the story that has waited for me.

Don't think. Do it.

I slash one wrist, hard and deep, and then the other. The glass slips from my hand as my wrists sink into the water and the streaming forth of my blood takes me through the skin of the Xhaaidla and into the depths where the five salmon wait. Tail first I let go of myself, to go with the streaming out of my blood into the depths that wait for me . . .

But the salmon are not waiting in the depths. Now fully within the streaming out of my blood, they swim toward me, swim past me, toward the sound of something beating, like the beating of Wesley's drum—

My heart. The beating of my heart calls out to me and with it, the last of my grandfather's words: *The river took Sinaan out to sea, but the well of the heart was what she was truly seeking.*

I begin to swim against the streaming out of my blood, but the stream of my blood rushes relentlessly past me toward its gashed open mouth. Fighting the current, I swim for the heartwaters of my life before the current runs out.

The crimson flow crests about me on its way to the endless sea, and I gather myself into myself for that one, last leap—

The letter is waiting for me when I come home from work, the only one that has found its way through the mail slot.

The handwriting on the envelope is my brother's. The stamp tells me it has come from the United Kingdom; however, the return address in the upper right hand corner of the letter isn't in English.

Sitting on the top step of the porch, I open the letter. It's late in the day, but I'll be on my own for dinner and I'm in no hurry. Cameron announced this morning that he was off to a sweat lodge somewhere north of Squamish—or the Arctic Circle, maybe—so I can take all the time I want to read this missive from Nathan Solomon.

I study the words at the head of the letter: Eglwys Lleu . . . Trwyn y Gwyddel . . . Pwllheli . . . Gwynedd, and then a postal code. Then I read on:

Dear Margaret,

Forgive me. I was aiming for me but took a shot at you instead. Not the first time I've done that. I don't know what I knew about Cameron, but it wasn't enough that night to make of it what I did . . .

Three years and two nights ago, the day the army and the Mohawk warriors took down the barriers on the Mercier Bridge. Now everyone on the south shore could drive straight to Montreal once again, as if the long summer of Oka had been only a bad dream.

My brother had been watching it all on TV since the middle of July, as if the drama in the Pines were a replay of his own life. That night he shut the TV off and gave me hell for not caring about any of it. I gave him hell right back for not putting his life where his words were. Then he suggested that Cameron had been out somewhere, putting himself into another woman, and I threw my teacup at him. Now he wants to tell me his words were more hot air than anything else.

93

I go on reading. So then, we have a sister, Erin, and Erin had a twin, Caitlin, only Caitlin is dead. Well, Dad, good for you. You got two for one with that pretty Welsh teacher who dropped in on Duxsowlas those many moons ago. Only it's one for two now, it would seem.

And we have a cousin, Wesley, only it sounds as if he wasn't ready for relatives to come walking into his life.

Ireland? Why Ireland, little brother? And then you say you'll go back to wherever all those Welsh words are and figure out what to do next.

A word of love to Cameron and me, and that's it.

My, my, Nathan Solomon—only you don't sign off with either name, just "Your Wandering Brother"—you do get around the world, looking for your grail.

I fold the letter and put it back in the envelope. The day around me is letting go of itself, letting the darkness in, but is not gone altogether. In these last hours of the first day of September, my husband is in a sweat lodge somewhere to the north of me, sorting out his life, and my brother is crossing the Irish Sea, figuring out his. In the meantime, "Forgive me," he says.

Forgive you, little brother? I don't know about that. But tell me, if you were aiming at you, not me, at which of your nine lives were you aiming? And how did you find your way to a relative in Alberta? Or even know we had a relative in Alberta?

What family secrets do you know that no one has ever told me? And on which side of the family are the secrets hiding? Mom's? I don't think so.

I get up, go inside and find the chapbook that I had hidden away in a line of books along the top shelf of a living room bookcase: *The Spirit of Haida Gwaii*, by Bill Reid. I take it with me out onto the porch where I have left my brother's letter, sit, and open the book to the flyleaf. A scraggily drawn raven stands on nothing at all and glares at the suggestion of a sun placed toward the upper right hand corner of the page. The words to my brother hover just beneath the sun, and below them is Bill Reid's signature.

I look at the picture, the words, the signature, and go back a year to a December evening. Cameron has taken me to an art gallery on Georgia Street. It's a benefit, he tells me, and Bill Reid will be signing prints that have become posters.

The night is clear and already filling up with stars. A moon nearly

94

full floats in the sky to the east. The mountains north of Burrard Inlet stand out clearly as the snow on them reflects the moon's light.

Inside the gallery, people mingle, including Native singers and dancers, some of whom make speeches. That's Robert Davidson, Cameron whispers in my ear, and names one or two other prominent bearers of Northwest Coast culture that he recognizes. Several of them glance with interest at my Native face, but I am already looking past them, at Bill Reid. He sits in a wheelchair, a blanket wrapped around his shoulders. Affected now by Parkinson's disease, his hand shakes even as he moves the pen as carefully as he can on the posters people bring for his signature. I walk closer and see that he is not only signing his name, but making little drawings, as well.

Looking about for Cameron, I see him engaged in conversation with a chiefly looking person who listens patiently. That's good, I guess. I decide I am not going to buy a poster and add yet another specimen of Northwest Coast art to my husband's gallery. That means I don't need to spend any money, or maybe I'll just make a donation.

I mull that possibility over as I stand at a bookrack toward the back of the gallery. Then I see the chapbook, tucked away shyly amid other, larger books. I take it in hand, the only copy of *The Spirit of Haida Gwaii*, and open it. The drawings by Bill Reid are of the figures in the canoe cast in black bronze that now sits in front of the Canadian Embassy in Washington, D.C. The text is also by Bill Reid, telling about each character of this journey transfixed in a moment of art.

I read the book through, to its closing words: "The boat goes on, forever anchored in the same place." Then I take it to a woman standing at a nearby desk, pay for it, and join the line of people waiting for Bill Reid's signature.

The person in front of me gets in a few more words before he turns away. Then I am standing before the man sitting in the wheelchair. His white hair sweeps away from the top and sides of his head, and his eyes are large and alert and filled with the readiness to give the pain its due but nothing more than its due. My heart relaxes and begins to open.

"Hello," he says.

"Hello. Would you sign this for me, please?"

He smiles as he takes the book. "This is easy to work with. Thank you."

"I don't need a poster."

He smiles at me again. "Nor do I."

"I'm Margaret Jacob. My father was Isaac Jacob. He came from Haida Gwaii. Maybe you knew him."

Why am I telling him this? What business is it of his who my father was? And why should he care?

But now he is looking closely at me. "You're Isaac's daughter?"

"Yes."

"I knew your father. He was a good carver." He pauses, still looking at me. "And he was a good human being."

And why did you feel you had to say that? I want to ask. But I merely nod.

"Your father's Haida name was Xuuyaa Gut-ga-at-ga. Did you know that?"

"No, I didn't. What does it mean?"

"Raven Splitting-in-Two."

Raven Splitting-in-Two. So what's that about, Dad? Anything more than wanting to love two women at once and tearing at least one of them in two while you did that?

"What should I write in your book?" he asks.

What?

"Draw a raven, please," I say.

And he does. His hand shakes as he exerts himself to control the shaking. The finished raven looks as if it has had a bad night in a garbage container and is ready to tell the world just how bad it was.

"Who is this raven for?" he asks.

"For my brother. Solomon."

"Solomon. Is he wise?"

His eyes twinkle up at me.

"I hope so," I answer.

He writes, To Solomon, and then looks up again. "And what else?"

My eyes tell him I don't yet understand.

"What else should I write to Solomon?"

What else?

"Chasing the sun," I say.

The twinkle in his eye deepens as he writes, Chasing the sun. Then he draws in the sun, above the words, and signs his name beneath it all.

He hands the book back to me. "Thank you," I say.

"Thank you, Margaret. I hope your brother and you find what you're looking for."

Then he gives his attention to yet another poster, and I step away.

Cameron is waiting for me at the entrance to the gallery. I had expected him to buy a poster and have it signed, but there is nothing in his hand.

"What did you buy?" he asks, as we go outside.

"Something for Solomon. If he ever comes back."

"Did Bill Reid sign it?"

"Yes."

I know he wants to see what I have bought, but I decide not to show it to him just then. I know I am being cruel, yet in that moment I choose to be cruel. I put the chapbook in my handbag and wait for Cameron to take me home.

Now I sit on the porch, gaze at the book in my hand, and realize I have never shown it to my husband. I stare up at the moon before I put my brother's letter in the book and go inside.

She stood in the kitchen, the receiver still dangling from her fingers, although Aunt Minnie had hung up a moment earlier. Your Adha is sick, very sick. We're bringing her to the hospital in Vancouver next week. Maybe you could come and see her. End of conversation. Auntie was never one to speak words unnecessarily, especially in the few phone conversations Margaret had had with her since she had left Aunt Minnie and Uncle Slim's home in Port Hardy at the age of eighteen.

So, Nathan Solomon is on his way to Ireland and my grandmother is on her way to hospital, and maybe her deathbed. What next?

Margaret sat in a chair at the kitchen table, started to rub at her eyes, and then stopped herself from doing that when she remembered the contact lenses that pressed tightly against her eyeballs.

I should go back to wearing glasses. These things are starting to irritate me, and who cares how I look now. Not my husband, it would seem.

Cameron had come home yesterday afternoon from his sweat lodge. The ceremony, as he called it, had gone on well into the evening. All of which was fine enough with her, only . . . only there was something that tugged at her about the way he had come home. At one time he would have wanted her to know about what had gone on in the lodge, about anything he had done that was remotely connected with things Native. Even if she had begun to tell him she didn't want to know as much as he wanted to tell, he would have at least started in on the telling.

But this time Cameron had said very little. It was a good experience, he said, and that was it for his day in Indian country. Then he had left early this morning, to go to SFU to prepare for the classes he would begin to teach next week.

But why do you need to prepare, Cameron? You open your mouth and the words start flowing like milk and honey. At least they were sweetness in my ears, those long years ago.

She straightened herself against the chair back. It was the same chair in which she had sat three and a half years ago after a similar call from Aunt Minnie.

Your mom died last night, Auntie had said.

It was Nathan Solomon's twenty-first birthday. He came home from SFU to find her sitting in the chair and sat down opposite her. They talked of going back to Duxsowlas before everyone else they cared about died on them. And then she told him she had never fully forgiven their mother for letting their father get away with loving himself into the teacher who dropped into their lives from Wales—the mother, it now seemed, of Caitlin, the dead sister, and Erin, the living one.

And there had been another night, some years earlier, when the two of them had sat late into the night at this table, after Nathan Solomon and his classmates, then in grade ten, had been rapped over the knuckles for the disruption caused by their extra-curricular pool playing. That night he had told her for the first time why he had left Duxsowlas: sexual abuse, more than she had known about the day she had left her village never to return, two years before her brother had left.

Margaret closed her eyes.

She is fourteen and this is the day she is to be confirmed. The bishop has arrived from Vancouver, and the whole of the village, except for her Uncle Charlie, has gathered in the schoolhouse for the event. Uncle Charlie will have nothing to do with the church, but then Uncle is a grouch, so who cares what he thinks.

She sits in the front row of chairs. Her cousin Billy Boy sits at her left, looking as if he wants to be somewhere else and would even die to go there. Auntie Lila, however, has been unrelenting. Billy Boy will be confirmed, even if being confirmed kills him.

Mary Silas sits to her right. Mary is her best friend, and Mary is as close to the angels as anyone she knows. "I'm going to become a holy person," Mary had said two days earlier. "I'm going to give myself up to God."

"Well, don't get so holy that I'll have to run a ladder up to heaven to find you."

"You won't need a ladder, Maggie, because you'll be a holy person, too."

"Getting confirmed isn't going to make me so holy, Mary."

"You'd be holy, Maggie, even if the bishop didn't confirm you. It's who you already are."

"I don't think so. I've too many mean thoughts crawling about in my head. So let's not get carried away about holiness."

Their families watch as the three of them kneel before the bishop: her mother and father, Nathan Solomon, now eight, and little Frank. Their older brother, David, watches warily from the back of the church. Mary's parents, Hazel and Harvey, also watch, as do Steve, Mary's brother, and her little sister, Naomi, Nathan Solomon's girlfriend. But Pam, Mary's older sister, is not there and has not come home from Port Hardy for two years. Why? Margaret wonders. Why doesn't Pam come home?

The bishop lays his hands on Billy Boy's head. As she waits for the weight of the bishop's hands upon her, Margaret's gaze penetrates the walls of the schoolhouse. She sees herself walking away into some distance she cannot yet fathom—walking away, her body unbending and her head refusing to look back.

Now she is seventeen, in grade eleven, and she stands with Mary in the park at Port Hardy. The rain pelts down on them, on the water of the bay beyond the park and the mud flats. But they are both oblivious to the rain as they square off against one another.

"What are you doing, Mary?"

"Living my life. So get out of my face, Margaret!"

"Why, Mary? Why?"

"Why what, Margaret?"

"You know what? You've become the resident whore of the high school. You want to get laid? Go to Mary. You want kinky sex? Go to Mary. She'll give you whatever you want and a thing or two you would never have dreamed up on your own. What do you charge, Mary? Or are you the Salvation Army of love?"

"Fuck you, Margaret—you righteous bitch!"

"What happened to my friend who was going to become a holy person? Where did that holiness go?"

"You really want to know? My father fucked it out of me! And out of Pam, and your brother David."

Then Mary's face collapses into the rain as her body crumples to the earth. Margaret goes to the ground with her, into earth gone to mud. Grasping Mary's sobbing body, she holds her friend to herself as her own tears begin to come.

Tell me, Mary! You have to tell me, goddamn it! Tell me—

A year later she went home for the Easter holidays. She stood in the kitchen with her mother, filleting salmon while her two younger brothers sat in the living room. As the knife in Margaret's hand cut into the fish with an intensity that brought a rebuke from her mother, the words in her chest could no longer be contained:

For Christ's sake, Mom! Can't you see what's happened to Pam, and Mary? And to David?

Don't you tell me what I can see or can't see!

Deny, deny, deny! That's how you live, that's how everyone here lives. Go to the potlatches, go to church, go through the motions, and always look the other way. Well, I'm tired of looking the other way . . .

She had packed what she wanted of her life there in her bag and spent the night with Sadie Moon, until the plane came for her the next day. All that long night Margaret sat on Sadie's couch and wept into her bosom. Sadie cradled Margaret and wept too. In all her years at Duxsowlas, Margaret had never seen Sadie weep until that night.

She opened her eyes and looked at the clock on the wall beside the stove. Cameron would be home soon, but there might be time enough to start a letter to Nathan Solomon. She looked for a sheet of paper, then for a pen, and started to write:

Dear Wandering Brother,
 You may have been aiming for you, but you sure hit me where it hurt. I've been trying to forgive you . . .

She put the pen down. Forgive you, little brother? I've spent the last years of my life trying to forgive more people than I want to think about. You're now one more on my list, and I don't know where to start. Where and how do I start forgiving?

The letter to Nathan Solomon stayed in its unfinished state all weekend. Margaret moved it here, then there, as she went about doing housework and anything else that needed doing.

"What is that bit of paper about?" Cameron had asked yesterday, as she slipped the letter in between a phone bill and the newsletter from their church. He had come into the kitchen suddenly as she had been looking at it, and her response had been as sudden.

"It's a letter to my brother," she said, even as she realized she could be setting the fuse to a powder keg.

"To Solomon?"

"Yes. He's in Wales, on his way to Ireland."

"Then you've heard from him?"

She nodded. "A letter came the day you were in Squamish." Her hand settled upon the phone bill, and she waited for what might come next. If he wanted to read the letter, she would say no, and then there could be a fight. They had fought about far lesser matters in recent months.

But he simply asked, "How is he?"

"Fine enough, I guess."

"When is he coming back?"

"He didn't exactly say."

"Say hello for me," said Cameron. And that was it.

Now Margaret opened the drawer and took the letter out. It was Labour Day, and Cameron had driven up to SFU just before noon.

"When will you be back?" she had asked.

"When I'm back."

Letter in hand, she walked into the living room, sat on the couch, and looked up at their wedding photograph on top of the bookshelf. Margaret stared at herself looking out at herself. God, I was so young, and so in love. What was I thinking of that day I walked into his office and told him I loved him?

For a while it had been a joke between them. "You chased me, remember?" he would say, as he reached for her and then took her. Yet she had decided as she sat in the lecture hall and caught him looking at her that she wasn't into it on her own. You're in love with me, Dr. McLean. You may not know it yet or want to know it, but you are.

At least that's what she had told herself and wanted to believe.

To her left stood the friend she had lived with in Port Hardy after she had moved out of Aunt Minnie's house. The friend she hadn't seen in years.

To Cameron's right stood Cyril Elspeth, Cameron's friend, colleague and aspiring mentor. Cyril smiled benignly at the camera and at her, as if being Cameron's best man had been one of the better deeds in his life.

The wedding done, the McLeans and the Elspeths had become friends. They invited each other over for fine dinners, went to certain events together, as Cyril continued to smile benignly, smoke his pipe, and be the good godfather to the younger couple.

And yet . . . what was it about Cyril that made her uneasy, every now and then. It was only now and then, but the nows and thens had a way of coming on her unannounced. It might be the way Cyril spoke as he stuffed his pipe, or something behind his eyes as he looked at Cameron, something that didn't square with the godfatherly smile.

"What's he like as a teacher?" she had asked Nathan Solomon once.

"He has his own way of seeing things," her brother had answered, "and that's all right. It gives you something to think about." Then he stopped speaking in a way that told her there might be something more to be said.

"But what?" she pressed.

Her brother smiled. "It's just that he's the sort of teacher that can take you only so far. Maybe because he himself can't go any farther . . ." He paused again.

"And?"

"And maybe he doesn't like it when someone wants to go farther than he can go."

She looked again at the unfinished letter: Dear Wandering Brother, I've been trying to forgive you . . .

But forgiving people doesn't seem to be something in my life that I've been very good at doing.

Alan had spoken about forgiveness in his sermon yesterday and had seemed to know what he was saying, although she had caught herself wondering if he had ever done anything for which he needed to be forgiven. Even so, she stayed with him.

Those who stand in need of forgiveness are those who can best forgive others. Those were the words that had gotten to her.

So then, for what do I need to be forgiven? What am I missing in all of this?

She stood up, letter in hand, and climbed the stairs to the room that had been Nathan Solomon's. Sitting at the desk, she opened the drawers, one by one, until she found the one she wanted.

Tunneling her way through the pile of books and papers, she found the essay she had remembered. Taking it in hand, she read the title: "The Healing Question and Why Parzival Didn't Ask It."

Nathan Solomon had written the essay in grade eleven for a main lesson on a medieval epic, but had become very reticent about it all as the main lesson went on, and had never shown her the paper. However, she had asked him once, what the Parzival story was about.

"Wounds, and wounding, and maybe forgiveness," he had said.

Margaret turned to the back page and looked at the grade and comment by Candace Waverly: "Thank you, Solomon, for trusting me with what you have written."

Above those words were ones her brother had written: "Mrs. Waverly, please don't show this to anyone else."

She turned back to the first page and began to read:

When Parzival first comes to the Grail Castle, he doesn't ask the question the wounded king needs from him. Why? Because Parzival is missing something in himself.

What is Parzival missing? That is the question for this essay, and maybe for my life.

The opening words were measured and careful, as if the writer were about to tread either on holy ground or ground aflame with peril, or both. Then the words began to pour forth:

Parzival had everything going for him. He was strong. He was beautiful. He had a beautiful wife, and his fellow knights esteemed him. Yet when he came to a person, his uncle, as he found out later, who needed a question from him, Parzival couldn't ask it.

What ails you, Uncle? That was the question. Why couldn't Parzival ask it? Maybe because he had never really suffered or failed at anything. How can a person who has never failed at anything ask someone who knows he has failed, what is hurting you?

Margaret turned the pages. Now the words were no longer the words of an essay, but a cry from the heart of a student to his teacher:

You talked in class about the Grail moon. You said that Parzival's name, who he really was, was hidden in that dark circle until he was able to shine a light on that place from earth and make his name visible. Even though you didn't quite say it like that, that's the way I heard it.

Well, that's where my name is, too, in that dark place, but I can't get to it because I am angry at someone—someone who hurt a member of my family and was about to hurt another member of my family. That someone is my uncle. So I know where Parzival is living when he rides away from the Grail Castle. In hell, that's where he's living, and all the success and esteem in the world can't change that.

That night at the kitchen table, when her brother was in grade ten, he had told her about their uncle and what he had come to believe about their uncle: Uncle Charlie was about to abuse their brother Frank and had probably abused David.

Margaret could say nothing about Frank, but Uncle Charlie abusing David? Harvey Silas had abused David, as he had abused Pam, then Mary, and who knows, maybe Steve and Naomi, too. But Uncle Charlie, an abuser? That didn't fit, somehow, though she had said nothing that night at the kitchen table.

Margaret turned another page:

So I ask myself, am I the person to bring a healing question to my uncle? But how can I do that if I feel only anger toward him and no compassion? Does someone need to stick a sword into me, or do I need to hurt someone I love, before I'll find that something that is missing in me?

Well, then, does Cameron need to cheat on me, or do I need to cheat on him, before I can get on with the forgiving I need to do?

She went on reading:

The story says Raven is the colour of hell. If so, then maybe Parzival needed to go through hell, hurt people who are related to him, to learn that they are related to him and what they need from him.

The Grail feeds people, whatever anyone wants to eat. Raven would like that, because he eats just about anything. But I think the Grail needs something from Raven, because Raven knows things the Grail doesn't know. The story says that Dove and Raven, the light and the darkness, have been split apart. Parzival had to bring the two together, to bring Raven to the Grail by making mistakes and shaming himself. Because he learned about Raven in himself, he could see through Raven to the Grail in a new way and find his way back to the castle with the question his uncle needed.

There were two concluding paragraphs but Margaret did not read them. She put the essay back in the drawer, took up the letter to Nathan Solomon, and went downstairs to the kitchen table. Pen in hand, she continued the letter to her brother:

. . . I've been trying to forgive you, and I guess I've covered some ground in doing that.

Along the way I've had to face some things about Cameron and me. I don't know how far I've gotten with that either, but it's time I looked at it straight on . . .

Then she told him about Adha's illness, and before she knew how it happened, she was writing about their Uncle Charlie:

. . . the only abuser I knew of when I left Duxsowlas was Harvey; he was the one who had abused David. I never warmed to our uncle, and he was a grouch much of the time, but an abuser? I wonder about that now.

She finished the letter, found an envelope and then a stamp. The sun was setting as she walked up to the mailbox on McGill Street and dropped the envelope through the slot.

Auxw!

Margaret looked up at the solitary speck of blackness and tried to remember when she had last seen a raven in the city. Yet there it was, winging westward in the high blue above her.

Chasing the sun.

I pause just inside the entrance of the Chinook Park Waldorf School on the Saturday of the Christmas Fair. I haven't been in this building since the day of Nathan Solomon's graduation.

Last night Aunt Minnie phoned me to tell me my brother had returned to Duxsowlas.

"When did he come back, Auntie?"

"Just before Halloween."

"Ooh! He didn't call me when he came through Vancouver."

My aunt is silent before she speaks. "No, I guess he didn't."

Well, thank you for the news, Auntie. And thank you, little brother, for not thinking of me! I guess you had other things on your mind.

"Hello."

I wake up to the young woman standing before me and know that I know her.

"I'm Sandra Carleton. I first met you the day Solomon came for his interview, in grade nine. Perhaps you don't remember."

But I do remember that day, seeing the fire hall that housed the high school as I crossed the street with Nathan Solomon and Cameron: *A high school in a fire hall? I don't know about this, Cameron . . .*

"Yes. I remember you. You were the one who disappeared down the fire pole before I could even say hello."

Sandra laughs. "I was quicker on my feet in those days. Have you heard anything from Solomon?"

Seeing something in my eyes, she goes on. "Sigune and Alex tell us they haven't heard from him for over three years, and neither has Izzy. We're planning a class reunion in June and we want him to be there, if he can get here from wherever he has gone."

"He went all the way to Wales and Ireland," I say, "but I've just heard that he's arrived home in Duxsowlas. Maybe some carrier pigeon can get word to him about your reunion."

She studies me, not sure what to make of those last words. "That would work for me," she says. "I want to see him again."

"So do I," I say, and then leave her, to go into the room where the handcrafted goods are for sale. I find the table filled with dolls and look them over one by one, picking this one up and setting that one down. Finally, I buy one with dark brown pigtails and tanned skin.

You could be a mix of just about anything, I say to the doll, as I tuck her into a bag and wait for the woman behind the table to give me my change.

So, why have I bought you? Is my womb tired of waiting for you to come in that way?

I make my way to the grade two classroom and into the tearoom, where it had been set up seven years ago when Cameron and I came to our one and only Christmas Fair during Nathan Solomon's time in the school.

Three people have just abandoned their table, and I sit down at it, placing the bag with the doll in it on the floor beside my chair. A high school student comes over to me and I order a cup of tea. When it arrives, I drink it slowly and remember that other Christmas Fair. Cameron was sitting with me at a table in this room, and then Paul Kane, Nathan Solomon's class guardian, joined us.

Even now, Cameron's words echo in my ear, spoken as he looked at a child's painting of St. Francis and the Wolf of Gubbio: *It must have been a wonderful thing to have had that kind of communion with an animal. Where did it go? I think the aboriginal peoples may be one of the few who are still in touch with that world . . .*

And then I turned on him: *Cameron, I am your wife. Your wife. Not a guide back into some aboriginal paradise you have dreamed up and which I have never known. And even if it did exist, I would not live there, or go there, even for the sake of taking you—*

"Hello, Margaret."

I look up and see Paul Kane standing at the table.

"Hello, Paul."

"It's good to see you after all these years. May I sit down?"

"Yes, do."

He pulls his chair up to the table. "Have you heard from Solomon?"

"That seems to be the question of the day. Yes, he wrote me from

Wales sometime in August, and he's now back at Duxsowlas. Or so I've been told."

"And have you heard from him since he's come back?"

"No. The only other news I've heard from what used to be my home was the word of my grandmother's death, late in September."

"From what used to be your home? You've not gone back to your village?"

The directness of his question nudges me off balance, but I recover and answer him just as directly. "No. Never."

He leans back in his chair, as if waiting for me to go on.

"Can I bring you something, Mr. Kane?"

The high school student appears beside our table and waits. Paul smiles and shakes his head. "No, Linda, but thank you, anyway."

"Okay," she says, and then she is gone.

Paul sits, waiting, and then I hear myself speaking: "Do you remember the last time you and I sat here, in this tearoom, with Cameron?"

He nods, and waits.

I straighten myself in the chair and place my elbows on the table, my startled eyes mirrored in his. I had not intended to open that door, but I have and am about to go through it.

"After blowing up at Cameron and leaving him here, I went into your hall and wondered at all those lovely dolls. My grandmother made me a doll when I was little—my mother wasn't sober enough in those days to make me much of anything—and then I lost it in the river. The water wasn't very deep where I was standing, but it was spring runoff and the river was moving fast. The doll slipped from my arms and the river took it right away from me. Someone tried to give me another doll later on, but that doll that the river took was the only one that could ever have been truly mine.

"So there I stood years later, in your hall, grieving for the doll I had once had and lost, and hearing inside my head my husband grieving for a world he had never had but somehow felt he had lost. And I asked myself, how can someone grieve over the loss of something he has never possessed? And how can he do that in such a way that makes me feel like shit because I can't give it to him?

"You know, Paul, I wanted to buy one of those dolls, even though I couldn't for the life of me think of a person to give it to other than me. But I didn't buy one, because I couldn't. How could I make up for my loss when I couldn't do a damn thing about the loss my husband felt?"

Then my words run out into the silence that hangs between us. He looks at me for a few seconds more, then at the bag by my feet and the head of the doll that sticks out from it.

"Is that the doll you might have bought on that day?" he asks.

I allow myself to smile. "Maybe."

"And how is Cameron doing now?"

"All right, I suppose. He's excited about a new course he plans to offer at sfu next term. And he's started doing sweat lodge ceremonies, which I guess is good."

"You don't sound convinced about the sweat lodge ceremonies."

I shrug. "Don't I? Well, maybe I'm not so convinced."

"At Solomon's graduation, I offered to lend Cameron a book," Paul says. "However, he has yet to take me up on it."

"Has he ever come back to the school to visit?" I ask.

"No."

"That's strange. Cameron was the one who got very excited about Solomon coming here. He'd come home from parent meetings full of what you and other teachers had said."

"And you weren't so excited about Solomon coming here?"

I blink at the question and then let myself smile. "No, I wasn't, not in the beginning, and even at the end, I wasn't ever as enthusiastic as Cameron seemed to be. I'm grateful for what you did for my brother . . . but there were things I wondered about, things I picked up between the lines."

"Such as?"

I draw back into myself and weigh up his question. Having opened a door impulsively a few moments ago, I don't intend to open a second door that way. He waits for me to decide.

"You believe in reincarnation, don't you?" I ask finally. "It's one of the between-the-lines things I detected."

He turns the question over before answering. "I don't know that 'believe' is the best word for it, but, yes, an understanding of reincarnation is part of our understanding of the human being."

"Is it part of what you teach?"

"No, not as such. Though if we did, many of our students would laugh at us, because they take reincarnation for granted."

"So we've all been here before? That's what you believe?"

"Or think. Yes."

"And we've all been together before and are together now for some reason or other? Karma, I think it's called."

"Yes, karma is one reason we're together."

I glance away from him. Well, I've pushed the door open. Now do I close it again or go right on through?

I come about in my chair and look straight at him. "All right, Paul. Here's a bit of karma for you. When I was nine and Solomon was three, a woman dropped out of the sky and landed in my father's lap. She had flown in from Wales and stayed in my father's lap long enough to conceive a child before her karma took here somewhere else. In fact, she conceived two children, girls. Solomon met them both in his travels, though it seems one of them died on him. Now was that meeting karma? Because if it was, a few people paid for it in the aftermath, my mother being one of them."

"And you, as well?"

"Yes, in a way. Maybe I asked for it in a previous life, if there was a previous life, but it's hard to see from here how that might have been so."

"Did you ever meet either of your sisters?"

"No. And one of them has now gone beyond that possibility."

"Would you want to meet the one still living, if that ever proved to be possible?"

"I don't know."

"What about the idea of reincarnation in itself? Does that ring true for you in any way?"

I think about it. "Maybe it's true. I may even have picked up hints of it in the thinking of my own people. But if it is true, Paul, then it can work in a damn cruel way, for everyone concerned. Or is there another way of looking at my little story?"

"I can't say, Margaret. I'd need to know more of the story. Is what you've told me as much as you know?"

"Yes. It's as much as I know. I suspect my brother knows more by now, but he hasn't as yet seen fit to let me in on any extended family secrets he may have in his pocket."

Paul is silent a moment. Then he smiles a little smile, almost to himself. "You're right. Karma can feel cruel, perhaps because we forget in the moment why we've set our lives up as we have. So we make a left turn when we had intended to go to the right. Then life does become confused and confusing."

I reach for the bag at my feet. "I've dumped a weight of stuff on the table between us. I'm sorry about that."

"Don't apologize. We're all in this together, as you just said. Tell Cameron I still have a book waiting for him."

As I stand, he looks again at the doll's head poking out of the bag.

"Yes, Paul," I say. "Seven years later, I've finally bought it, and I still don't know what I'm going to do with it."

I push the doll's head back into the bag as I walk out of the hall.

She touched the flaming match to the candlewick and watched the flame reach for the wick and embrace it.

The match burned right to the tip of Margaret's fingers before she blew it out. Behind her, Alan and Cyril sat on the couch. Mavis sat in an armchair beside her husband, and Cameron sat in a chair opposite Alan, as if waiting for the moment when he could square off with Alan yet again.

Somewhere in the room a chair waited for her, but she stayed at the window a moment longer and listened to the February rain slosh down on the roof over her head. Then she took the match into the kitchen and put it into the garbage container under the sink, giving herself another minute or so apart from what she could feel building up in the living room. Putting out the lights in the dining room, Margaret took a deep breath and went to her chair just as Cyril was raising the curtain on the next act of the drama.

"Now then, Alan, there must be a reason why Luke is so specific. Matthew says simply, fowls of the air. Luke, however, says, 'Consider the ravens: for they neither sow nor reap; which neither have storehouse nor barn; and God feedeth them.' Why ravens?"

But why not ravens, Cyril? Margaret asked herself. What are you about to stage, Mr. Director?

She started at the image she had conjured up. But, yes, the image was true. Cyril was setting something up, and this wasn't the first time she had witnessed him doing so, only she had not twigged to what she had been seeing until this moment.

Alan shrugged. "I have no idea, Cyril. I don't know much about ravens."

Cyril raised an eyebrow. "Really? Because there are numerous references to ravens in the Old Testament. As I recall, ravens brought food to Elijah in the desert after his duel with the priests of Baal on Mt. Carmel."

"And the raven was the first bird off the ark," Cameron interjected. Cyril raised the other eyebrow and nodded.

"I beg your pardon. I believe it was the dove that led Noah to land," Alan said.

"*After* the raven left the ark and didn't return," said Cameron, his cup and saucer resting in his lap. "I can bring you a Bible if you doubt me."

Alan tried to mask his confusion, then gave it up. "That won't be necessary. I can refresh my memory when I go home. I suppose if the raven didn't come back, I didn't consider it worth remembering."

"Ah! So, deserters don't deserve being remembered?" Cyril suggested.

"Well, yes, you could put it like that," Alan said.

"But suppose the raven wasn't a deserter?" Cameron said, committing himself to the line of thought Cyril had initiated.

"It didn't return to the ark. Call that what you will," said Alan.

"No, it didn't return, and for good reason." Cameron settled back in his chair and took charge of the conversation. "There was a Viking, Floki Vilgurdson, who traveled from Norway to Iceland. He brought three ravens with him because ravens don't like being out at sea and will head for the nearest land they see. Floki released his ravens one at a time. One flew back to Norway, the second returned to the boat, and the third didn't come back. Just like Noah's raven."

"And where did Floki's raven go?" Alan asked.

"To Iceland, and Floki followed along after it. When the raven didn't return, Floki knew he was near land, just as Noah knew when his raven didn't return. The raven wasn't a deserter; it was just doing its job."

"And where do you think Noah's raven went, Cameron?" asked Cyril.

"Perhaps to the Northwest Coast of British Columbia," suggested Mavis. Everyone laughed a little, and Margaret felt some of the tension slip away from between her shoulders. She looked gratefully at Mavis.

"I've read somewhere that a tribe of Indians on this coast used to put the placenta of a baby boy out on the beach," Mavis continued, "so the ravens could eat it and enable the child to see as clearly as a raven sees. Do you know anything about that, Margaret?"

As Margaret took in the question, her eyes went to the print on the wall called *Children of the Raven*. The face in the eye looked out at her and became the face of her brother.

I am six and Adha steps out onto the porch of our house, carrying a basin that holds Nathan Solomon's afterbirth.

Adha, what are you doing with Weesa's blood bag?

Ahh! I'm going to give Raven a good feed.

Then she walks along the bank of the river toward its mouth. In the sky to the west, a new crescent moon hovers above the sun. Adha empties the basin upon the beach, then goes on walking, past the mouth of the river, into the setting of the sun, and out of my life.

"Margaret?"

She came back to herself. "Yes, Mavis?"

"Do you know anything about such a custom?"

"Yes. My people used to do that." And then Margaret glanced over at her husband and knew she had set the fuse to another powder keg.

Have I never told you about that custom, Cameron? I guess not. Why in the world would I have thought of telling you? And now you're hurt.

"Did I just say something wrong?" she asked lightly.

"No," Cameron lied.

"Given that custom, Margaret, it's a pity the ravens didn't give anyone the foresight needed to avert this residential school mess." The words came from Cyril as he sipped casually at his tea.

"Yes, Alan, what about this residential school mess?" Cameron asked.

The room went silent. Mavis gave her husband a sharp look that Margaret couldn't quite fathom, as Cyril took out his pipe and began to stuff it with tobacco.

Margaret got up and walked over to a set of end tables where she had left the teapot. As she walked she traced her way back through the line of conversation. Consider the ravens: Cyril. The raven as deserter: Cyril. Then the sleight of hand and tongue that led Mavis's well-intentioned question into the residential school cesspool.

She poured herself a cup of tea and stood, her back to the wall and her eyes on Cyril, as if seeing him for the first time: Who are you, anyway? And what are you up to?

"The residential school mess. Well, what about it, Cameron?" Alan said after a moment.

"Physical abuse. Sexual abuse. And let's say, cultural abuse. A hundred years of abuse of Native children, at schools run by the Anglican Church."

"Yes, there were instances of abuse. I'm not denying that."

"More than just instances, it would seem," said Cyril.

"Considerably more," Cameron continued. Margaret pressed herself against the wall and went on staring at the back of Cyril's head. You're setting my husband up. Why?

She glanced at her husband to find him looking at her for help. You know something about this, his eyes said. I know you know something about this. Where are you?

Where am I, Cameron? I'm right here with my back to the wall, trying to stay out of the undertow that's about to take our living room away all the way back to the ark.

Alan set his cup and saucer down upon the coffee table and folded his hands in his lap. "All right, Cameron. There were many instances of abuse. Too many, because there shouldn't have been any. What are you trying to make of that?"

"What is the church going to make of it, Alan? Native parents entrusted their children to those schools, often against their better judgement, and the church betrayed them and their children. And don't tell me no one knew what was happening. The church has much to answer for."

"So I have learned in recent months. In fact, Margaret has told me a few things about the abuse her family suffered—more than I wanted to hear, at first. But who is the church?"

Margaret closed her eyes and then opened them to find Cameron staring at her with the look of one betrayed.

"Who is the church, Cameron?" Alan repeated. "Me? Are you blaming me alone?"

"You're the one wearing the dog collar," said Cameron, his voice hardening even more.

"So I'm the church, and you're not? I'm the one to blame because I'm the priest in this room, and I'm the one who has to answer for all that abuse?"

Cameron glared at Alan, and Alan stared back. Then Alan looked about the room, at Cyril, then Mavis, then Margaret. Only Margaret met his eyes and drank in the anger and pain she saw there.

"Well, if I'm the one to answer, I'd better go think about what answer I'm going to give. Excuse me." Alan stood abruptly and went into the hallway. The front door opened, then closed.

No one spoke. Margaret set her cup and saucer down beside the teapot and followed Alan outside. Closing the door behind her, she stood on the porch and listened to the rain pelting down upon the world around her. Rain rebounded from the walkway leading up to her house, from the sidewalk and street beyond. The ferocity of it reached right into the porch where Alan and she stood.

Alan stood at the edge of the porch, not directly in the cascade of water falling from the roof, but close enough to catch the wetness of it on the front of his shirt and pants and on his clergy collar.

Margaret stood in silence, watching him. You need someone to take you home, Alan, and tuck you into a warm bed, then get into that bed with you. I hope you find her soon.

She walked up to him and put her hand upon his shoulder. "You'll drown if you stand here all night."

It was a long moment before he looked at her. When he did, she gazed into naked eyes that wanted to cover over what they might reveal. "And where do I go, Margaret? Back in there?"

"Yes. If you want your coat, and if you want to leave here with some respect for yourself."

"Why is he out to get me?"

"Cameron? He's not out to get you. Cameron is out to get Cameron, maybe with some help from a friend. You just happen to be the most recent person in his way, that's all."

"It must be hard for you."

"Not so hard anymore. I've decided to take myself out of his way."

He looked long at her. "I see," he said.

"Let's go inside, Alan."

"Margaret, about the residential schools—"

"Not now, Alan."

"But I have to, because we haven't spoken about it since I visited your grandmother last September."

"We don't need to talk about it, Alan. You said what you had to say, and she said what she could say. I can live with that."

"But I don't know that I can, now that I know even more than I knew then. Cameron is right, and so is Cyril. We did terrible things to your people."

"I know that, Alan. And you know that I know it, because I have told you what I know."

"Yes, you did. Your telling me gave me the courage to say what I said to your grandmother. I should have done the same in there. I should just have owned up to what I know and let it pass. But something was going on in there that wouldn't let me do that."

"Yes, something was going on, and is going on, and it doesn't feel good to me any more than it felt good to you."

"What is it, Margaret? What's happening to Cameron?"

"I don't know, Alan. Or maybe I don't want to know. Let's go inside, please."

Back inside, Margaret offered everyone a fresh pot of tea, which everyone declined.

So then, how do we pull this out of the fire, so three of us can go home?

Then Cameron spoke. "Alan, I apologize. I put the blame for a hundred years of history on you alone and I was wrong to do that."

Alan stared at him. "Apology accepted," he said finally. "And I accept your critique of the church of which we're all a part. The history of abuse troubles me, too, more than you might think. But—"

"But what?" said Cameron.

"Why are you taking the situation on in such a personal way? Because that's what I feel you doing, Cameron."

Cameron was silent, as if the question had gone to a place within him to which he didn't want to go at that moment.

Cyril coughed. "It may have something to do with this new course Cameron is giving. The Inside of History, he calls it. Although from what you've said so far, Cameron, Trapped in History might be a more appropriate title. But you are taking up the experience of residential schools as one of your exemplary themes, are you not?"

Cameron looked at him sharply. "Yes, I am, along with Auschwitz. And you know I am, Cyril, because I've talked about it with you. Why bring it up here?"

Cyril shrugged. "It seemed pertinent to our situation at this moment. That's all."

"Indeed," Mavis said. "And how did our evening take the turn it did, to arrive at this moment?"

From her chair, Margaret sized Cyril up yet again. I'm on to you, Cyril. I don't quite know what I'm on to, but I'm going to watch you closely from now on.

"We began by considering ravens, as I remember," Cyril said. "So then, I have a rather whimsical raven story to lighten us up before we go home."

"No, Cyril, I don't think so," his wife said. "I will tell a story instead. The child Jesus asks the raven for a gift of one of her eggs for Him to send into the dark world. As the golden yolk shines in the egg, He tells her, so I will bring the birth of the sun to earth and the earth will not die."

As she stood, Mavis looked into the faces of those looking at her. "It's a dark world for all of us, but perhaps our raven is more than just a trickster. Good night, Margaret. Thank you, as always, for making us welcome."

Cyril turned to Margaret at the door to say goodnight, and Margaret looked him right in the eye. I don't often do that, Cyril, even after all these years of imbibing your culture, but I'm doing it to you to let you know what I now suspect. Cyril averted his eyes from hers. He took Mavis by the arm, and they made their way to their car.

Margaret walked out into the rain with them and stood a moment with Alan after Cyril and Mavis had driven away. Then Alan was gone. Margaret climbed the porch steps, her sweater half-soaked, her hair plastered against her forehead, and her mind anticipating what words might pass between Cameron and her when she walked into the house.

Cameron had not moved from the chair in which he had been sitting. Margaret sat opposite him and waited for him to speak.

"I'm sorry for the things I said tonight," he said finally, barely looking at her as he spoke.

Margaret took a deep breath and released it slowly. It had been a long time since her husband had apologized for anything he said in her presence.

I hear your words, Cameron, but where are you looking and what am I seeing in those eyes of yours? Pain, yes. And fear . . .

She took another breath and then risked her next words. "What is Cyril doing to you?"

Now he looked at her as if he didn't want to understand what he knew she was asking.

"Cyril has a hook in you, Cameron, and he's playing you on the line. What is that about?"

Cameron went on looking at her. A faint smile crept across his mouth, and he shrugged slightly. Then he got up and left the room.

Margaret sat a while longer, listening to the rain as it battered the roof overhead.

She stood in the doorway of her husband's office as if she had never stood there before.

Wrong, of course. I came through this doorway many times, once upon a time. But that was a long time ago.

Margaret looked at the empty chair behind the desk, willing Cameron to be there, but to no avail.

"Hello, Margaret."

She jumped within her skin, then turned to see Cyril smiling benignly at her.

You shouldn't creep up on people like that, Dr. Elspeth. It's most unnerving, she thought. But she said, "Hello, Cyril. Do you know where Cameron is?"

"Not at all. Was he expecting you?"

Did I make an appointment to see my husband? No, not exactly . . .

"No, he wasn't," Margaret said. "I dropped by on impulse. I thought we might have lunch at the pub."

I used to come by on impulse, Cameron, more and more, and you were always in. Where did that bit of serendipity go?

"Ah," said Cyril. "Well, I had the same idea, Margaret. It seems Cameron's Native friend has pre-empted both of us."

"Cameron's Native friend?"

"Yes. Lance. Surely you know about him?"

So that's his name. Lance. Well, now I know that much.

She stepped into the office and sat in the chair in which she had sat many times, long ago. Cyril entered behind her and leaned against Cameron's desk.

"Is something bothering you, Margaret?"

Margaret took him in, as if, yet again, she were seeing him for the first time.

"No, Cyril. Nothing is bothering me."

Then she took him in once more, remembering a recent evening in his company.

"Oh, but yes, there is something troubling me."

He had taken his pipe from his coat pocket as if he were about to stuff it, but then put it back as he considered the way she was looking at him.

"And what would that be, Margaret?" he asked.

"You, Cyril. You and Cameron. There's something about the two of you together that is starting to unnerve me. To give me the shivers, in fact."

Cyril settled himself more solidly against the edge of Cameron's desk. Yet his eyes betrayed a feeling that belied the impression of solidity. Something twitched in them as Margaret spoke, and then wanted to slip away.

"Something about Cameron and me that you find unnerving. And what would that mean?"

"Maybe I'm not yet sure what it means," said Margaret. "All I know is that my husband is fighting for his life right now, and that fight is taking him right to some edge in himself. I can't help him in the way he wants me to help him, I haven't found my way of helping him, so I don't know how to bring him back from that edge. But I'm not the only person nudging at Cameron's life. He gets many a nudge from you, as well, and I feel your nudges pushing him closer to that edge, not away from it. You may not see that, but please, Cyril, watch your elbows more carefully where Cameron is concerned."

Cyril contemplated her, like some plump guru who has insulated himself against dangerous nudges from anyone or anything, even as he guides others toward precipitous places in their lives.

"Do you understand what I've just said, Cyril?"

A trace of a smile flitted across his mouth, then vanished.

"I think so, Margaret. I shall take your words to heart. I'm sorry Cameron and you missed each other."

Then he walked out of the office.

Margaret stared into the space Cyril had just vacated.

Yes, you do understand. And so do I, now. You give me the shivers, Cyril. For all your jolly ways, there's no real joy in you and so you rob others of the joy in them.

You scare me, Cyril. You really and truly scare me.

The opening of the bedroom door awakened her. Cameron undressed as quietly as he could, then slipped into bed beside her.

She lay facing the window, waiting for him to fall asleep before turning onto her other side, but could feel sleep eluding him. Finally, she decided to take him on.

There are questions I want to ask you, Cameron, and this is as good a time as any.

She turned to face him. His eyes met hers, but were empty of any seeing of her. Cameron stared through her and beyond her, into some world beyond the walls of their home. And the stare was empty of Cameron.

Her questions evaporated—all but one.

"Where are you, Cameron?"

The question hung in the silence between them. Then his lips moved.

"I don't know."

A faint light at the horizon of his gaze flickered, then faded away. His eyelids closed and his breath became a brush of air against her cheek.

121

Water, water, wallflower
growing up so high.
We are all God's children
and we all must die . . .

I put down the form I have just completed as the verse from long ago sounds at my ear. Then I take it up again. The name at the top of the form is the name of a child.

You have leukemia, Mary, whoever you are. And your chances of making it don't look very good.

Except for little Mary,
the fairest of us all.
She can dance,
> *she can sing,*
she can wear a wedding ring . . .

But not you, little Mary. No wedding rings for you.

Kate looks up at me from her computer at the reception desk.

"I'm going to lunch now. I'll be back at one," I say to her.

She glances at the clock. "Sure. Have a good lunch. You should try the Chinese place around the corner. The dim sum is fantastic."

Kate has been pushing the Chinese place at me for five years. "I might do that," I say.

And then I head for the little park along the street from the lab. The sun has finally come to warm the last days of March, and trees are blossoming all around me. The trees are blossoming, and little Mary is dying of leukemia.

I find a bench and open the bag lunch I have brought.

I had a friend, little Mary, and *her* name was Mary. And she too has died. Or is as good as dead, for all I know.

. . . We are all God's children
and we all must die.

Except for my friend Mary,
the fairest of us all . . .

Emer brought that little rhyme to Duxsowlas, and the circle dance that went with it. Emer-Teacher, as Nathan and Naomi called her.

I can see her even now, as I stand on the steps leading into my classroom. I am nine, in grade four. Down on the soccer field, my brother stands outside the moving circle, his hand grasping Naomi's. She pulls him into the circle with her, even though he isn't sure he wants to go there.

Fie, fie, fie for shame,
turn your back to the
wall again...

And now Nathan has stopped moving with the circle and is on the edge of tears. My father walks across the field as Emer-Teacher takes my brother's hand and tries to comfort him. Then I watch as Emer and my father stand together, until my teacher calls me into the classroom.

Now my brother has told me I have two sisters, courtesy of Dad and Emer—or rather, one sister, because Caitlin is dead.

. . . and we all must die.

Except for little Caitlin,
the fairest of us all . . .

But I will not mock your death, Caitlin, sister that I never knew. I leave my husband to do the mocking of things, which he now does very well. Instead, I wish you peace in your place of rest, wherever your place of rest may be. And may the woman who bore you rest in peace, as I sit here knowing that being angry with her and the man who fathered you is no longer good enough. May he also rest in peace.

But then, is anyone at peace, really? Not my husband, that's for certain. He is off into the interior next week for another sweat lodge, he says, now that his classes are shutting down. Shutting down seems to be the word for it, because the new course he was all excited about doesn't seem to have gone well.

I could ask Cyril about the course, but I won't do that. Besides, I haven't seen much of Cyril or Mavis lately. We meet at church, but they don't stay around to talk with me. Are they avoiding me? Maybe.

In any event, Cameron will soon be off to be born again. There, Margaret, don't mock your husband's quest. But can a man enter the womb and be born again? And whose womb will you enter, Cameron, before or after your rebirth of fire and water? Because there is someone else. I know there is someone else . . .

Fie, fie, fie for shame,
turn your back to the
wall again . . .

No need to turn my back to the wall, because it's already there and my shoulders are getting sore. So what do I do? Leave Cameron?

To go where? Where would I go, little Mary? And besides, I love my husband. Yes, I do, as much as I did the day I walked into his office at SFU and told him so.

You chased me, remember?

Yes, Cameron, I did chase you. And then you made love to me, oh so willingly, telling me I was everything you had been looking for your whole life long. Were you lying to me? No, I don't think so. You simply didn't know me then, or yourself.

I almost went to Alan a while back, to talk out my marriage mess. Then I didn't go. Why didn't I go to Alan? I had gone to him without hesitation when Minnie and Slim phoned to say that Adha was in the hospital here, and I knew I had to face her after all those years away from Duxsowlas.

I sat in Alan's office, started to talk, and went on talking. The whole of Duxsowlas came spewing out once I opened my mouth. And Alan listened. Alan listened while I spoke of abuse and my anger about abuse, and my pain around the loss of the Mary who didn't die from leukemia, but who vanished from my life with a cancer just as deadly eating out her heart.

Then the words stopped coming. I stayed seated and waited for
Alan to say something. Anything.

"And you blame your grandmother for letting all of this happen?"

"Did I say that?"

"Yes, Margaret, you did. In so many words."

I looked away from him, at the crucifix on the wall behind his desk,
until I could no longer evade the truth of his words.

"I guess I do blame her. But not just her. There were others who
could have acted."

"Who else could have acted?"

I look again at the crucifix. It is bigger than the one Mom once had
on the living room wall of our house, until Dad told her she had to get
rid of it, but the figure of Jesus is pretty much the same—his head
gone slack at the neck, and the whole of him looking very dead.

David sits on the couch, beneath the crucifix. He is nine and I am
seven. Somewhere nearby, Nathan, still a baby, gives out a little cry in
the middle of his afternoon sleep.

Mom kneels before David, her hand on his shoulder. David's eyes
stare into the floor at his feet, as I stand in the front doorway and
watch.

What's wrong, David?

Nothing.

*Don't say, nothing. You look as if some ghost is following you around.
Where have you been all day?*

With Billy Boy.

All day long?

He hesitates. *No.*

Where else?

At Harvey's.

What happened at Harvey's?

*Nothing happened! He gave me some smoked salmon. Then we sat on his
couch and he told me a story.*

What kind of a story?

Just a story . . .

And that's all?

Yes . . .

David's eyes gaze toward the doorway, but he is not looking at me.
Instead he looks past me, out toward the gap between Sand Island and
Log Island where Raven threw the sun into the world and where the sun

is about to set. His eyes search out a way to go where the sun is going, so that he can leave the world closing in about him and never have to come back.

Mom's eyes follow his gaze until they find me. *What do you know about this?* her eyes ask me.

I shrug and stare back at her, into the sudden fear that erupts into her seeing, and which she pushes back down somewhere deep within herself.

"Who else, Margaret?"

I come back to Alan. "My mother, maybe. But my grandmother could have done more."

"Because she was the community matriarch. She was the keeper of your ceremonies, along with your uncle. She, more than anyone else, should have known what was happening and taken action to stop it, especially since your older brother was one of the abused. Others may have been culpable in letting the abuse go on, but she could have put a stop to it and didn't. Am I close to the mark? Or close enough?"

"You're probably right on the mark, Alan," I sighed.

"And now she's here, in hospital?"

I nodded, and felt the first tears run down my face.

"Are you going to see her?"

"Do I have any choice?" I said, holding something of myself at the back of my throat.

"There's always a choice, even if you do go. You could go, spend hours with her, and leave without having seen her."

"I know. Alan, what am I going to do?"

"Yes, what are you going to do, Margaret? If you don't go and she dies, how will that feel?"

"Terrible, I guess. But I don't even know that for sure."

"Would your grandmother like a priest to visit her?"

I thought about that. "Well, she did go to church when our priest came to Duxsowlas. Yes, I think she would like a visit."

"Then I will go and visit her."

"You don't have to do that, Alan. There are chaplains at the hospital—"

He took my hand. "I want to go to her, Margaret. After what you have told me, I want to go."

I shrugged, and then smiled at him. "Then I had better go, too."

My watch tells me it's time for me to return to the lab and let some doctor know the truth about little Mary. Yet I stay seated on the bench as the afternoon sun fills out the world around me and lightens the pink of the blossoms above.

So I went to the hospital to see my dying grandmother. I went prepared to forgive her, if I could do that. And then I left, in need of forgiveness.

. . . and we all must die.

Except for little Naomi,
the fairest of us all . . .

Forgive me, Naomi; forgive me, Nathan Solomon. Please, forgive me.

A hospital room, with a bed at mid-centre stage, its foot angled to-ward stage left. A stand with a single drawer is at stage right of the bed, holding a water pitcher, a glass and a vase of flowers. A chair is downstage from the stand.

Blaze Watson lies in the bed, her eyes closed, with a soft light on her. Margaret enters from stage right. She stands a moment, look-ing at her grandmother. Then she walks slowly, to the bed. She stands another moment, then sits in the chair, as if to wait until her grandmother awakens. The light on Blaze brightens.

Blaze: *(Eyes still closed.)* Ghe-la-kasla, Margaret. It's been a long time.

Margaret: Hello, Adha. *(Pauses.)* How did you know I was here?

Blaze: *(Opening her eyes.)* I felt you come in. Raise this end of the bed, please, and straighten up my pillows.

Margaret goes to the end of the bed and turns the crank that lifts the bed until Blaze is in a more upright position. Then she sets to straightening the pillows.

Blaze: You're thin. Thinner than I remember you being.

Margaret: So are you. Very thin. *(She returns to the chair.)*

Blaze: I guess I am. I try to eat, but the cancer they say I've got swallows up whatever I eat. I hope it starves itself to death on what they call food in this place.

Margaret: *(Matter-of-factly.)* What kind of a cancer is it?

Blaze: I don't know. An everything-coming-apart kind of cancer.

What does it matter what kind it is? I'm old and sick and dying, and the cancer is just helping me to die.

Margaret sits in silence.

Blaze: *(After waiting a few seconds.)* What's the matter? Has the cat run off with your tongue?

Margaret: Maybe. It's just hard for me to think of you dying.

Blaze: Is it? Well, it's not so hard for me. The mist is right in front of my nose, waiting for me to walk back into it.

Margaret: Ahh, yes! The mist that rose up about the Wanookqway, on the third day of their long trek down from the heights of Duxdzas to their river. The first light of Eagle had faded, along with the seeing of Mountain Goat. Now the Wanookqway were lost in that cold mist, until Grizzly appeared from wherever Grizzly appears, with the gift of his skin. Yet on the Wanookqway walked, through the long day into their long night, as the mist deepened—

Margaret stops speaking, gets up from her chair and walks down stage right, facing out toward the audience.

Blaze: You have a good memory.

Margaret: How could I forget? I sat and listened to you tell that story over and over to Nathan when he was in Mom's womb. I sat and waited for Raven to bring the sun, to bring all that mist to an end.

Blaze: What else do you remember?

Margaret: When Nathan was born, you took his placenta down to the river's mouth and put it on the beach, for the ravens to feed on. It was evening, a new crescent moon was hanging in the sky, and it felt so important, you doing that.

Blaze: Yes, it was important.

Margaret: Did you tell me that story when I was in Mom's womb?

Blaze: I did tell you that story. Many times.

Margaret: Did you put my placenta on the beach for the ravens to feed on?

Blaze: No.

Margaret: Why not?

Blaze: Because you weren't Nathan.

Margaret: *(Turning toward her.)* Who was I, then?

Blaze: *(Treading carefully, yet with resolve.)* What are you asking me, Margaret?

Margaret: Who was I, Adha? Why did I come down that mountain to the Wanookqway? Why did I come in this body, to Duxsowlas—?

Blaze: You knew why you came.

Margaret: Did I? Well, my memory is a bit confused right now, so help me out, please. *(She returns to the chair and sits.)*

Blaze: You knew up on the mountain, in the first light of Eagle. As we all know. We all know then why we're going down whatever mountain we go down. Then we walk into the mist and we forget.

Margaret: And what about Raven and the sun, at the other end of the mist? That should be enough to wake a person's memory up.

Blaze: No. That's when the remembering really goes to sleep. It takes some other things we meet to wake us up. Minnie says you're married.

Margaret: *(Rebalancing, with the sudden change of topic.)* Yes, I'm married.

Blaze: Why didn't you bring your husband to meet me before I die?

Margaret: Cameron is a busy man. He teaches at Simon Fraser University. And he's started going to sweat lodge ceremonies. Or so he tells me.

Blaze: A university professor who does sweats. He sounds like either an interesting person or a confused one. It's a shame I won't ever meet him on this side of the mist.

Margaret: Maybe you will.

Blaze: No, I won't. This would have been the moment, and such moments don't stick around. Do I have any great-grandchildren?

Margaret: No, you don't. I'm afraid there's just me, your granddaughter, here and now. *(Pause.)* But I've asked a priest to come and see you.

Blaze: Ooh! A priest! A husband someplace else and no great-grandchildren, but you do have a priest in tow.

Margaret: *(Now tight lipped.)* I thought you might want to talk to a priest right about now.

Blaze: I'm ready to talk to a priest at any time.

Margaret: Ooh, yes! I remember that, too. As long as the priest, or the church, doesn't interfere with your traditional way of putting the world in order.

Blaze: Margaret—

Margaret: *(Standing once again, then pacing back and forth downstage.)* Do you remember that Christmas after David became Hamatsa? I had come home from Port Hardy and I was making a wreath in the kitchen, while Mom and you baked bread. Uncle Slim was playing cribbage with Nathan, and Aunt Minnie was snoring away on the couch.

Blaze: Yes, I remember.

Margaret: *(Now calm, and deliberate with her words.)* I was making a wreath, with spruce boughs. Remember? I had spent a whole day up the river, scratching my hands and face on the fingernails of Mother Nature while I gathered those boughs.

Blaze: I remember. They were good boughs.

Margaret: They were good boughs? Is that all you remember? Then your memory truly is failing you, Adha. What I remember, to this day, is you saying to me, "Why are your hands working with spruce when there's cedar about?"

Blaze: Yes. I remember saying that to you.

Margaret: And why did you say that? Because my wreath fell apart
            in my hands when you said that, even though I got it as far
            as the living room table. I even stuck some cedar boughs
            into it when no one was looking, to make you happy, but
            for me it had disintegrated. What did it matter, Adha,
            whether or not my wreath had cedar sticking out of it?

Blaze: Cedar is very important to our people.

Margaret: As is spruce.

Blaze: Yes, spruce is also important.

Margaret: Then why did you tell me not to use spruce?

Blaze: I didn't tell you not to use it. I asked you why you were
            using it?

Margaret: And I said, "Because they use spruce at the church in Port
            Hardy." Wasn't that reason enough?

Blaze: Was it? Was that the only reason you used spruce? Or had
            you found a reason or two of your own? Because I would
            have been satisfied with a reason of your own.

Margaret: Do not do this to me, Adha! It wouldn't have mattered
            what reasons I had. No reason of mine would have been
            good enough for you: Axilaogua, the traditional
            grandmother. (She stops her pacing and looks coolly at Blaze.) I
            was afraid of you when I was little. Did you ever know
            that?

Blaze: Yes.

Margaret: And did it make you feel good, knowing your
            granddaughter was afraid of her esteemed grandmother?

Blaze: (Looking into a distant place and at the edge of tears.) No.
            Knowing that didn't make me feel good.

Margaret: Well, now, knowing you didn't feel so good about it
            almost makes me feel better.

Blaze: Margaret, don't do this to yourself—

Margaret: I damn well will it do to myself. And you will not die on me until you have heard me out. *(Pauses.)* Do you remember taking your drum in hand and dancing me about the house? But the feet that danced weren't mine.

Blaze: They were your feet.

Margaret: *(Almost shouting.)* No! They were not my feet, not when your drum was beating away at them. And my shoulders weren't mine when you put that button blanket around them. *(She catches herself, stops pacing, then returns to the chair and sits.)*

And it wasn't that I didn't love you. But is this me? I asked myself. Is this really me? Oh God, at times I wanted it to be me, button blanket and all, so that you would love me as I loved you, afraid of you though I was.

And then you asked me that Christmas why I wasn't using cedar, and Christmas became Good Friday. Then I knew that button blanket would never fit the shape of my back. Did I have my own reasons for using spruce? I don't know. Probably not. But I knew I didn't want your reasons.

(She stands again and walks slowly downstage. Very calm now, she stands, gazing out toward the audience.)

So I tucked my little question—Why did I come to this place and these people to get myself into this world?—into a remote corner of my life, and I waited. And then the answer came, that last Easter I was home. I had come down the mountain of the Wanookqway to blow the whistle, to name the abuse that was running rotten in our little village. The abuse everyone knew about, but which no one, you included, would name. So I named it. I stood in the kitchen with Mom that afternoon and I named it. I dropped it right it her lap, and when she tried to shake it away, I shoved it in her face.

And then I left.

(She turns slowly and studies her grandmother.)

You knew about the abuse, didn't you?

Blaze: Yes.

Margaret: You knew, and you said nothing.

Blaze: *(Very quietly.)* Yes, I knew.

Margaret: You knew and you did nothing!

Blaze: Please don't shout at me. I'm old and I'm dying, but I'm not deaf.

Margaret: Damn you, I will shout—

Blaze: We have a visitor, Margaret.

Margaret: *(Not heeding her.)* I will shout until the walls of this hospital—

Blaze: We have a visitor.

Margaret turns and sees Alan Eliot standing downstage to the right of her, as if in the doorway of the room. He is wearing clergy dress and holds a bouquet of flowers.

Alan: May I come in, please?

Margaret: *(Composing herself.)* Yes, of course. Adha, this is Alan Eliot, my parish priest. Alan, my grandmother, Blaze Watson. *(She returns to the chair and sits, as if that action will dissolve the tension in the air.)*

Blaze: Ghe-la-kasla, Mr. Eliot. And welcome to our display of family fireworks.

Alan: I apologize for interrupting. It sounded like an important conversation.

Blaze: Margaret and I haven't talked for a long time. It seems we have a lot to say to each other. *(She sees the bouquet.)* Do you deliver flowers when you're not at the altar or in the pulpit?

Alan: *(With a laugh.)* Only today. I've brought them for you. Where shall I put them?

Blaze: *(Glancing at the stand beside the bed.)* Not there, that's for sure. That bouquet is from Margaret's aunt, and she's claimed all of that territory. Here, let me have them.

Alan crosses to her bedside at stage left and hands her the bouquet. Blaze places them beside her, to her left, against the pillows.

There, now. I can die in a bed of flowers. *(She looks at Alan for a few seconds.)* You do know that I'm dying, Mr. Eliot?

Alan: Yes. Margaret told me. That's why I have come to see you.

Blaze: And what can you bring to a dying woman besides flowers?

Alan: *(Pauses.)* Not much, perhaps, though I will bring the sacrament if you so wish. But I haven't lived long enough to try to tell you how to die. As for dying in Christ, I think you may understand that as well as I do, if not better than I do.

Blaze: *(Moved by his words.)* Thank you, Mr. Eliot. Not all of your colleagues over the years have given me credit for knowing so much.

Alan: But I need to ask something of you.

Blaze: And what would that be?

Alan: Your forgiveness.

Blaze: Forgiveness? For what? What have you done to me?

Alan: I am a priest of the church that abused your people and perhaps abused you: the church that operated residential schools and abused children unfortunate enough to go to them, and that betrayed the trust of the parents who sent their children. That's what I've done.

Blaze: Ahh! I see.

Margaret: *(Quietly.)* Alan, please don't! You don't have to go there.

Alan: But I do, Margaret. I need to go there, even at the risk of imposing myself upon a dying woman.

Blaze: *(After a long pause.)* That was a very naked confession, Mr. Eliot. A little rehearsed, maybe, but admirable, nonetheless.

Alan: *(With candor.)* Yes, I did rehearse it, Mrs. Watson. And even the rehearsing of it took all the courage I could muster.

Blaze: *(Studying him.)* You are a very honest person. Your parishioners must love you for that. Or hate you, depending. *(She pauses again, now looking out at the audience and into another, remembered world.)* I myself did not go to residential school, but, yes, my four children did. So then, you are asking me to forgive you, or more correctly, the Anglican Church through you for whatever your schools may have done to my children and to all our children? Do I understand you rightly?

Alan: Yes, that is what I am asking of you. Please.

Blaze: That's a lot of forgiveness to ask from one old woman. And a lot of forgiveness to place upon the shoulders of one priest.

Alan: Yes, I know.

Blaze: Do you? I wonder. I wonder if you understand the thing for which your church and your people really need to be forgiven?

Alan: *(Hesitantly.)* I . . . I've tried to understand. I've tried to find out . . . what we did to you. I didn't like what I found and one time I wanted to turn away from . . . from what I was finding. But I didn't.

Blaze: I believe you in that. You don't look like a person who would bolt once he set his feet on a path. But do you realize the extent of the path you need to walk to know how the way you think about things has wounded us?

Alan: The way we think about things?

Blaze: Yes. The way you think. You told us about your God in the hope we would recognize Him as our God and then told us there was only one way of going to Him, yours. You told yourselves and us your schools would prepare us to live in the world you were creating, even as you put our world to death. Maybe we had to arrive where we all are now, in a world different from the one my people had once known, but you insisted my people travel here by the same road you were traveling because that was the only road you could comprehend. And that is where you abused us most deeply, Mr. Eliot. All the other abuses started from that one. Do you understand what I'm saying?

Alan: Yes . . . perhaps I do . . .

Blaze: But not fully. Not yet, anyway. *(Sizing him up again.)* Very well, Mr. Eliot. I forgive you and my church through you for the abuses you have understood. In fact, I have long ago forgiven my church, as did my late husband, even after we had learned of things that had happened to our children.

But I speak only for myself. Not for my children or for anyone else among my people. And my forgiving of you won't prevent the consequences of my church's abuse of my people from coming upriver to spawn. Do you understand me?

Alan: Yes. I do.

Blaze: Good. Then go in peace and take my forgiveness with you.

Alan: I will. And thank you, Mrs. Watson. May I bring you the sacrament?

Blaze: No, thank you, Mr. Eliot. There is a priest at Port Hardy who has begun to call in at Duxsowlas. It might not occur to him to ask my forgiveness, but he will be ready to bring the sacrament when I go home to die.

Alan: Then go home and die in peace, Mrs. Watson. Ha-la-kasla.

Blaze: And where did you learn Kwakwala, Mr. Eliot?

Alan: From Margaret. She's taught me a few words.

Blaze: *(With a glance at Margaret.)* Ooh! That was good of her. Ha-la-kasla to you, then, Mr. Eliot.

Alan: Goodbye, Margaret.

Margaret: *(Standing.)* I'll walk out with you.

They walk downstage right. Margaret stops and takes Alan's hands in hers. Blaze watches them, and then rearranges the flowers against her pillows.

Margaret: I had no idea you would do something like that.

Alan: Nor did I, for certain, until I stood beside her bed. *(He draws his hands away from hers, reluctantly.)* Goodbye again, Margaret, for now.

Margaret: Goodbye, Alan. Thank you for coming.

Margaret watches him exit, then returns to the chair beside her grandmother's bed and sits.

Margaret: Why were you so hard on him?

Blaze: *(Straightening out the bedclothes.)* Was I being hard on him? I don't think so. He wanted to be forgiven. I forgave him.

Margaret: After you put the screws to him. It did take courage for him to say what he said.

Blaze: No doubt, but there is still more to be said than he could say, and he needs to find out about that if my forgiving him is going to go anywhere. Don't ever ask for forgiveness, Margaret, unless you're really ready to know the thing for which you need to be forgiven.

Margaret: But Alan had the courage of what he did know. Please give him that much.

Blaze: Yes, I'll give him that. He has a good heart.

Margaret: I know he does. He's a good priest.

Blaze: I imagine he is. And he's fond of you.

Margaret: What do you mean, fond of me? Adha, he's a priest.

Blaze: That doesn't stop him from being fond of you.

Margaret shrugs her grandmother's last words away. A few seconds' pause.

Margaret: You didn't go to residential school?

Blaze: No, I didn't. Nor did your granddad.

Margaret: Why not? Wasn't there a school in Alert Bay when you were growing up?

Blaze: The school was there. But our parents chose not to send us. Not many children from Duxsowlas went to residential school during those years. We were too far away from the Indian agents for them to trouble themselves overmuch about us. And we were still a strong people then. Our parents kept the potlatches alive, and our dances, and all our ceremonies, even though the government had passed a law saying we couldn't do that. But we had a stronger law, a strict law of our own, and that law bid us dance.

Margaret: But you sent Uncle Charlie to residential school. And Aunt Minnie and Aunt Lila, and Mom. Why?

Blaze gazes once again into a remembered world. She places her hand about the flowers and holds onto them as she continues.

Blaze: The year before I turned twelve, my parents took me to a big potlatch at Village Island. I had never been to a potlatch like that one. Three hundred or more people came, and there were many gifts of names, and dances and goods: canoes, pool tables, gas boats, guitars, phonographs, and so much more. And cash. It all ended on Christmas day, and maybe Santa called in on the feast and left a few things of his own.

Well, that did it as far as the Indian agent and police were concerned. Over fifty people were arrested and twenty-two of them went to jail.

When Henry and I began having children, we saw them coming into a world that was closing in on ours, closing in for the kill. We watched our neighboring villages being stripped of their masks and ceremonies and knew Duxsowlas might not stay protected forever.

We told ourselves we were not a dying people, yet all about us, our people were dying. It's like coming down from Duxdzas, your granddad said, down into the mist. The old light is gone, Grizzly no longer has skin to give us, the oolichan have stopped running up our river, and the mist is only getting thicker.

The white people told us there was a new light for our children in their schools. So we asked ourselves, is this a new sun Raven is bringing? But why trust anything Raven brings? Yet we didn't see any other light, any other way out of the mist. So we sent Charlie, first, to see what would come of that. Then Minnie went to Alert Bay, and then Lila.

Blaze pauses and grips the flowers more closely to her before she continues. During the words to come, Margaret rises and walks slowly downstage right, where she stands, her back to her grandmother, and listens intently.

The three of them used to come home for the holidays, then the holidays ran out, and they had to go back. Your granddad would take them to the boat, stand on the landing that had now become the name of our village as far as the government was concerned: Doxology Landing, because no white tongue could say the true name of our village. He stood there and watched the boat pull away. He watched the faces of his children looking back at him from the boat, their eyes filled with questions and pain. Minnie told me years later she had decided we didn't really love them. Otherwise, we would never have put them on that boat.

Your granddad stood until the boat was way past the southern tip of Sand Island. Then he came back to our house, sat at the kitchen table and cried. For years he cried like that, every time Charlie, Minnie and Lila left us. I wanted to cry too, but I never did. One of us had to be strong, and besides, I have never been one to cry much. But your granddad cried for both of us, until the year your mom started getting on that boat. And then he ran out of tears . . .

(Blaze comes back from her remembered world and glances at her granddaughter.) Your priest does have a good heart, but he really knows nothing about the extent of the forgiveness he has asked for and received. Maybe it's just as well.

Margaret: *(Still looking out toward the audience.)* And what did happen to your children in residential school?

Blaze: Different things. *(She gathers herself in, her eyes now upon Margaret.)* Your Aunt Minnie was so tough and so mouthy that I don't think anyone ever came near her except to see whom she was going to clout next. She stood up for herself and that pretty much protected her.

Your Auntie Lila wasn't tough in that way, but she had another kind of protection. She had a good guardian spirit that kept mean and dirty things away from her. And if they did get close to her, they either ran off her back like water or she just walked out from under them and went on with her life. Your brother Frank is a lot like his auntie in that respect.

As for your mom, well, she started to pray even before she went to Alert Bay and I guess—I hope—her praying helped her while she was there.

Margaret: *(Now turning toward Blaze.)* Mary Silas prayed too, Adha. And her praying didn't help her when her dad decided to open her up.

Blaze: *(Slowly.)* Yes, I know praying didn't help everyone.

Margaret: Did Mom ever talk about what happened to her?

Blaze: No. Your mom didn't talk about much of anything. So your granddad and I could only hope things were all right for her at school. Though she did start drinking, just before you were born, and then I wondered . . .

Margaret waits for her grandmother to continue, then walks through the silence back to the chair and sits.

Margaret: And what about Uncle Charlie?

Blaze: *(Coming back to herself from somewhere else.)* What did you just ask me?

Margaret: Uncle Charlie, Adha. What about him?

Blaze: Well, he was abused some, maybe more than he ever let on, but not so much sexually. He was very proud of being the oldest and he became Hamatsa before we sent him, so he had already been out in one wilderness before he went into that other kind. But there were one or two staff that didn't like this Indian boy who was proud to be Indian, and I think they punched him about to knock the pride out of him. But Charlie was as tough as Minnie in his own way, and after awhile he got to be pretty big. Then people weren't so ready to shake a fist at him.

No, it's not what happened to Charlie, but what he saw happening to others that really hurt him . . .

Blaze lifts a hand to her face, to find she is crying.

Damn! What's this runoff all about? Hand me a tissue, please.

Margaret: *(Taking a tissue from the stand and handing it to her.)* I thought you said you didn't cry about things.

Blaze: I guess I have to get down to it sometime. And it looks like this is the time.

She wipes at her eyes, then continues, picking her way carefully.

Harvey Silas was Charlie's friend even though Charlie was several years older. When Harvey was little, Charlie would take Harvey by the hand, bring him to our house and make me feed them both. "My weesa," Charlie would call him, and Harvey would grin up at him through the teeth he had just lost.

Then Harvey went to Alert Bay, and Charlie was determined to protect him when Harvey walked through the door of that school. But there was somebody on staff who took a strong liking to Harvey that Harvey didn't need. For a time Charlie and Harvey were sleeping near one another and Charlie took Harvey into his own bed at night, just after the lights went out. Then the somebody who liked Harvey found a reason to cane Charlie and move him to another part of the building.

Finally, Charlie went to the head person at the school . . .

Margaret: And?

Blaze: And then the school sent Charlie home and wouldn't let
            him go back. We asked Charlie why they wouldn't let him
            go back, but he wouldn't say, not until years later after
            your granddad had died.

            Harvey came back to Duxsowlas, married Hazel, and then
            his children started to come.

            She pauses, looks at her granddaughter.

            You asked if we knew what was going on. Yes, because
            your uncle watched Harvey like a hawk even while he was
            helping Harvey put his life back together. But he couldn't
            be everywhere, and the children of our village were
            everywhere, because that's the way it was in our village.
            When he did find out that Harvey was abusing your
            brother David, Charlie stopped it.

Margaret: So, David wasn't abused that much?

Blaze: He was abused some, but it could have been worse.

Margaret: Then why was David so angry all those years before he
            took his life?

Blaze: The abuse may have been part of that, but he also had
            other reasons to be angry.

Margaret: Such as?

            *Blaze sizes her up and decides not to go in the direction of that
            question.*

Blaze: That's another story, for another time, Margaret.

Margaret: Then I hope someone other than you, with a good
            memory, will live long enough to let me in on it.

Blaze: Your brother might be that person, when he comes home.

Margaret: Ahh! Nathan knows the story. Nathan knows it, but you
            won't tell me.

Blaze: Nathan doesn't know it yet, but he will, when he comes
            home.

Margaret: *(Deciding to let the untold story go by her.)* All right. Uncle

Charlie bailed David out. What about others? What about Harvey's own children: Pam, and Mary, and maybe Naomi? What about my friend, Mary, Adha?

Blaze: We didn't find out about that, Margaret, until the damage was done.

Margaret: You didn't know? That's what you're telling me, right? But didn't you even suspect that David might not be the lone victim? What about Hazel? Was she wandering about the house stone blind?

Blaze: I don't know what Hazel knew, because Hazel has never said what she knew.

Margaret walks downstage and stands, turning it all over within her.

Margaret: Why didn't you call the police in as soon as you found out about David? Why didn't you see that Harvey was charged and taken away?

Blaze: We had a meeting to decide if we would call the police, and, in the end, didn't do that. Harvey was a hurt person. We decided that sending him to jail or anywhere else wouldn't have helped him heal. He was ours to take care of and we weren't going to turn our backs on him. Maybe that was a big mistake, but that's how we saw it then. Besides, in those days we wouldn't have entrusted any one of our people to the police or a law other than our own.

Margaret returns to the chair and sits. She wants to be angry, yet knows her anger can go nowhere and change nothing.

Margaret: So, you let your law take its course, while Harvey went on doing what he did.

Blaze: Harvey didn't go on abusing children, Margaret. We stopped him. Maybe it was too late for some, but we stopped him.

Margaret: Until he was moving in on Naomi. Nathan told me about that. Harvey was ready to go to work on Naomi. Getting drowned with Dad was the only thing that stopped him.

Blaze: No, Harvey had already stopped himself. Did Nathan tell you about that?

Margaret: You mean, putting a screwdriver through his testicles while coming out of a drunken stupor? Yes, Nathan told me.

Blaze: That was Harvey's way of stopping himself. And that's when your Uncle Charlie decided to stand back and let Harvey die on the beach, let the wound finish its work. Until your dad insisted on taking Harvey out in your uncle's boat and your uncle couldn't find a reason to say no.

Margaret: Why did Dad do that, when he knew neither of them would make it to Port Hardy?

Blaze: Because your dad knew that his work was done, or done as far as he could do it.

Margaret: *(Waiting for Blaze to go on, then knowing she will not go on.)* Is that, too, a story for another time?

Blaze: Yes, I think so.

Margaret stays sitting, her eyes searching out something above and beyond her.

Margaret: Did Uncle Charlie ever abuse anyone?

Blaze: I beg your pardon.

Margaret: Did Uncle ever abuse David? Or Frank?

Blaze: What makes you ask that?

Margaret: Nathan, Adha. Nathan left Duxsowlas because he caught Uncle with his arm around Frank the night Dad died and concluded that Uncle had also abused David. Did you know that that was why Nathan left?

Blaze: *(Slowly.)* No. Though maybe I did, in the way you know something before you fully know it. But if Nathan thought that, he was mistaken. Your uncle would never have abused David, or Frank, or anyone. Especially David.

Margaret: I didn't think so, either, and I've told Nathan as much in a recent letter. I hope someone else will back me up if you're not around to do that.

Blaze: Someone will, and that person may well be your uncle himself, when Nathan returns to have a conversation with him.

Margaret: What makes you so sure Nathan will want a conversation with Uncle when he returns—if he comes back to Duxsowlas at all.

Blaze: He'll come back. And he won't come back until he's ready in himself to have that conversation.

Margaret: *(From out of nowhere.)* Whatever happened to Nathan's little friend, Naomi?

Blaze: Naomi isn't so little anymore.

Margaret: I guess not. But what's happened to her?

Blaze: Why don't you ask her?

Margaret: What do you mean, ask her?

Blaze: She's standing over there. Ask Naomi what's happened to Naomi.

Naomi stands downstage right, as if she has just entered the room. She takes Margaret in and then walks around to the side of the bed, stage left. Blaze reaches out with her hand, and Naomi takes it.

Naomi: Ghe-la-kasla. How are you doing?

Blaze: About the same. Still old, still sick, and still dying. Not much change there.

Naomi: I've brought the medicine the doctor wants you to take.

Blaze: Thank you. I'll throw it away as soon as I'm home.

Naomi: You can go tomorrow. Slim has made all the arrangements.

Blaze: The doctor won't be pleased.

Naomi: Let Minnie take care of the doctor.

Blaze: I'll do that. Do you remember Margaret?

146

Naomi: *(With reserve.)* Yes, I remember Margaret. Hello.

Margaret: *(Now also reserved.)* Hello. It's been a long time.

Naomi: Yes, it has been a long time. *(To Blaze.)* What can I do for you?

Blaze: Take Margaret somewhere and talk with her, so I can get some sleep. Tomorrow's going to be a long day.

Naomi: *(With a glance at Margaret.)* And what should we talk about?

Blaze: Whatever you need to talk about. And you do need to talk, the two of you, as much as I need to sleep. So goodbye to you both, for now.

Margaret and Naomi look at one another across the bed as the light upon it begins to dim. They step away and walk downstage, eyeing one another as they do. Stopping at downstage centre, they face one another.

Margaret: Well, Naomi, what do we need to talk about?

Naomi: *(Deciding not to waste words.)* Why did you leave?

Margaret: What do you mean, leave?

Naomi: You know what I mean. You knew my father had abused your brother and my sisters and that he might be abusing others. Yet you left. Why?

Margaret: How do you know what I knew?

Naomi: Sadie told me.

Margaret: Ahh! And what else did Sadie tell you?

Naomi: *(Ignoring the question.)* Why did you leave?

Margaret: Because I had to.

Naomi: That's not a good enough reason.

Margaret: Maybe not, Naomi, but it was my reason at the time and it's all the reason you're going to get.

Naomi: *(Turns away for a few steps, then turns back.)* We all looked up to you. Did you know that? How much we all looked up to you: Vera, Angie, me, and others?

I remember the day you were confirmed, with Mary and Billy Boy. Mary was so nervous that no one thought she would make it through the service, and Billy Boy just wanted to be out of there and somewhere fishing with his dad. But you—you were right there, kneeling in front of the bishop, your eyes strong and seeing something we all wanted to see, but which you alone saw.

You were so strong that day, Margaret, and we all wanted to be like you. We wanted the strength you had. I looked at you and told myself, I'm going to be strong, like Margaret, and then nothing will be able to hurt me, ever. And then you left us. You left me alone with my father—

Margaret: I was seventeen years old when I left, Naomi.

Naomi: You left us—

Margaret: *(Firmly.)* I was seventeen years old and there was nothing I could do. Can you understand that? I told my mother what I knew and she didn't want to hear it. Nobody wanted to hear it. So I left. I had a life to live and I left to get on with it.

Silence. Margaret turns away for a few steps.

You mentioned Mary. How is she getting on?

Naomi: *(Her gaze still fixed on Margaret.)* I don't know. We haven't seen Mary since she left high school in Port Hardy.

Margaret: She hasn't come back to Duxsowlas, ever?

Naomi: Never. My disappearing and disappeared sister.

Margaret: And you have no idea where she went?

Naomi: A person in crisis doesn't think much about filling out a change of address form. *(Pauses, then relents a little.)* Someone said she had gone to Victoria. My mom went to look for her, but turned up nothing. That's all we know. But you left Mary behind, along with the rest of us, so why should you care?

Margaret: *(Wheeling about in a sudden fury.)* You snot-nosed little brat! What do you know about me? I loved Mary. She was my best friend, closer to me than any friend, ever. I did not leave Mary. Mary left me. I cried with her for a whole long year in Port Hardy. I held Mary, I pleaded with her, and I would have died for her, but Mary left me. Day by day she left me. Day by day I watched her go away and couldn't hold on to her. *(Now she is crying.)* I prayed for her, but I couldn't hold on to her. She slipped away from me into a current where I couldn't go, and then she was gone . . .

Naomi: *(Quietly.)* Mary loved you.

Margaret: And I loved Mary. But loving each other wasn't enough. *(Pauses.)* Maybe it's never enough, to help anyone.

Naomi: My father hurt her. Hurt her badly.

Margaret: *(Now looking at her.)* Did your father ever abuse you?

Naomi: No, he didn't abuse me, though he was getting ready to do that. Do you know who saved me, Margaret? Your dad. Your dad saved me.

She turns away and paces downstage right.

I told Nathan what was about to happen and he told your dad. Then my dad wounded himself. Everyone was ready to let him bleed to death, me included, but your dad packed my dad into your uncle's boat and set off in a pile of waves big enough to sink anything.

They both drowned, your dad and mine. And then I realized your dad knew that would happen. He knew he would never make it to Port Hardy. Your dad died to save me from my dad. Did you know that Margaret?

Margaret: Yes, I knew. Nathan told me one night after he had come to live with us.

Naomi: And where is Nathan now?

The question hangs in the air between them, the only question that truly matters to Naomi.

Margaret: I don't know.

Naomi: *(Stunned.)* You don't know?

Margaret: I don't know. *(She pauses, taken aback herself by the brutal matter-of-factness of her lie.)* I don't know where Nathan is.

Naomi: I can't believe that.

Margaret: Believe it, Naomi. We had a fight three years ago. Nathan stormed out of the house and out of my life and has been gone ever since. End of story.

Naomi: *(Faltering.)* But you must know something . . . you must have heard something from him . . . *(She looks away, feeling desperately for her next words.)*

I have to find him, Margaret. I have loved Nathan ever since we were little and there's no one else. I've tried to love others. I've even prayed that I could forget him and love another man, but I can't. I love Nathan, and there will never be anyone else. Help me, please!

Margaret: *(Resolute.)* I can't.

Naomi: Does he have friends here? Maybe they know something.

Margaret: I can't help you, Naomi.

Naomi: *(Sizing her up.)* You can't? Or you won't?

Margaret: *(With a shrug.)* Can't or won't—it comes down to the same thing right about now.

Naomi: Then why won't you help me?

Margaret does not reply.

Naomi: *(Quietly.)* My God! What a cold-hearted bitch you've become. And to think I once admired you.

Margaret: And you've become a self-righteous bitch. You and Nathan deserve each other.

Naomi: I'm sure we do, once I find him. And I will find him, Margaret.

Naomi walks to the bed and takes Blaze by the hand. Blaze opens her eyes as the light brightens.

Naomi: I'm going now. Ha-la-kasla.

Blaze: Yes. It's time for you to go. I love you, Makwalaga—Moon Woman. Ha-la-kasla.

Naomi: And I love you, Axilaogua. Thank you, for everything you have given me.

Blaze: Where will you go?

Naomi: *(Releasing her hand.)* To look for the other person I love.

Naomi walks downstage right, past Margaret, then turns before she exits.

Goodbye, Margaret. I hope you find out who you really are, before it's too late.

Margaret watches her go. For an instant she reaches out with her hand as if to call Naomi back. Then she goes to the chair and sits.

Blaze: *(Sitting up a little.)* You said Nathan had written you. Where is he?

Margaret: *(Lifting her head from her hands.)* In Wales, and maybe Ireland.

Blaze: And you didn't tell Naomi that.

Margaret: *(A question in her eyes.)* No . . .

Blaze: As I said, I may be dying, but I'm not yet deaf. Does he have friends here that she could have contacted?

Margaret: Yes.

Blaze: And you didn't tell her that.

Margaret: No, I didn't.

Blaze: That was a cruel thing to do, not to tell her any of that.

Margaret: Yes, it was cruel. I'll leave a note for her, when she comes back.

Blaze: She won't come back. Not until I've gone home and died, and she finds Nathan.

Margaret: Well, now, it seems I have made a big mess of things.

Blaze: Maybe not the worst mess in the world. Naomi is strong and she'll find a way of finding Nathan. In the meantime, I'm going home to die. As for you, Margaret, forgive yourself, please, for what you did just now, and for anything else you've done. And forgive me, and your dad, and your mom, and Nathan, and your people for what we might have done to you. Your life will be different if you can do that.

Margaret: I don't know if I can do any of that, Adha.

Blaze: Then your life will be different yet again. And now I must rest some more. It will be a long trip home, and I want to be well rested when I die.

Margaret: *(As she stands.)* Is there anything I can do for you? Now?

Blaze: Only what I've just asked you to do. That will be work enough. Ha-la-kasla, Margaret. It's been an interesting visit.

Blaze closes her eyes. The light upon the bed dims to a soft glow. Margaret stands, uncertainly, at her grandmother's bedside. Then she begins to exit, slowly, downstage right. Suddenly she stops, turns, and goes back to the bed.

Margaret: There is one thing I will do, Adha, as you once did it for me. *(She gathers herself together.)*

Listen!
Our story,
              yours
begins
        on the first day
high upon our mountain
when the great waters
had passed.

            The first light
was very high about us and
Eagle said to our ancestor
Duxzdas,
              He-whose-eye

sees-every-river,
          Go down
that one way to your River,
to that place where
you can be.

Down went our people
until the light became tired
and weak,
          until the mist
rose about them, grew
deep beyond any seeing . . .

Margaret takes her grandmother by the hand.

Ha-la-kasla, Axilaogua,
Holder of Names. Go through
the last of the mist,
back to the sun.

She left the lab at closing time and caught the Hastings Street bus. Getting off just before Nanaimo Street, she bought a few vegetables at a produce market, then found the little Greek restaurant where Cameron and she had often eaten.

There was no hurry to get home. Cameron was up in the interior at his sweat lodge, or so he had said, and wouldn't be back until late that evening. But why question what Cameron had said? Yet she sat, waiting for her dinner to come, and questioned.

Forgive us. We know not what we do . . .

Margaret took her time eating, allowed herself a second glass of wine, then started walking north on Nanaimo Street.

Maundy Thursday. They met for that last meal, and he told them things about himself and about themselves that they didn't understand or didn't want to know. Then one of them betrayed him and another denied him.

Yet he had given them his body and blood, and that made it a feast, despite everything else. The sharing of food and flesh and blood does something between persons that doesn't die away easily, unless you're dead set on killing it. And even then . . .

When she came to her home, Margaret sat on the porch steps and placed her handbag beside her along with the bag of vegetables. Leaning back, she rested her elbows on the top step. At her back the house waited for her to unlock the front door and go inside—funny, we never locked any of our doors at Duxsowlas—but she wasn't ready to go inside. Not yet.

Maundy Thursday: Betrayal and evasion, only both had started much earlier. Things had already started going wrong, but this was the night when the betrayed and betraying chickens came home to roost. Or as Adha had put it, when the salmon swam upriver to spawn.

You lied to me, Cameron, even though you were telling the truth. There is no other woman in my life, you said. The truth, yet a lie—how could that be?

Margaret looked over at the single garden bed she had begun shortly after they had scraped together a down payment for the house and moved in. She had had grandiose plans for gardens all around the house, but that one bed was as far as she had gone before other realities overtook her plans. Cameron had just laughed and told her to let the garden go, and then she too had laughed about it. They both had laughed a lot then.

She gazed up into the deepening sky. A few clouds had gone to pink, then red, with the sun's setting. Around them the blue of the sky dissolved its daylight mask toward a mystery beyond, which opened out into itself with the first flickering of stars.

You must get tired of things going wrong down here, she said to the mystery beyond the stars. Yet she prayed, Be as close to me now as you were to the man praying in the garden on that night. A better garden than mine, I hope.

So, where did I go wrong in all of this?

She let the question walk in and sit down, but didn't know what to do with it.

A small bird chirped drowsily from one of the trees along the street. To the south the traffic swished east and west along McGill Street, but her street was quiet, except for the bird that now fell silent.

Overhead, the stars brightened, yet spoke nothing. No dogs barked, and there was not even the sound of an ambulance or fire engine or police siren within earshot of where she sat. There was only the silence that wrapped itself around her questions and held them fast.

My skin is not my own anymore, Cameron had told her when they first began to make love. When I pour myself into you, the boundary is gone and I am no longer locked in my skin, in myself. That's never happened to me before . . .

Then the skin between them began to thicken. Why? Why is this happening to us? she had begun to ask.

Because you won't let me in, he said, and went on saying it with his eyes, long after he had given up speaking it.

Two nights ago, she had thrown herself upon him as soon as he got into bed. She had him erect and into her before he knew what was happening. Drawing him in, she could feel him losing himself in her, as he had done when they first loved—going down into her like one who has traveled through a wilderness all his life long and, suddenly, the wilderness plunges into a vast ocean.

She had taken her husband without warning, to plunge him once more into the ecstasy of losing himself in her. But then he pulled away from her, not with his body, but within himself. She felt him leaving her even as his flesh melted into hers.

Don't, Cameron. Please, don't—

But he had already left her. To go where and to whom?

Margaret gathered up her handbag and the vegetables, and stood. As she unlocked the door, she found herself thinking, well, Cameron, maybe you don't want to lose yourself in any woman's body anymore. Maybe you want to send yourself directly to heaven.

She turned on a lamp and dropped her handbag on the couch.

Or maybe you need a man to make love to.

She stopped short between the couch and the kitchen doorway.

Like your friend, Lance.

And now the silence about her turned upon her and held its breath. The bag of vegetables slipped from her hand to the floor.

Like your friend, Lance—?

And then she knew.

Her arms reached toward the wall beside her, took hold of the nearest of Cameron's prints and yanked it from the wall. The snap of the picture wire cracked the silence open. She screamed as she turned the frame ninety degrees and drove one corner of it into the wall.

The frame split apart and the glass splintered to the floor. Ripping the print from its crumpled frame, she tore it to shreds.

Her anger condensed, hardened and sharpened itself to an arrowhead of rage. Methodically, she moved from print to print. The plaster on the walls shivered, cracked and crumbled as it yielded to the onslaught of wood, metal and glass.

Her hands bleeding from edges of splintered glass and slivers of wood and metal, she grasped the last of the prints and reduced it to shattered glass and torn paper.

Now *Transformation #3* was the only print left hanging, the one print Cameron had not framed. Margaret stared at it. She drew her breath in, let it go slowly, and went into the kitchen. She put the kettle on the stove, then went to the sink and drew a splinter of glass from her left hand and a long sliver of wood from her right, as she had done when she was a girl and had been playing among fallen trees in the forest behind Duxsowlas.

She washed the blood from her hands with elaborate care, took the kettle from the burner, and made herself a pot of tea.

Sitting on the couch, Margaret drank the tea slowly, refilled the cup, and continued to drink, shutting out even the silence that pressed in upon her.

Sometime before midnight, she cradled the cup in her hands and stared into the tea that remained, as if looking for the answer to the riddle of her life. Then, turning the handle away from her, she gripped the cup firmly and threw it at *Transformation #3*.

The cup fell apart and a fresh tea stain seeped into the paper to join itself with the stain she had put there the day her brother had walked out of her life.

Margaret leaned her head against the back of the couch, watched the tea do its work, and waited until she heard Cameron's feet hurrying up the porch steps.

I brush pink blossoms from the windshield of the car. They float up from the glass, around my hand, out into the air around me. The blossoms hover long above the pavement, even though the air is very still, until they drop down to the street and the wheels of the car crush them as I drive away from the house.

Good Friday morning is forever still. At Duxsowlas, there was always a mist on the face of the river, like a gray shroud over the face of the dead, or the face of death itself. Nothing moved on Good Friday morning. No birds sang. No ravens croaked or belched or called seductively from the shadows cast by branches of cedar leadened with the weight of themselves.

Nothing moves now, even though a car or two passes me. Yet the cars seem to move in a world other than the world of suspended time in which I live.

All was still between us the whole of the night long, as we moved together, yet apart, picking up the fragments of glass, splinters of wood and metal, and shreds of paper. There were no words and always a space between us as we moved together.

Where I am, you are not. Where you are, I am not. Where I will be, you will not be . . .

And then we sat on the couch as the pale sun filtered into the living room, and we drank the tea I had made.

Suspended within myself, I left the house not knowing if I could or would ever reopen the door I had closed behind me.

I park in front of St. Cyprian's just before noon. Clouds overhead slide across the face of the sun, and then the sun momentarily breaks through.

The nave of the church is dim. What light there is strikes through stained glass that refracts and mutes its intensity, reducing it to a sluggish gleam.

We could not bear the full brunt of God's light, Alan had once said. Therefore, the church shields us from that impact, transforming the glare of divinity into the grace of colour.

Alan sits at the back of the church and will take the service from there. The cross is the focus, not me, he had said last Sunday, in preparation for today.

The cross is a crucifix, the one Alan had insisted on obtaining to replace the plain cross that was hanging above the altar, should he become the rector of St. Cyprian's. Alan became the rector and got his crucifix.

The head of Christ does not just slump to one side, but hangs so limply from the shoulders that his chin nearly touches his chest. Not simply a dead Christ, but a broken Christ, his body utterly abandoned by whatever man or God or both had stood it upright upon the earth.

My God, my God, why have you forsaken me?

The voice is Alan's as he speaks the opening words of the Good Friday service.

The Lord be with you.

And with thy spirit.

Let us pray.

My knees touch down upon the wooden kneeler, even as I tell myself, I shouldn't be here. I should be with my husband, trying to put our lives back together.

But why? Why should I be with Cameron?

I sit and try to listen as Alan reads the Passion story from one of the gospels.

Remove the cup from me . . . nevertheless, not my will . . .

The words open the first of Alan's meditations on the meaning of the cross: fidelity, and betrayal. We know the names of some who betrayed him: Judas, Peter . . . but do we stop with those names, or do we go on to name ourselves, as well? For betrayal starts with ourselves . . .

So then, Adha, what betraying have I done? Wherever you are now, please help me figure this out. I'm in the mist and I'm cold and I don't see much light. Maybe Grizzly will show up with his skin to warm me and maybe Raven will bring the sun before the time comes when it doesn't matter anymore. But right now I'm in the mist and I don't see a way through.

Forgive yourself, Margaret.

For what, Adha? For leaving Duxsowlas because I didn't know what else I could do? For finding it hard to forgive my father, or my mother for forgiving him? For cold-shouldering Naomi and not giving her the clues she wanted to find Nathan Solomon?

Forgive, Margaret. See through and forgive . . .

Let us pray.

Alan's voice calls me to my knees once again, but I do not kneel. Staying seated, I stare into the space before me.

I am kneeling in the schoolhouse at Duxsowlas on the day of my confirmation. My friend Mary kneels beside me: Mary, who wanted to become a holy person and has ended up on some city street, somewhere. Mary and my cousin Billy Boy bow their heads to the bishop, but my head stays upright as the bishop places his hands upon my head and confirms me.

"Did you see God, Margaret?" Mary asked later, because she had so wanted to see God.

No, Mary, I didn't see God. I saw my life. I saw it all coming toward me—the love and the pain and the betrayal that have become my life. It was as clear to me in that moment of confirmation as Raven's splitting the mist open between Sand Island and Log Island and letting the sun pour itself through the gap. Just as clear and just as blinding.

I told myself that day that I was going to meet whatever it was I saw, but I couldn't see through it, not then.

So, have I ever seen through?

And then I remember.

It is the Sunday after Easter. I watch Mom leave our house at Duxsowlas early in the morning to walk out to Bone Spit, where she will spend time at the grave of my granddad. She has done this every year on this day for as long as I can remember. But this year she is not taking David and me with her, as she always has done.

Emer-Teacher left our village in March with my twin sisters firmly implanted in her belly, and now Mom is pregnant with Frank.

I watch her walk toward the end of the village and do not understand how she could have let Dad come near her when he had hurt her as much as he did.

Standing at the edge of the soccer field, I see Mom pass Sadie's place, and then I follow her, taking care that she doesn't see me.

Mom crosses the wet sand that the tide has forsaken for the

moment, goes to Granddad's grave and kneels. Lying in the long grass that ends where the sand begins, I watch her as she stays kneeling, then as she sits beside Granddad's headstone and does not move.

The sun crosses the arc of noon and Mom does not move from where she sits. I want to go to her, but something more than the incoming tide separates the two of us at this moment, and I am all the more angry with my father for creating this barrier that I cannot cross.

Then Dad walks past me. Only feet away from where I lie, he stops and stands, looking at my mother's back. The tide is now well and truly in, and I do not expect him to cross over to her, but he does. Wading in the water up to his waist, he crosses, and then he is standing beside her.

She does not look at him, yet he does not move. Then he sits beside her. After a long time, Mom moves closer to him, rests her head upon his shoulder, and Dad puts his arm about her.

They stay there together until the sun is about to set and until I am tired of waiting for them to do something else.

I begin my walk home. Sadie is sitting on her porch when I pass her house. She smiles at me and I know she knows where I have been and why. I also know that she will ask me nothing and say nothing to anyone.

I do not understand what I have just seen, but I have seen it—my parents arm in arm in a life that has nothing whatsoever to do with what I think or feel about either one of them. I know I will not forget what I have seen, as little as I may understand it.

Until this Good Friday moment, when I'm able to see through.

Well, Cameron, your prints are gone and maybe our marriage, but if you're willing to put the pieces back together, so am I.

Psalm 130 . . .

Alan breaks the silence, asking us to read the psalm together. I reach for a prayer book in the rack attached to the back of the pew in front of me, then remember that there is a prayer book open in my lap. I look down at the page and see the words of Psalm 130:

Out of the deep have I called unto thee, O Lord . . .

Only the book in my lap is not open at the Psalter. My eyes go to the top of the page and my breath catches hold of itself. I am reading the words of Psalm 130 from The Order for the Burial of the Dead.

Cameron . . . ?

It is finished.

My body goes numb and I barely hear Alan speak the closing prayers of the service. The few others around me stand and leave, while I stay in the pew and cannot move.

"Margaret?"

Alan sits down beside me.

"Margaret, is something wrong?"

I place my hand on the back of the pew in front of me to steady the trembling that has come over me.

"Yes, Alan. Everything is wrong and may never be right again."

His eyes drink me in. "Do you want to talk about it?"

Now my widened eyes take him in. What am I seeing? Concern, yes. Compassion, yes. But there is something else I'm starting to see.

"I don't know, Alan. I don't know if I can talk about anything just now."

"Where will you go when you leave here?"

Where will I go? I had thought I knew, but now, suddenly—

"Home, I guess."

He looks intently between the lines of my words, my face, into the uncertainty in my eyes, and takes hold of what he sees.

"Come have a cup of tea with me, Margaret. Or let me make dinner for you. Perhaps you'll feel like talking then."

I look as fully into him as I dare. What?

And then I know. You're in love with me, Alan. Or you're about to fall in love with me, or have been falling in love with me, but haven't let yourself know that.

Yes, you're right at the edge and one word of encouragement from me, one flicker of response, one hint of a yes, will pull you over the edge. Even as I look at you, you're about to place your hand on mine—

I take a deep breath and place my hand firmly upon his, holding it to the pew back.

"Thank you for the service, Alan. What you said was what I needed to hear and you have already helped me, more than you know. Now I have to go home to my husband."

I squeeze his hand once, then release it as I stand and look into his eyes one last time: *I've given you an out, Alan. Please take it and don't betray yourself.*

Returning to himself, he looks up at me. "All right, Margaret. Please let me know if you do need me."

"I will, Alan. I will."

Having veiled the sun, the clouds begin to veil one another. There are more cars on the streets as I drive home, and the stillness of the day is evaporating. The deed of death done, the world around me wants to return as soon as possible to the way of things called normal.

Everyone, that is, but me. I don't speed, but neither do I waste time making for home.

I open the front door, close it, and stand still for a few seconds. There is no sign of Cameron.

What is it? What has happened?

My feet take me to the kitchen, then to the study. On the desk there lies a ceremonial pipe and a book, with a shred of paper linking them. I take the paper and read the words written on it.

Cameron—

The door to the bathroom off our bedroom flies open at the thrust of my hand, but there is no one there.

Where are you, Cameron?

I want to cry his name out, but cannot. Then I find myself standing at the foot of the stairs. My feet like lead, I climb them.

The bathroom door is ajar and I push it all the way open.

His body an island of white in a red sea, Cameron floats in the tub. I kneel beside him and my hand comes to rest upon his head.

After an endless moment, a voice speaks. My voice.

"I'm sorry, Cameron. I am so, so sorry."

Footsteps sound upon the stairs. I turn toward the door to see my brother standing there, and beside him, our cousin, Peter.

Then Nathan Solomon is beside me. His arms enfold me as my life comes to an end, then falls apart. His arms tighten about me as I rock myself against him and cannot stop myself from sobbing and sobbing.

III

Easter Monday—the day of my brother-in-law's funeral.

Cameron's coffin lies on a stand supplied by the funeral home, in the nave just before the altar. I sit with Margaret in the front pew and Peter sits beside me. A muffled silence holds everything else in my life at bay as I take in the space around me and the people who fill it—colleagues of Cameron from SFU, a few friends of Margaret's from work and some parishioners from St. Cyprian's.

And the crucifix above the altar, bearing a Christ heavy with death. Death—and more death. David, Dad, Mom, Caitlin, Adha, and now Cameron.

The service begins, spoken by the priest, Alan Eliot. I listen and don't listen to the words he speaks, until he begins to read from the Gospel for Easter Monday:

And it came to pass, that while they communed together, and reasoned, Jesus himself drew near, and went with them. But their eyes were held, that they should not know him . . .

No, they didn't know him and they probably didn't know each other, for all their communing and reasoning together. So, who of us really knows anyone else, let alone ourselves? Walking riddles, that's what we are, riddling one another as we go.

Then Alan Eliot goes to the pulpit and says what I am thinking: Who of us truly knew Cameron? Here was a brother human being in crisis, and who of us knew he was in crisis?

Or wanted to know? I ask myself. *Brother, what ails you?* Parzival's question, the question that dies on the lips, wanders astray—or comes home to heal.

Who are you talking to, Alan Eliot, as you look and don't look at each of us—Margaret, especially. You don't look at Margaret and she's not looking at you. What's that about?

And then there's me. I lived with you for six years, Cameron. I heard cue lines, lines that should have told me you too were trying to go through the dark light of this world. But I didn't understand them or didn't want to. I finally got it right with my Uncle Charlie, but I missed the mark with you. Me and my Raven heart.

Alan Eliot finishes his words and goes to his seat in the sanctuary. I glance at Margaret, but see no tears. Maybe she has cried herself dry. To the other side of me, Peter is still in shock from all that he has walked into, and I don't need to look at him to know that.

Cyril Elspeth walks to the pulpit to deliver a eulogy. As he speaks and goes on speaking, I get the feeling he has lost the address of the place to which he wants to deliver his words. He tells us what a good teacher Cameron was—creative, Cyril says—and how much his students and colleagues respected him. Then he tells us that Cameron was an idealist who could never be reconciled to the world as it is—an admirable, but perhaps unfortunate, character trait.

What are you really saying, Dr. Elspeth? That Cameron's corpse followed as the night the day from this unfortunate character trait? Or is there something else wandering around in your words?

After more words that walk around his meaning, Cyril Elspeth walks away from the pulpit to join his wife in the pew.

Alan Eliot speaks the prayers that commit Cameron's body to the elements from which it came and his spirit to the care of God. Then the service closes with all of us speaking the words of Psalm 130, because Margaret has insisted that these be the closing words:

Out of the deep have I called unto thee, O Lord; / Lord, hear my voice . . .

The pallbearers place the coffin into the waiting hearse, which will take it directly to the crematorium, while Cyril Elspeth invites the congregation to a reception at Margaret's home. As I leave the church, I glance again at the corpse on the cross.

Someone should bury him, too.

Back at the house, I stand in the kitchen with Peter, ready to do whatever needs to be done. Peter finishes washing another sinkful of dishes and I reach for a towel.

"Go and sit down, both of you." Margaret stands at my side.

"We're doing fine," I say. "Don't worry about us."

"I'm not worrying. I just want the two of you out of here and out

there, somewhere, sitting down." She reaches for the towel I am
holding. "You're not the only ones who can wash and dry a dish, and
you've done more than enough. So get yourselves out of here, please."

I put my arms around her and hold her.

"What was Cyril Elspeth trying to say, Margaret? Because he never
really said what he meant."

"I don't know what Cyril Elspeth meant to say."

"You do. I can feel it."

"Maybe. But I've never fully figured out what I know. So let it go,
Nathan Solomon."

"All right, for now." And I let her take the towel.

I pour myself a cup of coffee on the way into the living room.

"Solomon? What is that about?" Peter asks.

"It's my second name, Peter. You'd better get used to it, because it's
the name I'm known by here."

Cyril Elspeth comes toward me as I make for an empty chair beside
the living room window.

"Hello, Solomon. It's good to see you again, though I wish the
circumstances were different."

Circumstances? Is that what Cameron's dying comes down to?

"The circumstances are what they are, Dr. Elspeth."

"Well, your timing was certainly fortuitous for Margaret."

Circumstances . . . and now fortuitous timing.

I study his face as we speak. A round, cherubic face on a round,
though not fat, body, like the face of Santa Claus, only Santa looks ill at
ease right about now. I took two classes from Cyril Elspeth at SFU. He
knew his stuff, but I'd always had the feeling that it was all something
of a game with him, leading to one end, a big carnival of metaphors.

"It's a tragic end to an admirable life," he is saying. "I wonder what
he was thinking of when he got into that tub."

I glance at the door to Cameron's study, which Margaret closed and
has kept closed after showing me Cameron's note, the pipe from Wesley,
and the book by Rudolf Steiner with Paul Kane's name on the flyleaf.

"What do you think Cameron was thinking about, Dr. Elspeth?" I
ask, my eyes searching out his. Something is troubling you, good
Doctor. What? Are you more than just a concerned spectator in this
tragic end to an admirable life?

My question startles him. "I really couldn't say, Solomon." Then he
changes the course of our conversation. "Are you planning to return
to the campus sometime soon?"

"I don't know. Soon is a long way away, right now."

"Well, I hope I will have you in class again. You were a very interesting student."

"Was I? I guess that's a good thing to be, an interesting student."

Then Dr. Elspeth's wife takes him by the arm and, with a word of greeting to me, steers him toward the front door.

I look for Alan Eliot, to thank him for his few, good words, but he has already left.

A few women from St. Cyprian's stay to help us clean up, then they leave and the three of us are alone in this house that aches with Cameron's death.

"There's plenty of food still," Margaret says as she sits beside me on the couch, and as Peter sits on the chair by the window that I had started toward but never reached.

"My stomach is fine," I say.

"My stomach doesn't know where it's at," says Peter.

"I know," Margaret says. "This was a hell of a thing for the two of you to walk into."

"But we walked in," I say, "and it was time for me to come back."

"Why was it time to come back, little brother?" Margaret's eyes look up at me as I put my arm about her.

"To see you, and Cameron. And to find Hector Dawson if we can."

"Do you remember Hector?" Peter asks.

Margaret manages a little smile. "How could I forget Hector? The first in line at the feast table, whenever there was a feast. And the three of you running around the village, trying not to get into trouble and not always succeeding. The Three Musketeers of Duxsowlas, that's what you were. So, what is Hector doing here?"

"We don't know, Margaret," I say.

"And maybe we don't want to know," Peter adds.

"What do you mean?"

"Hector was in Nanaimo, the last we heard," says Peter. "He had been drinking heavily for some years and smoking pot, but had gone into a recovery program. He did well for a few months; then he slipped and vanished. The last person who saw him told us he was on his way here."

"I see," Margaret says. "And you hope to find him. Well, good luck to you. Vancouver is a hard place to find someone, even if he wants to be found."

"You and I found each other," I say. "Remember?"

"Yes, I remember. But you had a counselor at Fireweed who cared about you and worked her butt off until she found me. Who in this town cares about Hector?"

"Maybe only Peter and I, so far. But I'm intending to interest a person or two in caring about him."

"Such as?"

"Izzy, for one."

"Who is Izzy?" asks Peter.

"A classmate of mine at the school Cameron found for me. He had started volunteering at a food bank downtown just before I left."

Margaret's hand finds my shoulder. "Then luck may be with you. Stay here as long as you need to or until I decide to burn this place down."

"Then you'd better get some sleep before you join the homeless of Vancouver," I say.

"Sleep? What's that?"

"What you need right now. Go to bed, Margaret."

She smiles wearily. "Whatever you say, Nathan Solomon. Maybe I'll go out tonight and find my husband out among the stars." She starts to break down, then catches herself. "And if I do meet up with him, I'll have to think hard about what I'll say to him. Good night."

Peter and I sit in silence after she goes to her bedroom.

"Angie and the other girls always stood in awe of her, and maybe I do, too," says Peter after awhile. Then he glances in the direction of the kitchen. "And maybe I am hungry," he says.

"Then go talk to the fridge while I make a phone call."

"A phone call? To whom?"

"My friend, Izzy."

"Will he want to hear from you at this time of night?"

"Yes, because he's my friend. That's the last thing he told me before I left his place to travel the world. Go get some food, Peter."

"Nathan?"

"Yes?"

"Are you sure you're up to looking for Hector just now?"

"We have to look for him, Peter, whether I'm up to it or not."

I pick up the phone, dial, and let it ring until the voice at the other end of the line answers.

"Izzy? This is Solomon. I'm back and I need your help."

Izzy met them at the food bank. Solomon and Peter found him at the back of the nondescript building just east of the police station and provincial courts, unpacking a carton of donated food. A can of tomato soup in his hand, Izzy looked up and saw them. The soup fell back into the carton as he threw both arms around Solomon and hugged him.

"Oh man, is it ever good to see you!"

Solomon returned the hug, the memory of having walked out on his friend three years earlier without a word of thanks tugging at his heart.

"I'm sorry I split on you without saying goodbye. I wasn't having a good day."

"There are such days. What's up, Solomon?"

"This is my cousin, Peter. We're looking for a friend of ours, Hector Dawson. Here's a photo of him."

Izzy took the photograph and looked at it closely. "When did he come to Vancouver?"

"Late in February, maybe," said Peter. "He'd been in a recovery program in Nanaimo, but decided to put his recovery on hold and come here. At least that's the story Nathan and I got when we went to Nanaimo to see him."

"Nathan?" said Izzy, with an inquiring glance.

"That was my name at home, before I came here," Solomon replied.

"Okay," Izzy said, looking interested in what he had just learned. "And your friend came right to Vancouver?"

"As far as we know," said Peter. "About five weeks ago."

"Five weeks can be a long time in this city," said Izzy. He studied the photo again. "No, I don't recognize him, but that doesn't mean he's not in the neighbourhood. Would he come to a food bank?"

"Why wouldn't he come, if he were hungry enough?" Peter asked, with an edge in his voice.

"Some are too proud to come here, no matter how hungry they are. Did Hector come with money in his pocket?"

"He had been working for awhile, so he may have had money," said Solomon. "And Hector has his own kind of pride, for sure."

"Then if we see him here at all, it might be after his money runs out, which could be any time now. Why don't you both stick around for a few days, help out a bit, and wave that photo in front of those who come in the door. Then you can start hitting the local pubs and bars, the needle exchange and neighbourhood agencies. I'll back you up in any way I can."

Solomon turned to his cousin. "What about it, Peter?"

Peter's eyes widened as he took it all in. "Sure. I guess we've got to spread as wide a net as we can." He glanced at Izzy with a touch of a smile. "Thanks for being willing to help."

"Thank me when your net brings your friend to the surface," Izzy said.

When they came back to Margaret's house that night, she was sitting on the couch, holding a photograph of her wedding.

Peter went upstairs and Solomon sat beside his sister. One night shortly after he had moved here from his group home, Margaret had sat with him on this couch, holding the same photo. "I went into his office that day and told him I was in love with him," she had said. "I knew he was in love with me from the way he had been looking at me when I sat in his classes and when I sat in his office, every time I could cook up a reason to sit in his office. But he wouldn't cross the gap from teacher to student, so I had to make that walk and did. I wish I could show you a picture of the look on his face when I told him I loved him."

Then Margaret had smiled at him, the smile of a child who has crossed a slippery log spanning a river and knows she can never cross back over. "I couldn't believe I had done it, when it was done. And now here we are, the two of us."

Now Margaret sat beside Solomon, the photograph in hand, and told him about their drifting apart, and about Lance, Cameron's lover. When she had finished telling what she knew, which wasn't very much, she broke down, and Solomon held her as the tears and anger flooded forth.

Leaning back into the couch, his arms about his sister, Solomon listened. How could Cameron have turned to a man as a lover? And who was this man? An Indian, like Margaret. Someone who was supposed to be preparing to be a spiritual leader of his people, and there he was, screwing around with her husband.

And why? Had Cameron only been looking to another Native person for whatever he felt he couldn't get from her? Any Native person he could cuddle up to? How could he do that, when she had been ready to give him anything . . . everything? Except for that one thing she couldn't give, a doorway into a world where she had chosen no longer to live.

Solomon went on listening. Then, when the words had spent themselves and there were only tears, he withdrew a little into himself to find out how he felt about what Margaret had told him.

Who had Cameron been for him? The brother-in-law who had welcomed him into his home . . . the person who had gone out of his way to find a school that was not just any school . . . the person who had taken an interest in his life and the lives of his friends, and who had helped him with that huge grade twelve project. Maybe Cameron had done all of that, in part, for ends of his own, but he had been there for Solomon and Solomon could not be angry with him for what he had done to Margaret, no more than he could be angry now with his father for loving Emer and fathering two sisters who had become important persons in his life.

So how did he feel? Long after he had given Margaret a last, long hug and sent her off to bed, he stayed sitting on the couch. When his feelings did surface, he realized they had little to do with whatever relationship Cameron might have had with someone named Lance. Instead they revolved around a very different question: Where are you now, Cameron? What is happening to you right now?

For the next week Solomon and Peter stayed close to the food bank and showed Hector's photo to those not too proud to let their hunger lead them there. There were a few flickers of memory, of a night in a pub, of a cigarette passed from one hand to another, or of a casual meeting outside Carnegie Centre, but flickers of memory only. Hector's face eluded the kind of remembering that could place him clearly in space or time.

When they took to the streets the following week, they didn't fare any better. Bartenders glanced at the photo without really seeing it and shrugged. A few street workers could remember a young Native man who might have been Hector, but who had not stayed around to take whatever help they could have given.

No one at the needle exchange had any memory of Hector's face. That's good, thought Solomon, unless Hector isn't thinking much about the state of the needles he uses, if he's using needles. A glance at Peter told him Peter was having the same thought.

Well into their third week, Izzy joined them for a cup of coffee at a café called the Flaming Peacock, better known in the neighbourhood as the Ruptured Duck.

"Where did you go when you left Vancouver?" Izzy asked from out of nowhere.

The suddenness of the question took Solomon by surprise, yet released a fuller answer than he might otherwise have given. Izzy and Peter listened intently as Solomon told them about his cousin Wesley in Alberta, then of those three fateful nights in September of 1992 occupying a dam site that ended with the death of the sister he hadn't known was his sister. He then took them to Wales and his meeting with Sean, then to Ireland with his other sister, saying enough to indicate that the two of them were in search of something more than a holiday together.

Then Solomon stopped speaking. For a long moment neither Izzy nor Peter spoke.

"Jesus, Nathan!" Peter said, finally. "You never told me any of that, other than you tracked down two sisters, one of whom died."

"No, I didn't," Solomon said, "because some of it isn't easy to talk about and some of it I don't fully understand yet."

"It's funny, Solomon," said Izzy. "I thought I'd gotten to know you pretty well, those years we were together. I thought, in fact, I knew you better than anyone else in the class did, except for Anika, and maybe Alex, and later, Sigune. Man, was I ever wrong! You came with a past you kept pretty much to yourself, but which set you up for where your life took you these past three years. And none of us in the class was part of that. Now I'm wondering if I've ever really known you. But then, who of us really knows another person?"

"What do you mean?" Peter asked.

"What I mean is that I walk the streets of this neighbourhood and I see people hurting one another and helping one another. They share needles, shoot each other up, sometimes cover for each other, and other times screw each other around. This is the world into which your friend has disappeared and no one knows where or who he is. But then this whole city is a wonderland of enchanted strangers who touch shoulders, or eyes, even, yet never meet. Who really knows anyone else?"

Solomon looked out the café window at the faces walking past. "I was asking myself that question at Cameron's funeral," he said, as he tried to brush aside the stab of pain that had come when Izzy said Anika's name. "As for me, well, knowing myself has been pretty hard work, so I guess I don't make it easy for others to know me or for me to know them."

Outside the café, the late morning sun glared through the window at them, from the walls and windows of the buildings on the other side of the street. Peter leaned back in his chair and toyed with his empty cup. "What do you do when you're not at the food bank?" Peter asked Izzy.

"I'm working on a degree at Simon Fraser University, in sociology."

"As of when?" Solomon asked. "You weren't too excited about going on to school when we graduated."

"No, I wasn't, then, because I had no reason to go on. And then I found a reason to get a degree, although much of what I have to do is academic and dry as hell. But I want to work with people, and I want that bit of paper that will give me some room to shape the way in which I do that."

"And how do you want to work with people?" asked Peter.

"I want to help break the spell, if I can."

"What spell?"

"The spell that keeps people apart."

"That sounds like a big undertaking. Do you think you can do it?"

"No, and yes," Izzy said. "Sometimes there are miracles."

Peter nodded and said nothing more. Solomon looked out the window once again, then back at his friend. "What about us as a class, Izzy? Did we ever know each other, really?"

Izzy smiled. "I thought so at the time. Not always, perhaps, but often enough. And now? Well, we may have a chance to find out at our reunion."

"What reunion?"

"The one Alex and Sigune are hosting, in June. You'd better stick around long enough to be there. I won't be so forgiving if you walk out on us again."

"Well, while the two of you are thinking about your class reunion, where do we go from here in our search for Hector?" Peter asked.

"What about Commercial Drive?" Solomon said from out of nowhere. "There are Native faces walking around there."

"Why not?" said Izzy. "It's worth a try. We could always get a coffee at Joe's and shoot a game of pool if we need a break."

Solomon smiled. "I don't think so, Izzy. I haven't shot pool since high school."

"You'd get your game back quickly enough," said Izzy. "Watch your cousin, Peter, when he has a cue in his hand. He's a hustler behind that nice guy smile. By the way, old friend, who ever taught you to shoot that kind of game?"

Solomon came upright in his chair. "Someone who cared about me, and moved heaven and earth to find Margaret when I was living in the group home here. And she may be the person to help us figure out where to go next. Sit tight while I make a phone call."

They stood inside the entrance of the Adolescent Street Unit on Drake Street. Solomon looked about him, remembering the night eleven years ago when he had found his way into this building, then known as Emergency Services, a night when he had been wet and cold and lost.

Solomon went up to a woman behind a desk. "I'm looking for Judy, please."

But Judy found them before the woman got up from the desk. "Solomon!"

Without a second thought he reached out to her and she hugged him. Amazed at how short she was and how slender her body felt in his arms, fragile even, he wondered at the strength she had brought to his life during those months he had stayed at Fireweed.

"Come back to my cubbyhole, such as it is."

They seated themselves after Solomon introduced Peter and Izzy to Judy and shook their heads when she offered them coffee. "That's just as well," Judy said, "because I've drunk more than my share of that stuff today. So Izzy and you went to the Chinook Park Waldorf School together?"

"Yes," Solomon said. "How did you know?"

"I kept in touch with your sister for awhile after you left Fireweed, and I saw the notice of your graduation in the paper."

Moved by the fact that she had continued to be interested in him long after he had ceased to think of her, Solomon felt a sudden pang of remorse. "I should have invited you to our graduation, to thank you for finding Margaret. I'm sorry I didn't think of it."

"Don't spend too much time being sorry, Solomon. You simply got on with your life, and I went on with mine once I got used to the idea of you not being around and pushing my buttons the way you sometimes did," Judy said with a big grin. They both laughed. "Now, tell me about your friend."

Solomon handed her the photo and she looked at it.

"He's about your age?"

"Yes."

"Then I doubt that anyone in this building has seen his face. We deal mostly with adolescents. Where else have you looked?"

Solomon spelled out where they had looked.

"And you've turned up nothing?" Judy asked.

"Nothing that has taken us anywhere," said Solomon.

"But Hector came with money in his pocket," Izzy said, "so he may still be making it on his own."

"Are you sure he came to Vancouver?" asked Judy.

"He's here, for sure," Peter said.

Something in Peter's tone interested Judy. "Why are you so sure?"

Peter hesitated, then looked away from her and didn't answer.

"How would your friend spend whatever money he had, after making sure of food and a bed?" Judy directed her question to Peter.

Peter kept his eyes averted from hers. Then a thin smile crept across his mouth and he shrugged. "On women. On whores, to be more exact. There are more and better whores in Vancouver, Hector once told me, though I don't know where he got that idea."

Solomon and Izzy stared at Peter, while Judy sat and waited for Peter to continue.

"Hector likes women," Peter said after a long moment. "When we were growing up together, Hector liked food more than anything else. But when we went to high school in Port Hardy, his liking shifted to the girls. Then later to booze and pot, but he's never stopped liking women."

"And Hector would be ready to pay for what he liked?"

"Yes," said Peter.

Solomon glanced at his cousin and knew there was more to the story. Looking back at Judy, he found her looking at him.

"Then you and I, Solomon, know someone who might be able to help you, though whether she would be willing to help, I couldn't say. Do you remember Shannon?"

Solomon almost laughed at the question. "How could I forget Shannon? The world and everyone in it is fucked in the head. At least that was her working philosophy at Fireweed. The night she split from there, she was on her way to find a pimp called Diamond."

"She found him," Judy said, "but it's been awhile since she's worked for him. Diamond likes his employees to be young and pliable. At twenty-seven Shannon is no longer pliable, if she ever was, and is on the downside of her career."

"Where does she work?" Izzy asked.

"She used to work up here, on and off Davie Street, but a younger and stronger generation have pushed her and a few others out. The last time I ran into her she was working on Cordova Street."

Izzy's eyebrows lifted. "That far down on the pecking order?"

"Age and drugs are taking their toll," Judy said. "Would you recognize her, Solomon?"

"I think so. Shannon made lasting impressions."

"On all of us who knew her," Judy said, smiling. "I wish I had more leads to give you, but Shannon may be just what you need."

Judy walked them to the door and hugged Solomon one more time as they left.

"She did care about you," said Peter, as they stood in the sun once again.

"I know that," Solomon said. "And I knew it when I was at Fireweed, even though I couldn't let her know that I knew."

They spent that evening patrolling Cordova Street, from Gastown to Gore Street, then several blocks eastward, but there was no sign of Shannon.

"Maybe she doesn't keep regular business hours," said Peter.

"Or maybe she picked up an early client looking for a long night," Izzy said. "Let's try again tomorrow."

The next night, at the end of a sun-drenched Friday, Solomon spotted her. She stood under a street lamp that had just come alight as the dark of evening settled in about her. The light from the lamp touched down on her long blonde hair as if to lift up light from it if it could.

"Is that her?" Peter asked.

"Yes. Wait here."

"Are you sure?" asked Izzy.

"I'm sure. Wait here."

Solomon took his time approaching her. She turned toward him casually as she felt him coming. "Hello. Do you want some company?"

He stopped and knew that she didn't yet know him.

"Hello, Shannon."

Her eyes sprang wide open, then narrowed at the suggestion of recognition beyond the business of the moment.

"Remember me? Solomon. From Fireweed."

Then she remembered. "Solomon! Christ, what are you doing here? But what the fuck does it matter. A customer is a customer."

"I'm not a customer, Shannon. I need to talk with you about a missing friend."

"I'm a working girl, Solomon. I can't afford to talk about missing friends when I'm on the job."

He placed a fifty-dollar bill into her hand. "Now can you afford to talk to me? And a couple of my friends?"

She looked the bill over. "Sure. I'll talk to you."

"I'll buy you a coffee, too," Solomon said.

At a nearby café, Shannon sat with the three of them and lit a cigarette.

"You've taken good care of yourself, Solomon. And you're cute, too, now that you've grown up. And you're also cute," she said to Peter.

Peter squirmed in his chair and reached for his coffee cup.

"I like Native men," Shannon said.

"We can be likable enough," said Solomon, with a glance at Izzy, who was gazing pensively into some world beyond the plate glass window.

"No offense intended," Shannon said to Izzy.

"No offense taken," Izzy said, with a smile.

"So, what are we here to talk about?"

"Him." Solomon laid the photo on the table in front of Shannon.

Shannon became very still. She took a long pull on her cigarette, picked the photo up and looked long at it. Solomon watched her eyes, eyes not searching for recognition, but remembering.

"He's cute, too," she said, handing the photo back to Solomon.

"His name is Hector. Have you seen him?"

"I know his name. And yes, I've seen him, several times." She stubbed her cigarette out and stroked the rim of the ashtray with her finger. "His gut is getting flabby, but he has good strong thigh muscles and a good finishing kick. As I said, I like Native men. One night I was even tempted not to charge him."

It was Peter who broke the silence that followed Shannon's words. "When did you have these meetings with Hector?"

"The first was about a month ago. He was so sweet. He said he'd been looking for me all his life, that he loved doing it with white women, and that he'd pay me double if he could lay me down in the long grass, like he did it with girls back home. Down in the grass—it was a ripped and rotting mattress, but for him, it was down in the long grass."

"And you charged him double for that lay in the long grass?"

"I charged him exactly what he offered me."

Peter's knuckles went white as his hand gripped the edge of the table. "You bitch! You charged him double and told him how much you like Native men as you did it!"

Shannon's nostrils flared and her eyes flashed. "You're goddamn right I charged him double! He wanted a white woman, he paid for what he wanted, and he got his money's worth. I've got to survive down here and I'll take whatever I can get. And fuck you if you don't like it!"

Solomon put a hand on Peter's arm, and Izzy, a hand on the other arm. They released their grip when Peter settled back in his chair.

Shannon's eyes took Peter in as she lit another cigarette. "You're cute enough, Tan Man, and you're obviously an ignorant hick from some little hick town, so I'll let your mouth go by me this time without putting my fist through it. But you tense up too quickly and you could get burned fast in this part of town, right to the hole in your ass, if you keep on tensing up. So lighten up!"

Solomon looked out the window and watched the night creep through the streets of the downtown eastside. "Where did Hector take you?" he asked.

"To where he lives."

"Does he still live there?"

"He still lives there. Unless he's moved in the past few days."

"Would you please tell us where he lives?"

She considered her cigarette. "That might be a breach of client confidentiality, Solomon."

"Please, Shannon."

Shannon propped an elbow on the table and placed her chin in the cup of her hand. "'Please.' That's such a nice word. I don't hear it very often."

She took a paper napkin and the pen Izzy handed her. When she had written on the napkin, she folded it and gave it to Solomon. "Nicely written, because you said please when you asked."

Solomon took the napkin and stood. "Thank you, Shannon. Now tell me, are we all still fucked in the head?"

She smiled up at him. "Of course, Solomon. Double-fucked, in fact."

They left her sitting at the table and stepped out into the night. At the corner of the next street, they stopped beneath a light.

"Bitch!" Peter snarled.

"Peter, was Hector really that obsessed with white women?" Solomon asked.

Peter's rage suddenly drained away. "Yes, he was that obsessed. The more so when he found out white girls wanted him as much as he wanted them. He was good looking, kicked a mean soccer ball, and learned to wrap himself in a kind of Indian mystique. The white girls in Port Hardy loved it, and they didn't make him pay for it." He glanced back at the café. "Bitch!"

"Are you going to be all right?" Solomon asked.

Peter shuddered, then let it go. "I'll be all right."

"Good." Solomon handed the napkin to Izzy. "Do you know where this place is?"

Izzy looked at the writing. "Yes, I know where this place is and I'll even take you there."

The gray stucco building one block south of Cordova, near Oppenheimer Park, sat right at the edge of the sidewalk. As they entered it, Solomon could feel the despair and death that had seeped into its walls over the years.

A light bulb dangled from the ceiling at the foot of a flight of stairs, and its glimmer led them up to a second floor.

"Jesus!" Peter breathed.

The body of a man sprawled before them, his upper body propped against the stairs leading to the third floor. A needle stuck out at an oblique angle from his left arm. Izzy bent down, placing the palm of his hand close to the man's face.

"He's still breathing. Just step over him."

Izzy led them up to the third floor and along the hallway until they found Hector's room number. Solomon placed his hand on the doorknob, to find the door ajar. He pushed it open.

A slash of light from a street lamp came through the windowpane and across the body of a man lying on the bed. Solomon sat on the bed beside Hector and swallowed down the convulsion in his throat as the stench of vomit assaulted his nostrils. "There's a lamp on the dresser, Peter," he said.

Yellow light seeped through the room as Peter switched on the lamp. Peter stood at the dresser and stared at the bed, at Hector, and at the vomit in which Hector lay. Izzy went to the window and forced it open as far as it would go. "It's a good thing he went to sleep on his side and that there's a sink in the room," he said.

But there was no towel or washcloth. Peter took off his jacket, then his T-shirt, and soaked the shirt in the sink. Solomon and Izzy rolled Hector from the bed to the floor. Solomon stripped Hector's T-shirt from him, took Peter's wet T-shirt from the sink, and began to cleanse Hector's upper body as Peter took the blanket from the bed, rolled Hector's T-shirt into it, and tossed the blanket into a corner.

Solomon finished washing Hector and dropped Peter's T-shirt on top of the rolled blanket.

"We need to put something on him," said Peter. He looked into the chest of drawers, drawer by drawer. "Nothing here."

Izzy took off his jacket, then his shirt.

"He's pretty big," Peter said.

"This will fit," Izzy said. "I always wear shirts that flop around me."

Solomon put the shirt on Hector and then the three of them lifted Hector onto the bed. "Put him in the recovery position," said Izzy, "in case he vomits again."

Solomon sat on the floor, his back to the wall. Peter sat beside him.

"You don't have to stay, Izzy," said Solomon.

"But I think I will," said Izzy. He put his jacket on and sat beside Solomon.

Sometime after midnight Solomon awoke suddenly from a dull sleep to see Hector's body rising up from the bed.

"Peter!"

Then Peter was beside him. The two of them wrestled Hector to the bed. For a moment Hector fought them; his eyes filled with the light from the street lamp, he stared both into a world somewhere out beyond the last conceivable star and into the nightmare playing itself out somewhere behind his eyes.

Izzy stood beside the bed and watched. Then Hector collapsed into Solomon's arms. His eyes closed.

"Is he okay?" Izzy asked.

"I think so," said Solomon. "For now."

Peter and Izzy returned to their places on the floor and soon went back to sleep. Sitting between them, Solomon wanted to sleep but was too awake now to do that.

A few sounds drifted up from the street below the open window: a passing car, two voices that faded away into the night, and then little else, as the night crept into its silent hours.

Hector groaned faintly, turned onto his back, then was quiet. The street lamp dropped its light across his body like a shroud that veiled nothing of what it covered. Solomon stared at the body on the bed. Suddenly, the body was not Hector's but Cameron's, lying in a sea of blood in a white tub.

His head falling forward into his hands, Solomon began to cry. As silent as the night about him, his tears ran down his wrists and along his arms. Into the dead hours of the night Solomon cried, while Peter and Izzy slept on either side of him.

At last, the flow of tears began to ebb. Solomon lifted his head from his hands until the back of it rested against the wall.

I've found you, Hector, but lost Cameron. And my father. And my mother. And David. And Caitlin—and others who were part of me.

Death . . . and loss.

He wiped at his eyes with his fingers and looked again at Hector. But I have found you . . .

Loss, yet gain. I lost Caitlin, yet found Erin. Would I have found Erin if I hadn't lost Caitlin? Would I have found Margaret and Cameron, my school, my classmates and even Caitlin, if Dad hadn't died the way he did?

Losing . . . finding. I've found you, Hector. Now, can I also find the other person I'm looking for? Even as I grieve the loss of Cameron . . .

Soon, morning came. Solomon got up from where he had sat, went to the basin and washed the last of the tears from his face.

Hector stirred on the bed and his eyes opened. He stared up for a long moment at the person looking down at him.

"Nathan?"

"Hello, Hector."

"What are you doing here?"

"Visiting you."

Hector propped himself up on his elbows and tried to shake something out of his head. "It's been a long while since you visited me. And I'm out of shape when it comes to hosting guests."

"I'll take a raincheck on the feast. Peter came with me."

"So I see. And who is he?"

"This is my friend, Izzy."

"And he's visiting, too?"

"Yes, he is."

"Then I'd better sober up fast. Good morning, Peter. What are you doing in the big city?"

"Getting pissed off at you," Peter said, as he and Izzy stood up.

Hector swung his legs from the bed and tried them on the floor. "Save your urine, Pete, because I'm just as likely to get pissed all over again on my own. But not before I find that clean, white toilet down the hall. Only it's not clean or white, but that's life."

Hector stood and wobbled toward the door. "I'll come with you," said Solomon.

"I don't need a baby sitter, Nathan. You just take your cousin in hand and tell him to think kindly of his friends."

"Go to hell," Peter said, as he went to the sink to wash his face.

"I'll go for a piss instead," said Hector.

Solomon stood in the doorway until Hector came back to the room. Hector washed his face, looked around for something to dry it with, and then shrugged. "It stinks in here," he said. "Let's go outside, to the park. We can lie in the sun and watch other drunks lying in the sun. And maybe there'll be children playing. I like to lie in the sun and watch children play."

When they came to the second floor landing, the body that had been lying there the night before was gone.

"There was someone lying here," Peter said. "With a needle sticking out of his arm."

"Oh yeah, him," said Hector. "The stupid fucker can never wait until he gets to his room to shoot up."

They made their way along Cordova to Oppenheimer Park and sat down on the grass near a play area for children. Solomon and Peter sat side by side with their backs to a grassy knoll. They helped Hector lower himself to the earth, then cradled him between them. Izzy sat beside Solomon.

The sun climbed toward noon and then passed over into the afternoon. All that while they sat together, watched the children play and said nothing. Then Hector broke the silence.

"Do you remember how we used to run around Duxsowlas, playing?"

"I remember," said Solomon. "You and Peter and me. The Three Musketeers of Duxsowlas—that's how Margaret remembers us."

"We'd gawk at the totem pole, or at Sisiutl on the front of the big house, or watch our big brothers and sisters out on the soccer field. Or we'd go to where your Adha stayed and watch her weave cedar. It was good, the way we played then."

Solomon smiled. "Yes, it was good."

"Where did you go, Nathan, when you left us?" Hector asked.

Solomon watched a small boy tackle a big climbing frame. "I came here, found Margaret, and went to school with Izzy. After that I went to Alberta, found a cousin and a sister, and then went on to Wales and Ireland and found another sister. Then I came back to Duxsowlas, but you had gone by then."

"I guess I had. And you came here to find me?"

"Yes, Peter and I came to find you."

"And that was the only reason you came?"

Solomon looked down as Hector's eyes searched his. "It was a good reason to come."

"Then I hope you're not disappointed." Hector looked away, at a man shuffling across the far corner of the park. "Are you still angry at me, Peter?"

Peter shifted his weight to deal with a muscle that had started to cramp up on him. "No, I'm not angry at you."

"That's good. It doesn't feel good, having friends angry at you."

They went on sitting as the sun slipped down the sky toward the west. The children also slipped away, and for a few moments the park seemed to be empty of people.

"I need a smoke and a coffee," Hector said.

"I'll get you a coffee and cigarettes," said Izzy.

"I think I'm out of money." Hector took out his wallet and inspected it carefully. "Yeah, I'm broke. The last whore I laid must have rolled me."

"The smokes and the coffee are on me," Izzy said. "What do you take in your coffee?"

"Cream and sugar. As much as you can pour in."

"And what brand do you smoke?"

"Anything that will burn."

"I'll be back in a few minutes."

Hector settled back in his friends' arms as Izzy started across the grass. "He's a good person," Hector said.

"Yes, he is," Solomon agreed.

"Do you remember the first time we went drinking? At Bone Spit, with Robbie and Steve?"

186

Peter groaned. "And my sister, and your sister, and Violet. Yeah, I do remember that night."

Solomon twisted some grass around his finger. That night had been in the fall after David had burned up Log Island and himself with it.

"Robbie bought the beer and then we sloshed out to Bone Spit just after sundown. Violet bitched all the way there because the tide wasn't right out," said Hector. "Remember, Nathan?"

"Yes, I remember."

Robbie wanted the tide right out, he said, because he didn't want to carry drunken girls through bounding waves in the middle of the night. Naomi's older brother, Steve, wisecracked about boozing among the spooks and about his squeaky clean sister who had decided not to come along. Angie and Vera worried about what their fathers would do if they found out what they were doing, while Robbie promised to stuff Violet under a bush if she got drunk and come back for her in the morning.

And then only the sound of popping cans greeted the descent of darkness upon the graveyard of Duxsowlas.

"And then Peter started to come on to my sister," said Hector.

"I did not come on to Vera," Peter said.

"After your third beer, you snuggled up to her and became a serious lover. I would call that coming on to her," Hector grinned.

"So what do you think you're doing?" said Vera.

"Vera, I love you," Peter mumbled.

Angie and Violet exploded in a fit of giggles. Vera put her arm around Peter. "Well, Peter darling, I'll tell you what. You just keep your zipper high and tight to the mast, and you can love me all you like."

"High and tight. That's me," said Peter happily and started to hiccup.

"Then Steve got on your case, Nathan," Peter remembered. "Because you weren't keeping up with him."

"Are you going to take that can to bed with you, Nathan?"

Nathan looked at the can he had stopped drinking from moments before, thinking about David. Nathan had thought getting drunk might deaden the pain, but knew as he looked at the beer in his hand that the pain wouldn't go away, no matter what he did. He put the can down in the grass and stood up to leave.

"What's the matter, Nathan? Can't you keep up with the big boys and girls?"

Hector asked Steve if he had a problem, and then Steve asked Hector if he had a problem. A season on the soccer field had moved Hector's weight from his belly up to his arms and down to his thighs. But Steve was older and decided not to back down. He stood up and Hector stood up.

"Your mouth is my problem, Steve. It's never closed."

"Then maybe you'd like to come over and close it for me."

"Maybe I would."

Then Vera jumped to her feet, both her hands sweeping Hector and Steve apart—

"Whatever happened to Steve?" Hector asked.

"He went off to school, got a degree in something and came back to Indian country with a suit and tie," Peter replied. "He's one of our negotiators, whenever we negotiate about something."

Hector laughed. "So his mouth is still never closed?"

"Hardly ever," Peter said.

Izzy appeared with the coffee and cigarettes. Hector sipped the coffee and found it to his liking. "Thanks, Izzy. Did you remember to bring matches?"

Izzy gave him a packet of matches and Hector lit a cigarette. He settled back against Solomon and Peter and let the smoke stream out from his nostrils. "That's good," he said.

Hector finished the cigarette, drank the rest of his coffee, then lit another cigarette.

"I'm going to need a drink soon."

Solomon watched an old man get up from a bench on which he had been sitting, check out a nearby garbage container, then hobble his way from the park. "How about sobering up?" he said.

"And what would I do then?"

"Go home, with us," answered Peter.

"Did we leave any beer at Bone Spit?"

"I think we drank it all."

Hector thought about it. "Sobering up and staying clean isn't something I've done well at. I'll need some help."

"There's a detox centre not far from here," said Izzy. "It might be a day or so before a bed is available, but I'll get you that bed as soon as it does come free. I just need to talk to some people."

"Well, Hector?" Solomon said.

"Let me think about it," said Hector.

They walked Hector back to his room and Peter took him upstairs while Solomon and Izzy stood outside.

"He should stay at least a month, if I can swing it," Izzy said. "Which would keep you in town for the reunion. Everyone within reach will be coming."

"I guess that would work out," said Solomon. Then he hesitated as a lump suddenly rose to his throat. "Who isn't coming?"

"Catherine, for one. She's in England. And Lorne is in Calgary." Izzy paused. "And Anwar."

"Why not Anwar?"

Izzy stared at him, then shook his head. "Of course. How would you have known? Anwar was killed when the Americans bombed Baghdad in 1991."

Solomon stood very still as the sound of traffic along Cordova Street passed by him—only within himself he was no longer standing on Cordova Street but was sitting beside Anika at Third Beach in Stanley Park, nearly four years ago. *Have you heard any news of Anwar?* she had asked.

Why are you asking about Anwar? he had wondered, and then remembered that Anwar had moved back to Iraq and that Iraq had just occupied Kuwait. But Solomon had pushed aside any thought of Anwar and what might be happening to him because he had already decided he wanted to lay Anika down in the sand and get from her what he hadn't taken earlier on. Then she realized what he was doing and threw sand in his face: *You ravening bastard! You were going to fuck me! Fuck me! And that was all, wasn't it?*

He hadn't cared a damn at that moment for Anika, or Anwar, or anyone but himself.

"Solomon, where have you gone?" Izzy asked.

"To another place in my life," Solomon answered, with a shake of his head. "I'm sorry about Anwar. He was too good a person to die like that."

Izzy nodded, and then the two of them stood in silence.

"Has anyone heard from Anika?" Solomon hadn't known he was going to risk the question until it sprang from his lips.

"No one has seen anything of Anika for several years," Izzy replied. "Her mother moved away and we don't know if Anika went with her or stayed."

Peter came down the stairs. "I'll stay with Hector tonight," he said to Solomon. "You go home and spend some time with Margaret."

"I'll go to work on that bed," said Izzy, "and I'll call you, Solomon, when I know something. In the meantime, call Alex and Sigune when you come up for air. I've told them you're back and they're waiting to hear from you. Okay?"

Izzy hugged him, then walked off into the evening.

"He is a good person," said Peter. He stood for a moment, hands in his pockets, then said, "Now that we've tracked Hector down, when are you going to start looking for Naomi?"

"When did I say I was going to look for Naomi?"

Peter looked at him and did not answer. Solomon shrugged. "Where do I start looking for Naomi, Peter? Aunt Minnie knew I was living with Margaret. Why hasn't Naomi called Margaret? Maybe Naomi isn't that interested in finding me or in me finding her."

"That's bullshit, Nathan, and you know it. Maybe your auntie never told Naomi you were living with Margaret. Are you afraid she'll be in the same shape as Hector, if you find her?"

"No, not that, but—"

"But what? What's holding you back? It's as if you need to do something else here before you can find Naomi and she can find you. I've felt that in you ever since we left Duxsowlas. Am I right?"

"Maybe so," Solomon said. "I think I should stay with you and Hector tonight."

"No way. I can look after Hector, now that he's sobered up a bit. Go home and be with your sister."

Peter turned and vanished up the steps that led to Hector's room.

Solomon stood in the evening that was darkening about him and peered into that gathering darkness, as if he might see Naomi on the street corner, or Anika. But he saw only a dog lifting its leg against a streetlight.

Margaret sits at the kitchen table, staring into the cup of tea she has barely touched. She looks up at me as I walk in.

"Any luck?"

"Yes. We found him yesterday in a stinking little room just off Cordova. Izzy is going to try for a bed at the detox centre."

"How is he?"

"He could be worse. Now we have to figure out how to keep him straight and sober until we can take him home."

"Does he want to go home?" Her question snags me and won't let go.

"I hope so," I reply.

"You'd better find that out before you buy him a bus ticket." Her eyes drop to her cup as she pushes it away from her.

"I'll make a fresh pot," I say.

"Thank you."

I stand with my back to the stove as the kettle heats itself toward a boil. Margaret stays sitting, where she had sat across from me the day Mom died and also that night I was in grade ten and a little crisis in my class that began with a pool cue found its way to a crisis between the two of us.

How many crises in people's lives come to a head at a kitchen table? I wonder.

As I make the tea, I remember the night Mom smashed a bottle of ketchup against our sink at Duxsowlas, set a dish filled with ketchup and glass in front of Frank, and told him to eat it. Then came Mom's angry words to Dad—*Don't you preach to me, Isaac. You have no grounds on which to preach to me*—before she went out into the night. Frank and I sat at the kitchen table and waited for our world to end in a cataclysm of ketchup, broken glass and words.

I bring the pot to the table and wait for the tea to steep, and for Margaret's silence to play itself out.

Sadie Moon always had bread and jam on her kitchen table and so did Aunt Lila. Peter and I always ended up at one of those two tables at the end of long summer days and on cold winter nights, when we should have been on our way to bed, only by then it was too late to worry about being in bed.

"Do you remember sitting at Auntie Lila's table and Sadie's and stuffing yourself with bread and jam?" I ask as I pour the tea.

She looks blankly at me, her cup on the way to her lip. Her eyes ask, And where is all that coming from?

"Do you remember?"

Then her eyes brighten. "Yes. More so Sadie's bread and jam than Auntie Lila's. Mary and I would go to Sadie's with Vera, Angie and Violet in tow, because Sadie never cut us off. She knew we'd figure out for ourselves which bite should be our last."

I laugh. "Sadie did cut Peter, Hector and me off, while Auntie Lila never did."

"Maybe each had learned a lesson by the time the three of you came along," Margaret says. Now her eyes become moist. "Then Mary and I would go to Sadie's on our own, when we were in grade eight. Sadie filled us with food and tea, and mothered us as if each feed might be our last. As if she knew what might be coming our way when we went to Port Hardy . . ."

Margaret lowers her cup to the table and starts to cry. I reach for her hand, and her other hand reaches for mine.

"And then I saw the pain. Abuse and pain, hidden under the table, then right in my face—and I couldn't take it any more. So I left, came here and met Cameron. Now the pain will stop, I told myself, but it didn't. Cameron wanted into my world or into his dream of my world, but my world was filled with pain and I didn't want to take anyone there. It was then Cameron and I got down to hurting one another because he couldn't understand and I couldn't tell him. In the end he leaves me a note telling me it was all his fault, and would I please return a book to Paul Kane and a pipe to my cousin Wesley, whoever my cousin Wesley is."

I release her hands. "Do you want to know who our cousin Wesley is?"

She thinks about it. "Sure, little brother. Why not? Now is as good a time as any for untold family secrets."

So I begin. Wesley, our cousin, had a grandfather named Wounded Drum, the brother of our grandfather whose name I have never learned. Our grandfather had a dream two nights before the battle of the Little Bighorn, a dream of a crescent moon with a white raven in the dark circle above the crescent. He came to the northwest coast of Canada and to Haida Gwaii to search out a people who might know the secret of his dream. Our father told me all of that after I had spent three days on Log Island—before David burned it up—and had seen my own vision of that crescent moon. Ever since then I have been searching out the meaning of that dream and my own seeing of what our grandfather saw. Along the way I found you and Cameron, and my class and teachers at school, and then Wesley when I ran my life here into the ground and had nowhere else to go.

Two years later Caitlin walked into my life and her dying led me to her twin, Erin, and their uncle, Sean. Sean told Erin and me of his meeting with Dad during the war and of Dad's first meeting with Emer, who became the mother of Caitlin and Erin when she came to Duxsowlas that year as a teacher and met Dad again.

And then my telling is done.

Margaret drinks it in slowly, as she drinks down her tea until the cup is dry.

"So that's what your grade twelve project was about. Really about."

"Yes, along with many things in my life."

"Did Adha know anything of what you have just told me?"

"I think she knew something, though I couldn't say how much she knew."

"She didn't tell me anything before she died. I was there in her room in the hospital and she told me nothing. No one has ever told me what you just told me."

She stands, goes to the sink with her cup and saucer, and turns on the tap.

"Maybe she never felt you asking for that story," I say.

"It seems there were many things I didn't ask for," Margaret says.

She returns to the table, sits and starts to go back into herself, but I tug at a thread I think I see. "What did Adha tell you when you went to see her?"

She sorts through her remembering, deciding what she will tell me. "She told me about Uncle Charlie and his time at residential school. And Aunt Minnie and Aunt Lila, and Mom, but mostly about Uncle Charlie."

Then she tells me how Uncle Charlie had tried to protect Harvey Silas, Naomi's father, from being abused. Uncle had tried to protect Harvey and had failed.

"Did she tell you about Uncle Charlie and David?" I ask.

"No. What about Uncle and David?"

"David was Uncle Charlie's son. That's why Uncle lavished gifts on David the way he did."

She stares at me. "How did you find that out?"

"Uncle told Frank and me, when I went home last October. I had walked out on him after Dad died, thinking he was another village abuser. Then you told me you didn't think Uncle was an abuser, when you wrote me in Wales. Maybe if I looked at him with different eyes that night I stood in the doorway of his house, I might have seen what you told me and not spent years judging him."

"Perhaps," she said, "but you were filled with Dad's death and how close Naomi had come to being abused by her father. How could your eyes have been other than what they were?"

"I guess that could be true. Erin said as much to me when we were in Ireland. Stop thumping your craw about it, she said. Maybe I should pass those words on to you. You've spent years within yourself beating up on Dad and Emer and Mom, but I think it's yourself you've really been beating up on. Give yourself a break from doing that."

"That might be a good idea," she says, with a touch of a smile, "but stopping myself from banging against myself may not be easy. I may need some help in doing that."

"What about your friends, Cyril and Mavis?"

"Cyril and Mavis? I don't think so. Mavis wouldn't be up to taking on the thorns in my life, and I wouldn't confide anything to Cyril because I'm convinced he helped grease Cameron's slippery road."

"And your priest?"

"Alan?"

"Yes. What about him?"

Her smile goes inward, leaving but a faint trace of itself on her mouth. "Alan is a good person, but no, I wouldn't bring any of this to him right now." She gazes into what wants to be a new seeing of herself, and then gives up trying to see anything new. "Perhaps I should go back to Duxsowlas, with Peter and Hector and you."

I hear the resignation in her voice and see it in her eyes. I can also feel it in my own heart. Why not go back, when no way of going forward appears? Yet I also know in my heart that my sister can't go back until she has gone forward, somehow, somewhere . . .

I get up and take my cup to the sink. "That would be a good thing to do, one day. But maybe you need to do something else first."

"And what is that?"

"There's a book that needs to go back to Paul Kane and a pipe that needs to go back to Wesley."

"So?"

"I'll take the book to Paul, because I want to see him anyway. You take the pipe to Wesley."

"Me? Why me?"

"Because I think you need to meet Wesley and learn what he knows about Cameron's lover, Lance."

Standing at the sink, I go on thinking. "Then consider going east even more, until you come to Wales and to Sean Davies, the uncle of the sisters you have never met."

She folds her arms. "And why, pray tell, should I take my life to Wales and to the uncle of the sisters I have never met?"

"Because he knows the story of their mother, probably more of it than he has told me, and maybe you need to know her story to be at peace with her and with Dad. You'll find Sean living in a church that's about to be pulled down."

"A church that's about to be pulled down?"

"Yes. A very old church called Eglwys Lleu. It sits on a nose of land that juts into the Irish Sea. Other churches nearby are also being pulled down. Sean's friend, Dafydd Jones, took me to one at a place called Sarn Mellteyrn."

Margaret's mouth has fallen open. "Why are they pulling down churches?"

"I asked Dafydd the same question as we stood in the graveyard beside what had once been the church at Sarn. The roof was already gone and a backhoe had ploughed its way through the east end where the altar had stood. The rafters were stacked in a field to the north of the church and the pulpit stood on its own amid the sheep. A concrete cross had been placed before the front door, but it too looked as if it was on its way to some dumping ground. 'Sarn Mellteyrn means the causeway of the lightning,' Dafydd said to me, 'and this is where the lightning has struck most recently. They saved the bell, however; it's hanging in a nearby pub.'"

"But how could that happen?" asked Margaret. "How—"

"How could the church let a church be torn down? Well, that's something you might want to ask Sean when you meet him."

Margaret shakes her head as she takes it all in. "You have the next step of my life all figured out for me, it seems."

Her words stop me short. Is that what it sounds like, Margaret? When it's all I can do to figure out the next step of my life?

My eyes take her in. My sister, who once took me in and cared for me. And now, here am I—doing what?

"I don't know what I've figured out," I say. "I'm just playing a hunch."

"And that is?"

"That your falling apart right now might be something bigger than you or me or even Cameron's suicide. At least it's been that way with me. When I left here four years ago, I thought it was just my world coming apart and the world of our people. Now I know all that is part of something bigger still."

Our eyes touch, then she drops hers to her fingers as they lace themselves together. She stands and goes to the fridge. "Do you want something to eat?"

"No, I don't think so."

"Neither do I, now that I'm here." She closes the door. "And where will you be, if and when I'm over yonder sorting myself out?"

"At Duxsowlas, I guess. Working on a pole Dad and I left unfinished a long time back."

"Now that you've pretty much done what you needed to do here." Her statement, as casual and deliberate as a hand brushing a fly away, catches me off guard.

"No, I haven't done all I need to do."

"What else do you need to do, now that we've cremated my husband, and you've found Hector and counseled your sister?" Margaret asks as she sits.

"I need to find Naomi. She came down here with Adha and then stayed. To look for me, Frank thought."

"Ooh, God!" Her eyes go wide with the shock of remembering something.

"What is it, Margaret?"

She stares into what she remembers, as if wanting to turn away from it.

"I met Naomi in the hospital, when I went to see Adha."

Her eyes meet mine, as I search for words to take me beyond the shock I feel.

"You met Naomi?"

"Yes."

"And?"

"It was not a good meeting. She had some things to say to me, and then I had things to say to her. It all ended with her going off to look for you."

Her eyes stay with mine, hoping I will see into her and understand.

"Was that after I had written you?"

"Yes."

"Did you tell her where I was?"

"No."

"Did you tell her how to contact Izzy or Alex and Sigune, in case I had been in touch with them?"

"No, I didn't."

She holds her gaze steady and does not mask whatever her eyes might tell me.

"In the letter you wrote me, you said you were trying to forgive me," I say finally. "I guess you hadn't quite done that at the time you met up with Naomi."

"No, I was still working on that little matter." She pauses. "It's just that I went to a group home years ago after a call from a counselor, brought you to this house, helped pay for three years of school that gave you something of your life back; then you walked out on me, after hitting me with some words about my husband that I didn't need to hear there and then. And you stayed gone for a long time without a word. Besides, I don't remember you doing anything to get in touch with Naomi all that time you were here."

I look away from her. "I wanted to, but I couldn't."

"Then it seems there were things neither of us could do," Margaret says. "The only consolation I can give you comes from Adha. She was convinced the two of you would find one another."

"Thank you for that much, if I can figure out what to do with it. Good night, Margaret." I stand and make my way to the stairs.

"Nathan . . ."

I turn toward her. "What did you just call me?"

"I can't call you by the other name anymore. At least not on its own. It's not you."

"It was my name all the time I lived here."

"But it's no longer you. Not anymore."

Then we stand together, arms about each other.

"Forgive me, Nathan Solomon."

"Forgive me, Margaret. Go to Wesley, then to Sean."

"I'll think about it. Good night."

Upstairs, at the window of my bedroom, I look out at the mountains along the North Shore, now fully dark against the stars above and beyond them. Below the mountains the black water of Burrard Inlet is a sea of floating lights reflected from the ships anchored and waiting to discharge or take on cargo.

In the window my own face looks back at me, and then it is not my face but Naomi's. The face and form of Naomi when I knew she was no longer just my childhood friend. We were in grade eight and stood together on the soccer field during a break in the game between the Sisiutls and the Thunderbirds during the spring tournament. The rest of the team was priming Peter to put the winning goal into the net, but I looked at Naomi, my eyes lingering on the soft curves of her body. Then she looked right at me, caught me looking at her, and my eyes panicked and my tongue went numb.

My tongue stayed numb the rest of that month while Dad and I worked on David's pole, and as Naomi and I started bumping ourselves against one another because neither of our tongues would come loose.

Going to my desk, I sit and look at the carving on the wall above my bed. The head of Raven gestures to me from the circle above the crescent moon as the two heads of Sisiutl embrace it from either side.

I took up my carving tools when I came back to Duxsowlas and began to work on the pole, completing the figure of the Raven at the bottom, then going to work on Sisiutl just above it. But it is the last stretch of the pole that holds me at bay, not because I don't know what I will carve there, but because I cannot cut into that place until I know I have lived through what I will put there. If I can live through it . . .

But Cameron didn't live through his darkness, whatever his darkness was. What were you thinking of when you got into that tub, Cameron?

Moments later, I am downstairs, sitting at Cameron's desk in his study. Looking up at the Sisiutl print, I see the two heads stretching away from the central face, away from one another. Not meeting, but pulling apart. Pulling the central face apart—

Shocked, I keep my eyes on the print. Was this the knowing you lived with, Cameron, for all those years I lived here with you and looked at this very print? While I struggled to turn those two heads about and bring them face-to-face with each other? Your young, naïve brother-in-law, trying to reshape his world to fit his own quest . . .

Was this knowing what led you to slash your wrists open and let your blood loose into the tub?

Don't spend time with that centre face, Adha said to me on the day I turned fourteen, until you've learned what those end faces are about.

What did you know, Cameron, that convinced you there was no point in knowing any more? And what do I still need to learn?

I look again at the two heads stretching apart from one another. Cameron—Margaret?

Yes, and no. Try again, Nathan Solomon.

Naomi—Anika. I love Naomi. I have always loved Naomi, yet I wanted to love Anika once. Why? Because Anika loved me? Yes, and no. Because I despaired of ever seeing Naomi again? Or because the Raven in my heart wanted to play around with loving in two directions at the same time?

Was that why I never contacted you, Naomi? And why I never came clean with you, Anika?

My eyes drop down to the desk. Wesley's pipe lies beside Paul Kane's book. Connecting them is Cameron's suicide note, lying where Margaret had found it and where she replaced it after reading it.

And how did you and Wesley meet, Cameron? At a sweat, Margaret intimated, and that's all she knew. Or would say.

The pipe—the book . . .

I pick the book up. *The Philosophy of Spiritual Activity.* Thumbing through the pages, I find a sliver of paper at the beginning of Chapter Two.

I start to read the chapter. The night deepens and turns toward morning as I read. Then I put the book down.

A world split apart . . .

A world split apart because I split it apart, and the split begins within me—

Nathan—Solomon.

Raven—me.

I—Raven . . .

Suspended within the silence around me, I gaze again at the print on the wall.

Izzy calls to say he has secured a bed at the detox centre for Hector. Peter and I go with Hector when he checks in.

"A month," Hector says over a cup of coffee at lunch. "I guess I can manage that."

"You'd better manage it, at least until all those arms Izzy twisted for you straighten themselves out again," Peter says. "Then we'll take you home."

"Yeah, home," Hector says, with a touch of irony. "I've forgotten what being home might feel like. I hope everyone can handle it, me being home."

"Grace will handle it," I say. "She'll stuff you with salmon and anoint it and you with grease."

"Sure. My mom down at the river killing the fatted oolichan for her prodigal son." Hector lights a cigarette. "Well, we'll see about all of that. In the meantime, what are the two of you going to do with yourselves in the big city while I hang my insides out to dry?"

"Learn how to become a city person, I guess," Peter says, "and remind you that I can beat you at cribbage. As for Nathan, I think he has some things of his own to catch up on."

"Is that so, Nathan?" Hector asks, with a sharp look in my direction. Several days sober by now, his eyes are clearer and more penetrating.

I look back and see the friend who stood before me in the big house the night my uncle shamed me because he had caught his nephew playing with the Humsumth masks in his house. Playing at being Raven. Hector stood before me, having become Hamatsa, and gave me a paddle and a hat: *This is for you, Nathan . . .*

"There are things I need to do," I say.

"Then you'd better start doing them," says Hector. "I may dry out sooner than you think."

An hour later, I stand outside Joe's. The day is warm and sleepy. A few people walk past me along Commercial Drive, but only a few.

Joe's is also empty of people, except for a lone pool player at one of the back tables.

Why have I come here, I ask myself, as I rack up the balls, then break the formation wide open? Do I think Naomi will walk through the door out of nowhere and buy me a cappuccino?

Or do I want Anika to materialize beside me and take me on in a game?

It takes me awhile to steady the cue, but I work at it and my game begins to come back. I go after the coloured balls first, then the others, imagining there is someone squaring off against me. Finally, the eight ball alone is left. I sink it just as the voice at the other end of the table speaks.

"Good day, Solomon." I look up to see the face of Cyril Elspeth. "What a surprise! I didn't expect to meet you here."

"Nor I you, Dr. Elspeth," I reply, as I return the cue to the rack, then the balls to the front counter.

"May I buy you a drink, Solomon?"

I look for a second or two at the face of Cameron's colleague and friend. Is this the person I came here to meet?

"Sure. I'll have a cappuccino, please."

We sit at a table near the door. I sip at my cappuccino as he stirs his latte.

"How is Margaret getting on?" he asks.

"Okay, considering. She has a lot on her mind."

He nods. "It's just that we haven't heard from her since the funeral."

Did you expect to hear from her? I wonder.

He gazes around the room as if waiting for me to say something. I sit back in my chair, tempted to let him go on waiting, because there is nothing I want to say to him.

Then, suddenly, the question forms itself.

"Something's eating at you, Dr. Elspeth. About Cameron's suicide. What is it?"

A look of relief, even gratitude, flashes up in his eyes.

"Yes, Solomon. Something is eating at me. I have the feeling Margaret blames me in some way for what Cameron did."

So there it is. What now?

I take my time and choose my words with care. "Margaret might have some feelings about you, but she's the only one who could tell you what they are. What about you, though? How do you feel about what Cameron did?"

"I wish I could have prevented it. I wish—"

He pauses, palms extended as if in supplication. Then his hands drop to the table and his words with them.

"You said at the funeral that Cameron was an idealist who could never be reconciled to the world as it is. What did you mean by that?"

He thinks about my question, then says, "Cameron was forever wanting to read between the lines. I think he became stuck there, trying to find meaning that wasn't there to be found. We had long talks about that. He even offered a course called the Inside of History just before he died, and the course didn't go well. He didn't come right out and admit that, but what he didn't say spoke volumes. It was hard on him, and, I suspect, on his students, as well."

"And what went on in your long talks with Cameron?"

"I suppose I tried to talk him free of his desire to look for meaning the world doesn't give us, for his sake and the sake of his students. And even for Margaret's sake. He was punishing her as well as himself."

"Punishing Margaret?"

He looks at me, very surprised. "Yes, punishing your sister. He wanted a doorway into her Native world, to find something he couldn't find in this one—a doorway Margaret didn't seem disposed to open. Surely you were aware of that?"

"I was aware of it. But why were you so concerned about Cameron's students?"

He sips at the last of his latte, searching me out as he does so.

"Students arrive on our doorstep entangled in illusions about the world and themselves. Disentangling them is part of our task. Cameron, however, was entangling them even more, in aid of his own need for meaning. It wasn't fair to them."

"Was I entangled in illusions when I arrived on your doorstep?" I ask, pushing my cup and saucer to the centre of the table.

He starts, and then smiles. "A very direct question, Solomon."

"We're having a direct conversation."

"So we are. Well, to be frank, I was never sure about you. You had lively ideas and an engaging way of stating them. I was intrigued by you, but whether or not you were—"

"Trying to find more meaning in the world than is here?" I suggest.

He smiles again. "Yes. I never quite experienced you doing that."

"Maybe there's more to what is here than we've seen," I say. "And maybe that's what Cameron was looking for, something more than what he had been able to see."

His eyes stay with mine and the smile stays on his lips. "Cameron once told me about a poem by Yeats that you read to him: 'Gaze no more in the bitter glass—'"

"'For there a fatal image grows. And the ravens of unresting thought go flying, crying, to and fro.' I know the poem. You taught it to me."

He fingers his latte glass, as if uncertain how to respond.

"Do you think," I ask, "that you might have pushed Cameron off balance, in trying to talk him free of what you thought were his fatal images?"

Now the smile fades from his lips. "It's conceivable I might have done that. The thought has been haunting me."

He falls silent. Two young men come into Joe's and go to the cue rack. Moments later the sounds of their playing reach our table.

His eyes come back to mine. "It's just that . . ."

I sit and wait for him to go on.

"It's just that a teacher once freed me from some of my illusions. As painful as the experience was, I was grateful."

"And you thought Cameron would be grateful, too. One day."

"Yes, I did. Perhaps it's a difficult thing for you to understand."

Now I look away. The day has mellowed toward sunset and for the first time I can feel for this man and for his pain.

"Not so difficult," I say. "Accept life as it comes, take whatever meaning lies on the surface of things, and let death have its way—that would make things simple and easier to bear. Life comes and goes, and death has the last word: Cameron's death; my father's; a dead sister who grew up in Wales, and a brother who killed himself when I was young—even a great-grandfather who died at the Little Bighorn. All a person needs is enough meaning to wait life out until death comes along. Why should anyone ask for more?"

"Do you ask for more?"

"Yes, I do."

"On what grounds, Solomon?"

I draw back into myself, his question in hand, even as my eyes stay with his.

What grounds would you accept, Dr. Elspeth, or understand? And then, as the sound of a cue ball striking home reaches my ear, the words come.

"I turned on the TV this morning before going out into the day. The news was full of the election taking place in South Africa. There was Nelson Mandela putting his ballot in a box. There were black people and white people standing in line together, ready to spend the whole day under a hot sun until they could vote in an election that seemed beyond possibility when I was in high school learning about South Africa. Yet this morning I saw it happening and wondered, what's made this moment possible? And now I know: This election happened because Nelson Mandela didn't spend twenty-seven years in prison waiting life out until death came along. Today, that's grounds enough for me, Dr. Elspeth."

Once again, a touch of a smile lights upon his mouth. "You can call me Cyril, Solomon."

I shake my head as I stand. "I don't think I can do that. But I hope you can make peace with the thought that is haunting you."

His eyes mist over. "Thank you. And I hope you find that something more than what you've seen."

I walk along Commercial Drive to a bus stop, but it's not until I change buses at Hastings Street that I can free myself from the look in his eyes.

The following Sunday, I knock on Paul Kane's door. Paul leads me through his house into the garden at the back, where we sit at a table piled high with main lesson books.

"Student payback time," Paul says, with a laugh, "but it's spring and we're all winding down and lightening up, so I'll make it through the pile before the year comes to an end."

I smile. "It was hard to take school seriously at this time of year."

"I even remember two members of my first class playing hooky the day after they had finished their projects," says Paul.

"I remember that, too, and painting a classroom for you when you caught up with us. But you never asked what Anika and I did that afternoon."

"Didn't I? How remiss of me. Can I get you something to drink? Coffee, perhaps?"

"Yes, please." I sit and go on remembering that afternoon with Anika while Paul goes inside to make the coffee:

I had a dream about you, before you came to the school. You were sitting alone in a canoe, like the one Bill Reid made. It was so big and you looked so alone in it as you tried to paddle it by yourself . . .

I pick up one of the main lesson books. Projective Geometry: A line running out to infinity sooner or later rays back into the point from which it began. So far out, it just has to come back, Izzy had quipped in class. Sooner or later, depending. But changed—nothing goes through that infinite point without being changed . . .

Paul places two cups of coffee on the table, then sits.

"I'm sorry about Cameron," he says.

"He left a note, asking Margaret to return this book to you."

Paul takes the book, turns it over in his hands, and sits a moment without speaking. I sip at my coffee and wait.

"I remember the day Cameron came for this book. I had offered it to him the day you graduated, but never heard from him about it. Then late in January he knocked on my door. We talked, and he was eager to have the book. Too eager, it seemed. I wasn't sure about giving it to him there and then, but did when he pressed me. Why was I uneasy? Perhaps I was afraid Steiner would open doors Cameron wasn't ready to walk through."

"Maybe so," I say, "but don't blame yourself, Paul. Cameron was walking some edge of his own all the time I lived with Margaret and him, though I didn't fully see it then. He was like a person pacing in a cage, looking for something or someone to let him out."

"Many people spend their lives pacing one cage or another," Paul said, "but at least your brother-in-law was conscious of his cage and had the courage to question it. Did I ever tell your class the meaning of *spina*, the Latin root for spine?"

"You may have told us," I say, smiling, "but I don't exactly remember what you might have said."

Paul laughs and then goes on. "*Spina* means thorn. The spine is the thorn in our bodies that brings us to consciousness, and consciousness is the thorn that wakes us up enough to question the cages we put ourselves in. Cameron had the courage of that kind of consciousness, even if he couldn't sustain his courage right through to the end."

A bee weaves itself past my ear toward the honeysuckle that is flowering along the trellis a few feet from where we sit. A wagon and a toy truck stand apart from one another on the lawn, abandoned by Paul's children.

"You're saying we put ourselves in cages?"

"Yes."

"I'd never thought about it in quite that way, but I think you're right, and I think that's what that book I gave back to you is also saying."

Paul glances at *The Philosophy of Spiritual Activity*, then back at me. "You've read it?"

"The first couple of chapters. I liked what Steiner said about doing things consciously. I've sometimes felt that something bigger than myself was looking after me; otherwise, I'd have cracked myself up on myself a long time ago. But now I also know it's up to me to figure out what I'm going to do next, out of my own questions. I think that book might be about doing things more consciously."

"Then I'll give it back to you," Paul says, with a funny look in his eyes. He takes a pen, opens the book to the title page and writes something there. Then he hands the book to me. I start to thank him, then know the words aren't necessary. I look over at the trellis and the honeysuckle, but the bee is gone.

"Steiner was the person who started the Waldorf schools?"

"Yes, he helped start them."

"I remember you telling us that, but you didn't say much more than that about him."

"What else do you want to know, Solomon?"

What more do I want to know? And then the question forms itself.

"Did he ever say anything about what it's like on the other side for a person who takes his own life?"

Paul takes his time with my question.

"Yes, he did. It seems such a person goes through a difficult and painful time right after death. He has to stay with the life he would have lived, right to the end, but isn't able to live it out as he could have."

I think about that. "Is there any way to help such a person, from here?"

"Yes, you can send him healing thoughts and prayers, if doing that makes sense to you."

"It makes sense. A person I met in Wales also told me something like that. But is there anything else I could do for Cameron?"

"You could read to him," Paul says.

"What would I read?"

"Whatever might have meaning for him. Do you have a Bible?"

"Cameron had a Bible."

"Then start with the Gospel of John, a chapter at a time."

"What about the book you just gave me?"

"Yes, you could read from that, and from anything that you think would have meaning for Cameron."

I nod. "Thank you, Paul."

"You're welcome, Solomon. Would you like more coffee?" I shake my head and he settles back in his chair. "How long will you be in Vancouver?"

"Until a friend of mine dries himself out at the detox centre downtown, which should take me into June. So I guess I'll go to the class reunion that Alex and Sigune are hosting."

"That would be good. You became an important member of the class. Do you know about Anwar?"

"Yes, Izzy told me."

And again I see myself sitting with Anika at Third Beach: *Have you heard any news of Anwar?*

"Have you seen anything of Anika?" I ask Paul.

"No, Solomon. I haven't seen Anika for several years."

I let the matter go, and so does he. If he knows anything, what he knows doesn't show itself on his face or in his eyes.

"What will you do with yourself after your friend dries out and the class reunion is over?"

I shrug. "I'm not sure. Maybe go on looking for someone else I know who is down here. Then go home and finish working on a totem pole that has been waiting a long time to be finished up. After that? I don't know, Paul."

"What about going back to SFU?"

"I don't think so. Finishing a degree in English doesn't interest me anymore."

"Then what does interest you?"

What? What else? "Light, and darkness, and light," I reply. "The way light and darkness work together and don't work together, but could work together. That's been the question of my life. Doing English helped me go into that, but now I need to find another path. I remember you talking about Goethe's ideas of light and darkness in grade twelve physics. Maybe I should read him."

"You could do that," Paul agrees.

I think some more. "And maybe I should even consider doing physics. You have a degree in physics, right?"

"Yes, I do."

"Well, then, how would I go about getting a degree in physics?"

"Would you like more coffee first?" Paul asks.

"Why not?" I say.

When he arrived home, he went into Cameron's study and found Cameron's Bible. Taking the book in hand, Solomon opened it to the Gospel of John. The first words were familiar, but he tried to put that familiarity aside and hear them in a new way:

In the beginning was the Word . . .

Then he paused. This was your Bible, Cameron. You must have read it many times, yet doing that didn't stop you from killing yourself. So why should these words help you now?

But maybe it can be different. Then, you were here. Now you are somewhere else and it might be different.

Solomon continued to read:

What has come into being in him was life,
life that was the light of men;
and light shines in darkness,
and darkness could not overpower it . . .

He glanced up at the print of Sisiutl on the wall above the desk.

What are you grinning at? he asked the central face, his eyes following one head then the other as they stretched away on either side, as if they would never dream of meeting one another.

That's how it was with Erin and me, until we sat back-to-back in the darkness of a passage grave and told our stories to each other. Then the light came, from our hearts, and the darkness couldn't swallow it away, even when we put the darkness behind us and went through the back wall of the head chamber out into the daylight once more.

So that's where I'll read from, Cameron. From the heart.

Solomon read to Cameron daily for the next two weeks, while Hector dried out at the detox centre. Hector's skin began to shine again from eating good enough meals and from the sun that broke through the clouds often enough to lighten him up. Solomon and Peter visited him every day, and on some days Izzy joined them.

"You're crazy," Hector said to Izzy after a long day walking around Stanley Park. "As crazy as I am and even crazier. Two crazy people like us aren't a good thing for the world."

"The world can handle it," Izzy said. "The world needs more crazy people like us, who don't spend time looking over their shoulders at themselves."

"For sure," Hector agreed. "It's better to look at yourself straight on, even if doing that cracks you up."

"Well, don't crack up," said Peter, "or at least wait until we're home before you do."

Back at the detox centre, Izzy turned to Solomon. "Have you phoned Alex and Sigune yet?"

"No, not yet."

"Don't keep putting it off, Solomon. Alex is waiting for you to call."

He called Alex that night and arranged to meet him the next day at the Museum of Anthropology at UBC. Then he continued to read to Cameron:

I am the light of the world . . .

He seated himself and contemplated the Raven while the Raven contemplated him.

I am the light of the world . . .

Don't you wish! Yet you are. You're the wannabe light of the world and that's the funny thing about it. Or not so funny, depending on a person's point of view.

Footsteps sounded faintly along the carpeted corridor leading to Bill Reid's carving of *The Raven and the First Men*. The steps came closer and then Alex sat down beside him.

"Renewing an old friendship?" Alex asked.

"Two old friendships. I'm sorry I didn't call sooner."

"That's okay. Izzy told us about your friend."

"My friend's troubles needn't have stopped me from calling you."

"Let it go, Solomon. You called and that's what matters. It's good to see you again."

"It's good to see you, Alex."

They sat together while the Raven gazed at them from his perch on the clamshell. Beneath the clamshell's upper lip, the human figures crept forth into the daylight: Bemused, mesmerized, entranced, hesitant, terrified, stricken—the six human beings emerged into a world riddled with light. The Raven, in turn, contemplated their emergence like a god resting on the seventh day of his creation.

And it was good . . .?

"I remember the night you presented your project," Alex said. "You strung everyone in that room together, word by word, and walked us around this carving and into the work of Bill Reid. When you were done, it was as if we were inside Bill Reid's eyes, looking out at the world he had created. And inside the Raven's eyes, too."

"I thought I had him figured out then," said Solomon after a moment. "And then I learned the hard way that you never have him completely figured out. Do you remember that day in grade ten when we were reading the *Odyssey* in class? I had to go to the washroom all of a sudden, and then you found me sitting under a tree in Chinook Park?"

"Yes, I do. Something got to you."

"It was Anika reading that passage where Odysseus plunges the red-hot olive beam into Cyclops's eye and twirls it around. That's when I bolted. I stood in the washroom, looked into the mirror and expected to see Raven looking at me, with one eye shot out of his head."

"Shot out of his head?"

"Yes. Before I left Duxsowlas, I took a rifle my father kept in the house and went upriver to a beach where my friends and I had seen twelve eagles. My dad had just died and I had concluded something was rotten in the state of my village and in my family. I wanted to shoot it all away and thought I would kill the eagles. But instead I tried to shoot the hell out of the sun. When I had emptied my rifle and the beach about me was littered with the feathers of terrified eagles, I met up with my friend Raven in the shadow of a cedar tree. One of his eyes was gone and I knew I had just shot it out of his head when I tried to kill the sun. Odysseus bringing Cyclops's eye to the boil brought all of that back to me. Do you remember saying to me as you sat down, 'There's a shadow on your tail?'"

Alex nodded.

"Well, that was the shadow, Alex, or a piece of it. So I took on the Raven, to throw some light on that shadow, and thought I had done that pretty well. Then along came the summer of Oka, with the Quebec police, then the army, against the Mohawks, and back the shadow came."

"Is that why you left Vancouver? Because you were upset about Oka?"

"About Oka, and being Indian, and about other things." Solomon stopped, because he wasn't ready to tell Alex about Anika.

"Where did you go?"

"To Alberta, to look for family I hoped still existed. When I got to where I thought I wanted to be, I walked along a road into the Nakoda reserve. The morning sun threw my shadow way to the west, but I knew then that the real shadow wasn't the one walking alongside me. The real shadow was the one inside, tailing my heart."

Alex took his time before speaking. "That day at the park you asked me how I knew so much about a shadow being on someone's tail. Do you remember?"

"Yes. And you said, 'It takes one to know one.' What did you mean by that?"

A man and woman walked up the steps that led to the carving. Alex remained silent until they had gone around to the other side of the Raven.

"My father left my mother the year I turned nine," Alex said quietly, "and my world fell apart. Do you remember what your life was like when you turned nine?"

Solomon thought about it. "Sort of. Everything was farther away from me than it had once been, and I began to see things differently. My uncle gave a potlatch for David, my brother, and I sat through it all watching everything closely, asking questions about what I was seeing and trying to figure out what was really going on. It was like being inside something, yet outside of it and looking in at the same time. Then a few months later my dad put me on Log Island for three days. Those three days became a vision quest that kick-started the rest of my life."

"I remember you telling us about that on the Stein Valley trip in grade ten," said Alex. "I only wish somebody had dreamed up a vision quest for me when Dad left, because everything went so far away from me I couldn't even see where it had gone. I only knew that my mother was angry, so angry she never told me why he had left."

"Where did that leave you?"

"Angry, too, because she was angry. Being angry was easier to handle than being hurt. So I imagined all kinds of reasons for Dad's leaving, reasons that would justify my being angry with him. And my anger became the shadow on my tail. I was angry when I came to the Waldorf School in grade seven and stayed angry right into grade ten. Then I fell in love with Sigune in grade eleven, as you may remember."

Solomon let out a laugh that turned a few heads in his direction. He smiled at the faces looking at him and they smiled back at whatever his laugh had been about.

"I guess I remember! You fell in love during the Parzival main lesson. I had more phone calls from each of you than I could count. I didn't know whether your falling in love would end as a tragedy or a comedy. No one in the class knew."

"I-wasn't sure either," mused Alex, "until that afternoon in Rebecca's art class when you pulled that painting out of a mess of watercolour, the one that led on to your carving for your project. The whole class stood and watched you, and suddenly Sigune and I were holding hands. We didn't look at each other, but we held hands and I knew we had found each other. And right then I stopped being angry."

"Did you like Sigune when you were both in the grade school?"

Now Alex laughed. "Are you kidding? I thought she was a barefoot freak, and she thought I was arrogant Mr. Know-it-all. And I suppose I was the class brain until Anwar came in grade eight and took over that role. No, falling in love with each other had to wait until high school, and until you came to the class."

"Me? What difference did my coming make?"

"It made a difference, that's all I can say. Perhaps because you were who you were. There were eleven of us who went into grade nine, and then you came through the door that spring day, told us your grandfather had been at the Little Bighorn and had fought with Poundmaker. We didn't know what to make of that story, but as soon as you opened your mouth we knew you were one of us."

Solomon looked away and didn't know what to say. In his heart he felt the truth of Alex's words, yet he doubted them in the same instant. Why? Somehow, the Raven's light and doubt seemed to go together.

"Are you coming to the class reunion?" Alex asked.

"The one in June? I guess so."

"What do you mean, you guess so?"

"Don't work up a sweat, Alex. I'll come. Why wouldn't I come?"

"I don't know. Maybe it's something Izzy picked up from you and passed on to me."

"Izzy should be more careful about what he picks up and passes on."

Then they seemed to run out of words. Solomon looked at the Raven once more, to see if the Raven would give any hints as to where to go from here, but the gaze in his eyes had gone to some faraway place.

"Do you know how Anwar was killed?"

Alex shook his head. "Only that he died during one of the bombings of Baghdad. His mother wrote Astrid as soon as the Gulf War ended and the smoke over the city cleared away."

"And what about Anika?" Solomon asked, looking directly at Alex to gauge what effect his question might have. "Izzy said no one had heard from her for a few years."

"We haven't heard from her." Alex's eyes gave no hint of knowing more than his words said. "I thought she might stay in touch with us or at least with Sigune. But not so."

Solomon nodded, as the Raven now gazed knowingly at him.

"How is your sister?" Alex asked.

"She's all right," said Solomon. "She's trying to decide where to go next with her life."

"I'm sorry about your brother-in-law. He was always interested in us, whenever we got together at your house, and wanted to know what we thought about life."

"Yes. He was a good person."

"Why did he do it, Solomon?"

Solomon shook his head, wondering what he could say. He glanced at the Raven as the Raven's knowing look deepened.

Do you know why Cameron did it?

Why would I know? The Raven grinned. And why would I care?

Because you know something about it. Not the whole of it, maybe, but something . . .

"I think the daylight was more than he could bear," Solomon said at last.

Alex nodded, let the question go, and then had another question for him. "Did you ever see Anika after we graduated?"

Solomon was tempted to lie, but didn't. "Once. Just once."

Alex turned to him. "Look. I don't know what happened between Anika and you the night of our graduation party at Catherine's. We all thought the two of you had finally gotten it together and then discovered it was otherwise. That's between the two of you. Anika might not even know we're having a reunion, but you do and we want you to be there. So please don't skip out on us."

"What about Sigune? Does she want me there?"

Astonished, Alex stared at him. "What a dumb question, Solomon! Yes, she wants you there. She's even been on my case, along with Izzy, about making sure you come. Why would you think otherwise?"

"I don't know, Alex. The question just popped into my head."

"Well, pop it out of your head, Solomon. Do you want a ride into town?"

"Sure. My feet have gone to sleep from sitting here."

"We'll stop at my place on the way. Maybe Sigune will be home."

Solomon glanced back at the Raven as they walked away from the carving, but the Raven was no longer interested in the two of them.

"And that's about all I want to say tonight, except that I've had a hell of a lot more fun in my few months of being sober than I had all those years being drunk. Thanks for my sobriety."

The man with the grizzled beard and stark blue eyes returned to his seat, amid a round of applause.

Solomon applauded too, or half-applauded, because he kept going back to the moment a few hours earlier when Alex and he had walked through the door of the apartment in Kitsilano where Alex and Sigune lived. Sigune had been sitting in a chair, reading. She stood slowly when she saw Solomon, and as her eyes met his, he saw them veil themselves over. A thin veil, yes, but it was a veil. He reached out to hug her and she returned his hug, but with a touch of restraint.

Sigune made coffee, and the three of them sat and talked until it was time for Solomon to leave and join Hector and Peter at the AA meeting, where he was now sitting. As he turned in the doorway to say goodbye, he met Sigune's eyes once again. You know something, he realized, something Alex doesn't know. What do you know, Sigune? And do I want to know what you know?

Peter stirred beside him and he realized the man chairing the meeting had just called Hector's name. Hector stood up and walked to the front of the room.

"Ghe-la-kasla, everyone. I'm Hector, and I'm an alcoholic."

A chorus of voices from around the room greeted Hector. He stood, hands thrust down into the front pockets of his jeans, and thought about what he would say next.

"The greeting I just gave you was in my language, Kwakwala. It's a greeting from the heart and I want to speak from the heart. I haven't been clean or sober very long this time around, but each day counts and I want to make this moment count.

"I grew up in a village up the coast from Port Hardy, along with two old friends who are here with me tonight. I was the fat kid who always took two or three extra helpings of food at any feast that was happening.

When there were no feasts, I would invite myself to my friends' homes and sit at their kitchen tables until someone took the hint and fed me. I guess I was addicted to food and that was the first of my addictions. My people put up with my appetite because they loved me, though I got a lot of teasing along with that love.

"Then I went to Port Hardy to do grade ten. By then I'd dropped much of my fat away, learned to kick a soccer ball when it counted, and was also learning to drink and have a good time alongside my soccer game. The fat little Indian kid had hit the big city of Port Hardy, and you know what? He discovered girls. He had known about girls back home, but only that they put up with him like everyone else did.

"But at Port Hardy I had girls coming to me, wanting to be around me, and then hitting on me. Man, that was heaven on earth! And not just Indian girls, but white girls, too. To find myself at a party with a glass in my hand and a white girl leading me in the direction of her bed—that was heaven plus!

"So I changed addictions, from food to booze and sex, and that led me on to drugs. This threesome became the god of my life and I put my faith in that god, because I no longer knew who I was apart from it."

Hector paused, as if thinking about something.

"When I was twelve, I became Hamatsa. The Hamatsa for my people is a person who shows his community what they have to struggle with to be themselves. I was supposed to have lived that struggle through for three nights out in the forest, alone, preparing for the Hamatsa ceremony. But I didn't live it through, not all the way through. I crossed creeks and went through rough places with my body, but not with my spirit. So even though I came in from the forest and did the ceremony that made me Hamatsa, I left something of me out in the bush, waiting to come through. And something of me is still out there, waiting.

"Maybe this time I'll come through to myself. Maybe. And be able to say, Nu gwa am—I really am becoming the person I could be. People here tell me I can do it, my friends tell me I can do it, and maybe I will, though I can't say that for sure. All I know is that I'm standing here to-night and that's a start. Thank you for my sobriety."

Then the meeting ended with the words of the Serenity Prayer:

God, grant me the serenity to accept the things I cannot change,
the courage to change the things I can,
and the wisdom to know the difference.

Solomon and Peter walked to the coffee urn at the back of the room.

As Peter started talking with someone, Solomon looked around to see Hector going outside through the fire exit. He left Peter and followed Hector out onto a ramp that sloped up to street level. Hector was leaning against a metal railing, smoking. His white T-shirt gleamed in the light from the single bulb above the exit door.

"You didn't bring me a feast, Nathan. You're slipping."

"I thought you'd gotten clear of that addiction. But I'll bring you a coffee."

Hector shook his head. "I've had all the coffee I need today. Maybe I'll go back to feasting when we get home. When is your class reunion?"

"Three weeks from this coming Friday. Hold on until then."

"I'm holding, one day at a time."

A quarter moon sat in the sky overhead and the street alongside the building was silent, though they could hear the city sounding a few blocks away. Hector drew on his cigarette and took his time releasing the smoke.

"Any luck in finding Naomi?"

"No. Not yet."

"Where have you looked?"

"Everywhere we looked for you. And a few other places. I went to the Friendship Centre yesterday, but nobody there knew of her."

"Don't spend too much time looking where you looked for me. Naomi was never one for hanging around bars."

"I know that. I only hope that's still the case."

Hector looked at him sharply. "Don't give up on her, Nathan."

"I'm not giving up, Hector, but I'm running out of places to look next."

"Yeah. This city is like a forest, in its own way. A person can get lost here without too much trouble."

"I know. I almost did get lost here years ago. Those were good words you said in there."

"Thanks."

"Do you remember coming up to me at the end of your family's potlatch, after you had become Hamatsa?"

Hector squashed the last of his cigarette against the railing. "Sure. Your uncle had just shamed you, and I guess Peter and me too, for playing around with his Humsumth masks. You in particular were playing at being Raven, and your uncle didn't think much of that. But he was hard on you that night, too hard, I thought. And I wasn't alone in thinking that."

"Uncle had expectations of me and I let him down. And maybe I asked for what he gave me. All I knew that night was that my world had fallen in all about me. Then I saw you standing before me, with a paddle in one hand and a baseball cap in the other. You were my friend and you had brought me gifts. I couldn't look at you that night or thank you, but I'm going to thank you now, for helping me come through a forest inside of me."

"I guess I'm sober enough to be thanked. What happened to the paddle?"

"It sat in our house all the years I was away from Duxsowlas. Then Frank nearly killed me with it at Bone Spit the night I came back. But your paddle broke on the one I had in my hand and I survived. I'll tell you that story another time."

"And the hat?"

"I left it at the Asking Rock at the trailhead of the Stein Valley when I was in grade ten. It was my way of saying thank you to whatever it was that had helped me find that school and my class."

"It sounds like it came to a good end," Hector said. He started to light another cigarette, then changed his mind. "The stars are really something, eh?"

Solomon followed Hector's gaze into the sky beyond the moon.

"Do you remember that teacher we had who loved talking about the stars?" Hector continued. "He even got us to go out at night and spend time with them. I had a hard time figuring out what was going on up there, though you were quick enough about it, and Peter was even quicker. But I liked just looking at the stars, whatever they were doing."

Solomon nodded. "Me, too. When I was on Log Island for those three days, I spent a whole night just watching the stars travel the sky."

Now Hector did light another cigarette. "You didn't ever tell me much about that time, when I was getting ready to go out into the forest."

"I guess not. I didn't feel like saying that much, then."

Hector squinted at the sky above him, as if trying to puzzle something out. "Maybe if you had said something about how it was for you, I might have gone into the forest in a different way."

Solomon stared into the night. "What are you trying to tell me, Hector?" he asked.

Hector rolled a mouthful of smoke past the railing and through a cluster of small insects that hovered at the edge of the darkness. "Probably nothing much," he said. "It's just that we were sitting together on Sand Island and I asked you what it had felt like to be alone for that many days. I guess I was looking for support."

"And I didn't give you that?"

"You had a lot going on inside of you, that's all. You've always had a lot going on inside of you that you keep hidden from your friends."

Solomon turned to Hector. "Yes, I have my hidden lives. But if I could have said something, anything, that might have supported you, and didn't, then I'm sorry."

"You don't need to be sorry, Nathan. That's just the way it was, so let it go." Hector looked at the last of his cigarette and flicked it away. "I think I'll have that coffee now," he said.

Solomon and Peter arrived home just before midnight. Solomon turned out the porch light and the lamp in the living room Margaret had left on for them, and started to follow Peter upstairs.

Then he heard Margaret speak his name.

Turning about, he saw her standing in the doorway of her bedroom with something in her hand.

"It's a plane ticket," she said. "To Calgary, then on to Wales."

Solomon took the ticket from her and looked at it. "Are you sure?"

"Yes. Once I began to find my own reasons for going." She smiled at the question that stayed in his eyes. "They're my reasons, Nathan Solomon, and I'll keep them to myself until I understand them more than I do now."

Then she looked at him more closely. "Are you all right?"

"I guess so. Why do you ask?"

"I know that look in your eye, the look that tells me you're coming up to another edge in your life."

He smiled. "Maybe so. When are you leaving?"

"Sit down for a minute and I'll tell you," Margaret said.

A few moments later, Solomon climbed the stairs and into the bathroom. As he stood at the mirror brushing his teeth, he saw that uncertain look in the eyes that looked out of the mirror into his. It had been a while since that look had been there, but there was no mistaking it now.

"Hector's looking better," Peter said from his mattress on the floor as Solomon got into bed.

"Yes, he is," said Solomon and turned out the lamp beside his bed.

They lay in the dark of the room as the night sounds drifted through the half-opened window. Down at the inlet something clanked and then something else squealed in protest. Freight cars, maybe, being dragged away somewhere. From his bed Solomon could see the last light of the moon touching down on the leaves of the linden tree in the back yard. Then he told Peter about Margaret's plans.

"She's leaving the day of your reunion?" said Peter.

"Yes. Her tenants will move in that night. We can stay with Alex and Sigune until we go."

"And when do you plan on leaving?" Peter asked.

"As soon as the reunion is over."

"Maybe Hector should stay here longer. He's dried out, but I don't know if he has really sobered up," Peter said.

"No way, Peter. It will be seven weeks by then and Izzy can't stretch Hector's stay any further."

"I guess not. I just hope he can keep things together once we get home. If we get him home."

"We'll get him home, Peter."

But even as he spoke, Solomon could feel a doubt gnawing at the edge of his words. He turned on his side and waited for sleep to gather him in.

"Nathan?"

"Yes?"

"Do you remember one night when we were in grade four and learning about the stars and the planets? The three of us were out one night, with Naomi, and we had a long discussion about what up there moved and didn't move."

"I remember. Hector was confused because he hadn't listened to any of it and you were full of it all and so sure of yourself."

Peter chuckled. "I guess I was. But you were insisting that both the stars and the planets moved because that's what you thought you were seeing. Then Naomi said there is a difference. The stars shine and move by staying at home, and the planets don't."

Solomon lay on his side, his eyes upon the leaves of the linden tree.

"You and Hector have been wandering planets," Peter went on. "You came home when you could do that and maybe Hector will do that, too. But Naomi has never left, not really. Even though she got tired of waiting for you and decided to do some wandering of her own, she's still a fixed star. Naomi is waiting for you to find her, somewhere. And if you don't find her, she'll stay put until she finds you."

I hear you, Peter. But will I be there in myself, in the moment when she finds me, to see her seeing me?

Nu gwa am . . .

Some hours later he awoke and sat upright in bed, into the dream that still hovered about him. He had been standing in the water at Duxsowlas, the line connecting him with the boat slipping through his fingers as his father pulled away from the beach. Harvey Silas, wrapped in a bearskin, lay in Uncle Charlie's boat, a lifetime of pain and shame weeping from the lines in his face.

Then the line left Nathan's hand. Isaac brought the boat about one last time and spoke:

Ha-la-kasla, Gwawinastoo. See through.

But there were other words in the dream, words he had not heard that day when he had stood on the beach and watched his father disappear into that chaos of wind and water—words he had read that day or yesterday . . .

He got up and made his way downstairs to Cameron's study. Turning on the light at the desk, he opened the Bible and looked for the passage he had been reading from when he had last read to Cameron. As he turned the pages, he remembered another night years ago when he had sat in the dining room at Fireweed with a Bible, researching his discovery that Jesus had been killed. And why had Jesus been killed? Why had his father died as he had died?

He found the page and then the lines from the Gospel of John:

. . . I lay down my life
in order to take it up again.
No one takes it from me;
I lay it down of my own free will . . .

Maybe that was the answer. They had killed Jesus, but only because he was ready to lay down his life. As Isaac had been ready when he looked out at the tossing water, then down at Harvey, and asked Uncle Charlie for the use of his boat.

Things come to you when they are ready to come, trusting that you're ready for them.

He closed the Bible. Turning out the light, he went on sitting in the darkness.

Margaret tucks her boarding pass into her handbag and takes out something else before she closes it.

"Here. This is for you."

She places the paperbound booklet into my hand and watches my face as I open it to the flyleaf. As a disembodied voice announces the departure of yet another flight, my eyes leave Bill Reid's words to me and meet hers.

"I bought it a year and a half ago at a benefit Cameron took me to. Then I put it away and forgot about it until last night. You may be interested in this as well."

I take the clipping from The Vancouver Sun. The photograph shows a second casting of *The Spirit of Haida Gwaii* being lowered into the courtyard of the Vancouver Museum.

"It's destined for here, eventually," Margaret says, looking around the airport. "I guess they'll find a place for it when the construction workers have had their day."

"Thanks for thinking of me," I say. "I'll stop by the Museum on my way back to the house."

"And you know what to do when you get back to the house?"

I laugh. "Yes, Margaret, I know what to do. I pack my gear and anything Peter has left behind, wash the last of the dishes, and leave the keys to the house and car where your tenants will find them."

"You can use the car, you know. Until you leave."

"No, I don't think so. I can bus it to the reunion. Stop worrying about me and get on that plane. Wesley will meet you in Calgary."

"How will I know him?"

"Look for an Indian underneath a cowboy hat. Don't worry. He'll know you."

Then her arms reach out to me, and I hold her.

"I think I'm somewhat scared about doing this," she says. "Calgary, then Wales. And for what, really?"

"For you. Trust what you really want to know, and being scared will take care of itself. That's how it was for me. Give my love to Wesley and Sarah, and to Sean."

"Will I meet Erin?"

"That depends on Erin. She wants to come this way, sometime, and make that journey to Haida Gwaii that I never made. She may already be on her way. You'll meet her when the time for that comes."

"You sound so sure of it all."

"Do I? We'll both see soon enough just how sure I am."

She glances in the direction of the security gate. "Sure or not, I'd better get going before that plane gets tired of waiting for me. Goodbye for now, Nathan Solomon. I love you."

"I love you, Margaret."

I take my time driving back into Vancouver. The late morning traffic is thin and the faces behind the steering wheels look less stressed than they do at other times of the day. I have the rest of the day to pack, lock up Margaret's house, and then join Peter and Hector at the detox centre. At the close of the day I will go to the reunion of my class, to meet whatever I may meet there.

If it be now, 'tis not to come . . .

Hamlet's words come to me as I turn into the parking lot of the Vancouver Museum. Inside, the woman at the desk directs me to the room where *The Spirit of Haida Gwaii* is on display.

The casting in green-tinted bronze, counterpart of the first casting in black bronze that now graces the Canadian Embassy in Washington, D.C., stands at the centre of a room filled with plants. I walk around it once, then again, taking in the figures as I go.

At the stern, the Raven is trying to steer the canoe. The tiny face of Mouse Woman peers out from under the Raven's wing. Then the Dogfish Woman and the Beaver, each grasping a paddle, lead me on to the Bear Mother and Bear Father, with their two cubs, in the prow of the canoe.

Coming around to the starboard side, I see the Eagle biting at the Bear Father's paw, then the Wolf biting into the Eagle's wing. The Frog stares out from beneath the beak of the Eagle.

I sit, open the booklet Margaret has given me, also titled *The Spirit*

of Haida Gwaii, and something falls into my lap. I open the folded
paper to find that it is the letter I had written to Margaret from Wales.
Funny, how things keep coming back to you.

I set the letter aside and begin to read.

Bill Reid has named the figure sitting behind the Eagle, the Ancient
Reluctant Conscript. The expression on his face says, what the hell am
I doing on this boat?

And then there is the figure in the centre, robed in a blanket,
wearing a cedar hat, and holding a talking stick—the figure, Bill Reid
suggests, that seems to have a vision of what's to come . . .

I had a dream about you, before you came to the school.

Anika and I were sitting together on the sand at Third Beach, the
afternoon we played hooky from school.

*You were sitting alone in a canoe, like the one that Bill Reid made. It was
so big and you looked so alone in it as you tried to paddle it by yourself.*

I walk around the casting again. The Raven is steering the canoe.
The Raven is trying to steer the canoe. Of course the Raven is the
steersman, Bill Reid observes. Who else? Raven is taking charge and
so the canoe could land just about anywhere.

*And I dreamt about you that night we came down from Prince Rupert on
the ferry, only this time there were people in the canoe with you. Some
members of our class and others I didn't know . . .*

Did you see yourself in that canoe, Anika? I wanted to ask you that
question, but didn't. And then I betrayed you that second time we met
at Third Beach. If you were in the canoe, I pushed you out.

I sit, open the booklet to the flyleaf, and read what is written there:
To Solomon. Chasing the sun. Then I read through Bill Reid's words
again, right to the end: The boat goes on, forever anchored in the same
place.

What about the class of 1987? Are we still anchored in the same
place? I hardly think so, which means that you might be in the canoe
once again, Anika, tonight.

. . . if it be not to come, it will be now . . .

I close the booklet and make my way back to the car.

I have given myself several hours to pack but find I don't need them. I stuff my clothes into my backpack and then the carving from the wall above my bed. The carving takes some stuffing to fit it into the pack, but eventually it goes where I want it to go.

My main lesson books, my project and Parzival essay, and the photographs of our class are something else again. I look them all over, pack the photographs, then place the rest of it in a cardboard box and put the box in the closet of my room in the hope that it won't be in someone's way. Maybe I'll see the box again, and maybe not. If Margaret decides to send it on to me when she gets back, that'll be fine. If she sends it off in another direction, well, that's all right, too, because I realize I no longer need to keep anything that's in it.

And then I'm done. I go downstairs with my pack and walk around the house to make sure everything is left the way it should be left.

The kitchen is clean. The car key is on the kitchen table, alongside a note from Margaret to those who will use the house until she returns.

Standing in the living room, I gaze at the walls that had been covered with prints by Native artists. Now the prints are gone and the walls are empty, except for *Transformation #3*. Covered with tea stains, the figure of Raven trying to slip free of himself to become himself hangs where it has hung since the day I first walked into this room. Why has Margaret left it there, when she has packed away nearly everything else with any trace of personal meaning?

I glance over at the top of the bookcase where the wedding photo used to be, but that is now packed away somewhere. In fact, Margaret has packed away everything.

Except for a scarf draped over one end of the couch.

I take the scarf in hand and go into Margaret's bedroom. Opening the closet door, I look for an empty hook, and then I see the doll. She looks up at me from a paper bag that leans against one wall of the closet. Bending down, I look more closely. I have seen her before, or at least dolls like her, at the Christmas Fair at my school. But what is she doing here?

I cup one hand about her brown face and pigtails. Who are you? The child that Margaret and Cameron never had? Then I stuff the scarf into the bag along the doll's back and close the closet door.

Back in the living room, I look again at *Transformation #3*. Maybe I should take it with me . . . But no, that's for Margaret to deal with, that and the Sisiutl print in Cameron's study, when she decides to pack everything up—because she will pack everything up when she comes back.

I look about me one last time, knowing I will never return to this house and that my sister will never again live here.

. . . if it be not now, yet it will come . . .

Then I lock the front door and slip the key through the mail slot. Tightening the pack against my shoulders, I walk toward the bus stop on McGill Street and my meeting with Peter and Hector.

Peter is waiting for me at the detox centre.

"Drop your pack, Nathan, and sit down."

"Where's Hector?"

"Drop your pack and sit."

I do as he says and sit beside him on the front steps of the centre.

"Hector's gone," Peter says.

"What?"

"Hector's gone, Nathan. He went out last night and didn't come back. I came this morning after I found your friends' apartment and left my things with them, and I've been waiting in case Hector showed up. But I don't think he's coming back here."

"Are his clothes still here?"

"They're here, what clothes he has."

I glance up and down the street, as if expecting Hector to round a corner or emerge from an alleyway.

"Can I leave my pack here while we look for him?"

"I've already arranged for that. Inside the front office, beside the copy machine."

We scour bars, pubs and other likely places until late into the afternoon. One bartender vaguely remembers the face of Hector buying a bottle off sale sometime last night, though the bartender doesn't want any other ears listening while he remembers. However, it had been late, and when it's late, it's hard even to take in, let alone remember the face of the person doing the buying.

There are no other leads. As afternoon drifts toward evening, we make our way to Oppenheimer Park and sit. A few children come to play. A few old and tired men come to thank the day for ending.

"We could look for Shannon," I say, as the sun slants along my shoulders.

"Why would he go back to her?"

"Why wouldn't he go back to her?"

Peter rubs his fingers into his forehead, as if to rub that question away. "I guess he might have done that. Let's look for her."

We find her on Cordova Street, three blocks east of Gore. Overhead, clouds have begun to thicken together, though the sky to the west where the sun will soon set stays clear. Shannon stands a few feet from the street corner and does not yet see us.

Peter stops halfway along the block, and I walk on.

Shannon looks over her shoulder and sees me standing beside her. Her blue eyes are misted over with something other than herself and it takes a moment for her to know me. Then the mist begins to lift.

"Solomon. What brings you back into my life?"

"I'm looking for my friend, Shannon. My friend Hector."

"I told you where to find him. Why are you still looking?"

"Because he walked away from us again, last night."

"Did he do that, Solomon? Then maybe he doesn't want to be found."

"And maybe he does. What do you know, Shannon?"

"I know where he was last night."

"And now?"

"Who knows about now? Who knows where someone like your friend goes with his life, once the sun rises?"

"Please, Shannon."

"That word only works once, Solomon."

And then I run out of words. Her eyes are very clear now and very blue, as her hand closes gently around my arm.

"There's no point in looking, Solomon."

A smile brushes at her mouth, the smile of some ancient goddess who knows a man better than he can ever dream of knowing himself.

"There's no point now, Solomon."

Her hand brushes lightly up my arm, then down. Her eyes grow until they become a depth of blue, a welling up of primal water into which Hector has plunged and vanished.

And now I am standing at the edge of that well and on a traffic island in the middle of Dublin's O'Connell Street, looking down at a female figure sculpted in metal lying in a metal tub. Water flows down her body and her eyes stare vacantly into some haunted place, while Erin's voice tells me the story:

Sinann stood at the edge of the welling water where in the deeps the five salmon waited to eat the nuts of knowing all things, the nuts that fall into the deep from the nine hazels. Wanting that knowledge, she plunged into the beckoning blue and became the river Shannon . . .

I pull my arm away from Shannon's hand and walk back to where Peter waits for me.

"What did she say?"

"There's no point in looking."

"What does that mean?"

"That there's no point in looking. Let's go back to the detox centre."

Back at the centre, Peter turns to me. "Maybe that whore knows what she's saying, but I'm not ready to give up on Hector. Not yet."

"Then let's get some dinner and we'll keep looking."

"I don't think so, Nathan. You go to your reunion and I'll keep looking."

"Forget it, Peter. Hector is my friend, too."

"But you have other friends here and you need to be with them tonight."

"Why are you so sure about that?"

"I just know you need to be there and you know why, even if I don't. Your friends will be hurt if you don't go, and there's no good reason that I can see why they should be hurt. I'll find you at the apartment tomorrow when I think there's no more point in looking for Hector."

"All right, Peter. Take care of yourself tonight."

"I'm not Hector and I'll be fine. Ha-la-kasla, Nathan. Go to your reunion."

I strap on my pack and catch the Hastings Street bus.

God, grant me the serenity to accept the things I cannot change . . .

On Granville I change to the Fourth Avenue bus. The sun strikes the horizon to the west, and the sky above me goes blood red.

. . . the courage to change the things I can . . .

The bus turns onto Fourth Avenue as the last rays of the sun flare toward me from the horizon and the buildings on either side of the street turn to walls of flame. Then the flames soften to a glowing red as the sun sets.

. . . the readiness is all.

The action takes place in the living area of Sigune and Alex's apartment. A dining table stands upstage left, with dinnerware, cutlery, glasses, cups and food. At stage right stand seven chairs arranged in a half-moon around a coffee table. Downstage left, the dining area runs out into a balcony that overlooks Kitsilano Beach, English Bay, and beyond, West Vancouver.

The lights come up on Sigune giving the finishing touches to the spread of food on the dining table. Sandra and Izzy sit and watch.

Sandra: That's four.

Izzy: Five, in fact.

Sandra: Five?

Izzy: First, at centre table. Then down beside the coffee urn. And then the long trip to the other end, beside my hors d' oeuvres. Then back to the centre. And now, removed again from centre stage into exile beside the cheese plate and dessertspoons.

Sandra: Okay, five. I missed the move to the coffee urn.

Sigune: *(Looking up.)* What are you two talking about?

Sandra: The number of times you've moved the salad around the table.

Izzy: I'm watching for it to vanish into the kitchen and from our sight forever.

Sandra: Yes, Sigune, you have changed.

Sigune:	How have I changed, Sandra?
Izzy:	Tell me, too, while you're at it. In grade three, she moved her desk seven times around the room before the year was out. That salad bowl has at least two moves left by that reckoning.
Sandra:	Yes, but the attention to detail, Izzy—
Izzy:	True enough. That is a new dimension of Sigune.
Sigune:	*(Hands on her hips.)* You guys, what is this all about?
Sandra:	It's about expending so much effort on making a table of dishes and food look just so. How long is this going to go on?

Alex enters with two bottles of wine.

Sigune:	Until it all looks just so. It's not every day we have a reunion.
Izzy:	*(Reaching for one of the bottles and looking at the label.)* My, my! This is vintage goods.
Alex:	As Sigune said, it's not often the class of 1987 reunites on the heath. We deserve better than the usual witches' brew.

He places the bottles on the table.

Sigune:	Not there. Over by the cheese plate.
Alex:	There's a salad bowl there.
Sigune:	*(Moving the salad bowl to the centre of the table.)* Now there isn't a salad bowl there.

Sandra and Izzy break into laughter, as Alex places the wine where the salad bowl had been.

A knock at the door, stage right.

Alex:	*(Raising his voice.)* Come in. It's open.

Jason enters, a casserole in hand.

Jason:	What? No butler? I'd have thought the two of you would have had a butler by now.

Sandra:	My goodness! Jason!
Izzy:	With a casserole in hand. Another change in character.
Sandra:	*(Hugging him.)* When did you learn how to cook?
Jason:	*(Returning her hug.)* I've always known how to cook, Sandra.
Sigune:	*(Taking the casserole.)* Then you kept the secret well hidden.

She hands the casserole to Alex, moves the salad to a spot beside the coffee urn, and places the casserole where the salad had been.

Izzy:	And that's move number seven.

Juliet sweeps through the open doorway, carrying a basket of fry bread.

Juliet:	Hello! Hello, everyone!

Balancing her offering from one hand to another, she gives and receives hugs from everyone else in the room, then hands her basket to Sigune.

Juliet:	An indigenous offering, courtesy of my mother's recipe. My mother got it from my very traditional grandmother, who probably got it from a Hudson's Bay Company cookbook. Enjoy, one and all!
Alex:	I thought Astrid was coming with you.
Juliet:	Not so. She had an extra rehearsal dropped in her lap. Who else are we missing?
Sandra:	Lorne is married and living in Calgary. And Catherine is in England.
Juliet:	And Anika? Does anyone know where she is?

Glances pass from one to another, with a few shrugs.

Sandra:	Sigune?
Sigune:	*(Putting the finishing touches to her table.)* There's nothing for me to tell.
Alex:	Solomon is coming.

All voices: Solomon?

Jason: Is he back in town?

Alex: Solomon is back in town.

Juliet: Is he okay?

Sandra: Why wouldn't he be okay?

Juliet: I'm not sure. It's just he left so suddenly. He was upset about the standoff at Oka. So was I, but it was different for him somehow. Then he vanished.

Sigune: *(With a glance at Alex, as she gives her table a finishing touch.)* He seems okay.

Alex: *(Deciding to say more, as he opens one of the wine bottles.)* Do you remember Solomon's brother-in-law, Cameron?

Jason: Sure. He's a good guy, even if he does live in an art gallery filled with Native prints.

Alex: Cameron committed suicide, just before Easter.

A stunned silence.

Juliet: *(After a moment.)* O God! How did I know?

Izzy: *(Quietly.)* What do you mean, how did you know?

Juliet: Cameron came into the gift shop where I was working late last summer. He wanted to know where he could take part in a sweat lodge ceremony, so I gave him a lead, and then almost wished I hadn't.

Sandra: Why not?

Juliet: *(With a shake of her head.)* Because I suddenly felt I was talking with someone about to run his life off the edge of a cliff.

Sigune: *(Pouring herself a glass of wine.)* Well, it seems that's what he did. Thanks, Alex, for getting the cork out in one piece. I usually blow it.

Izzy: *(Going to the table and picking up the plate of hors d'oeuvres.)* Let's put this plate to work.

He moves from person to person, as each takes food from the plate. Then, one by one, they go to the table and pour themselves glasses of wine, except for Juliet, who stays seated.

Has Solomon called you, Alex?

Alex: No. Why do you ask?

Izzy: He phoned me this afternoon to say his friend had gone missing again and that he and his cousin, Peter, were going to look for him. He wasn't so sure he would get here tonight.

Jason: What friend?

Izzy: Hector. From the village where Solomon lived before he came here. I helped Solomon and Peter find him and get him into the detox centre. He was doing well for a while.

Jason: It doesn't take much to knock you back on your ass if you've been on the skids.

He looks around to see Solomon standing in the doorway. Everyone falls silent.

Alex: *(After a few seconds.)* Izzy told us about Hector. Any luck?

Solomon: *(Taking a chair.)* No. Peter is still downtown looking, but I think we've run out of luck. *(He looks around at the faces looking at him.)* Hello, everyone.

They look back at him, almost tongue-tied, each taken back to that moment when he walked into their lives in the spring of their grade nine year.

Sandra: *(Finally.)* Hello, Solomon. It's good to see you again.

Solomon: It's good to see you, Sandra. *(Then also remembering.)* Have you got a locker that needs opening?

Sandra: *(With a laugh.)* No, thank you. The only stuck locker in my life was the one you kicked open the day you came to suss out our class.

Solomon: *(Gazing at her.)* How do you know that word?

Sandra: Suss out?

Solomon: Yes. It's Irish.

Sandra: I know. My mother is Irish. How do you know it?

Solomon: I have a sister who's Irish.

Sandra: Another sister? Besides Margaret?

Solomon: Yes, another sister. Two sisters, in fact. But one of them
          died on me. And now my brother-in-law has died. There's
          been a lot of death in my life.

          *He falls silent. The others in the room are at a loss as to where to go
          next.*

Sigune: *(Standing at the table.)* Would you like a glass of wine,
          Solomon?

Solomon: No, thank you. But a glass of juice would be good, if you
          have it.

Sigune: I have juice but forgot to put it out. Would anyone else like
          juice?

Juliet: Yes, please.

          *Sigune exits upstage right. No one speaks. She returns momen-
          tarily with a juice jug and pours a glassful. Solomon gets up and
          goes to the table. He takes the full glass to Juliet and then pours a
          glassful for himself.*

Juliet: Thank you, Solomon.

Solomon: You're welcome.

          *He returns to his seat. The room falls silent again. The members of
          the class of 1987 glance at one another, thrown off balance by Solo-
          mon's arrival and his reserved politeness, except for Juliet, who
          gives him a knowing look.*

Sandra: *(Looking around the room.)* So, I guess most of us within
          reach are here.

Juliet: Except for Anika—if she's within reach.

          *Another silence. They are aware they have run out of greetings
          and small talk.*

          *Sigune stands at the table, taking in the situation. Then she goes to
          the coffee table. Kneeling at it, she takes a folder in hand.*

Sigune: Come; gather around me, my merry choir.

Juliet: *(With a laugh that breaks the tension.)* Sigune, what is this about?

Sigune: A trip down memory lane, guys. *(Opening the folder.)* Come; gather round.

            They gather around her and look over her shoulder.

Sandra: Oh, my God!

Izzy: Sigune has raided the archives.

Juliet: Is that you, Izzy?

Izzy: That's me. In kindergarten.

Sandra: Standing beside Lorne. You both are so cute!

Izzy: Yes, we were, as a matter of fact.

Juliet: And there's Anika—

Sandra: Looking as Anika has always looked, centred and ready for anything.

Jason: And the little girl with no shoes—

Sandra: Is our Sigune.

Juliet: Grade one, and two more familiar faces. Jason, with his baseball hat, and Catherine.

Sandra: *(To Jason.)* You were wearing a baseball hat already, in grade one?

Alex: I think Jason was born with a baseball hat on his head. Where are you, Sandra? Didn't you come in grade one?

Sandra: *(Quietly.)* No. I came toward the end of grade three, after a horrible year. You'll find my face in grade four. There—

Alex: Beside Anika.

Izzy: Grade five. There you are, Juliet, with Astrid.

Juliet: *(Taking the photo.)* Yes, so we are. I was so shy when I came to our class that I didn't think I would ever find a friend.

	Then on our first day Astrid and I ran smack into each other on the playground. Remember, Sigune?
Sigune:	I remember. You two rounded the same tree at the same moment, only from opposite directions.
Juliet:	And bang! Down we went and there we sat, consoling one another for the rest of recess and into the next class.
Sigune:	Grade six—
Sandra:	And grade seven. And there you are, Alex.
Jason:	You look angry, Alex.
Alex:	I was angry, but not at any of you.
Sigune:	Grade eight.
Sandra:	The year Anwar came.

Pause.

Izzy:	Maybe that bomb had Anwar's name on it, but I've never understood why his father went back to Iraq.
Alex:	There was a family obligation of some kind. Anwar felt he had to go, too. My family needs me, he said, and you don't walk away from family.
Solomon:	*(Quietly.)* Some of us do, and have.
Jason:	*(Glancing at Solomon.)* Bad timing for family loyalty.

Silence. Sigune brings up another photograph from the stack. The stage lights begin to dim.

Sandra:	And here we are in grade nine.
Jason:	Grade nine. Outside the Chinook Park Waldorf High School fire hall.
Juliet:	With the fire pole just visible through the open doorway . . .
Izzy:	And not a fire engine in sight.
Alex:	The photographer wanted a group action shot of all of us sliding down the pole, but Paul nixed that idea.

Sigune: Yes, grade nine

Solomon: May I see it, please?

            He reaches for the photograph as he kneels beside Sigune at the coffee table. As the stage lights dim, spotlights brighten to a soft light upon the chairs on either side of the one in the middle of the half-moon and upon the coffee table.

Jason: *(Sitting.)* You're not there yet, Solomon.

Solomon: No, but I was on the way and this photograph was my first meeting with you, the day I came for the interview.

Sandra: *(Also sitting.)* The day you kicked my locker open.

Izzy: *(Also sitting.)* Then you came to class the next day and sat down beside me, as I was scrambling to catch up in my main lesson book.

Alex: *(Also sitting.)* In time to tell us that your grandfather had fought alongside Poundmaker at Cutknife Hill.

Solomon: And then Sigune got on my case for trying to bullshit you with far-out stories.

Sigune: *(Rising and taking a seat.)* You were angry when I said that, weren't you?

Solomon: Yes, I was. And then I tried not to be angry.

Juliet: *(As she sits.)* Instead, you and Anika paired off during eurythmy class and couldn't stop throwing copper rods to each other, even when the time for throwing was done.

            Silence. The stage lights are now out, leaving only the muted spotlights falling upon those sitting in the chairs and a fuller light upon Solomon, still kneeling at the coffee table.

Sandra: Anika didn't phone?

Sigune: She didn't phone.

Sandra: That's not like Anika.

Jason: Then again, maybe it is like Anika.

Juliet: Meaning?

Jason: Probably nothing.

Izzy: But it is odd, for her to vanish just like that.

Alex: Perhaps she vanished for a reason.

Jason: What reason?

Sigune: Any number of reasons.

Sandra: But it doesn't fit. With Anika, things fit.

Juliet: Except when they don't fit. Remember *Romeo and Juliet* in grade ten? Anika wanted to be Juliet, always. I wanted to be Juliet, for God's sake, but her hand was always up first: "Romeo, Romeo, wherefore art thou?"

Sandra: "Come night. Come, Romeo. Come thou day in night . . ."

Juliet: "O serpent heart, hid with a flowering face!
            Did ever dragon keep so fair a cave?
            Beautiful tyrant! Fiend angelical!"

Sandra: "Dove-feathered raven! Wolfish-ravening lamb!
            Despised substance of divinest show!
            Just the opposite of what thou justly seemest . . ."

Juliet: Yes, Anika got into the skin of Juliet, all right. She wanted to be in love but didn't know what to do to make that happen.

            A sudden, awkward silence. Solomon places the photograph he has been holding on the coffee table.

Sandra: Why didn't Anika come tonight?

Solomon: Because of me.

            He gazes upward, the light upon his face, suddenly relieved that he has said what he has just said.

Izzy: What do you mean, because of you?

Solomon: Do you remember the summer of 1990, Izzy? The summer of Oka?

Izzy: I remember. You appeared on my doorstep one night, very suddenly, after a fight with your sister.

Solomon: It was more than a fight with Margaret. All that long summer I'd come up against being Indian in a way I had never done before. I was angry.

Juliet: So was I, Solomon. So were many other Native people. We all were angry.

Solomon: Maybe. But you joined in on a blockade. You did something with your anger. Me? I sat in front of the TV and let it stew. I watched it all unfold, right to the day the army reopened the Mercier Bridge, then blew up at Margaret because she wouldn't own up to being Indian. After pissing her off, I came to your house, Izzy, and got mad at you because you couldn't pronounce the Kwakwala name of my village.

A pause as he gathers together the words that want to come next.

Alex: (*Prompting gently.*) And then?

Solomon: I phoned Anika. We met at Third Beach, sat and talked, and then I got angry with her for handing back a feather I had given her the day we graduated. I guess it's too Indian for you, I said.

In my anger, I found myself wanting what she might have given me once. So I moved in on her. Then when I almost had her down in the sand—

He pauses.

She caught on to me, threw sand in my face and ran.

Alex: And then you ran.

Solomon: I ran.

Silence.

Sandra: Is this the first time you've told this to anyone?

Solomon: Yes . . . but you already knew, Sigune, didn't you?

Sigune: I knew.

Izzy: How did you know?

Sigune: I knew.

Silence.

Jason: *(Finally.)* That was one hell of a thing to do, Solomon.

Solomon: Yes. I betrayed her.

Juliet: You were angry.

Alex: You were angry when you came in grade nine. Even though you tried not to be angry, you were angry.

Solomon: Yes, I was angry: angry at my dad for dying, at my uncle for letting my dad die, and for something else he had never even done.

           Anger was the shadow on my tail all through high school. You saw that shadow, Alex, and told me what you saw.

Alex: It takes one to know one.

Silence.

Sandra: Did you love Anika, Solomon? Ever?

Solomon: I don't know, Sandra.

Jason: You don't know? Christ! What do you mean, you don't know? Anika fell in love with you with the first throw of that eurythmy rod and stayed in love with you right to the night of our grad party. I tried to tell you that, one night, but you didn't get it. You told me once *I* didn't get it much of the time, but when it came to Anika you never seemed to get it.

Sandra: Love doesn't always go both ways.

Jason: Then get out of the way. Step aside and let the other person walk on. But you stayed put, Solomon, and kept Anika stuck in her tracks while you were meditating on how you felt about her.

Izzy: Let it go, Jason.

Jason: I don't think I will do that, Izzy.

Alex: Jason—

Solomon: Jason is right.

Pause.

(Quietly.) Jason is right. I did keep Anika from moving on, right up to that night on Third Beach. She still loved me, somewhere in herself, and I played on that. She could only move on by running from me.

Then I ran, angry, and still not knowing how I really felt about her.

Silence.

Sandra: Where did you go, Solomon, when you ran?

Solomon: To Alberta. I met a cousin there. And a sister, Caitlin. I didn't know she was my sister until a stray bullet killed her. I held her body in my arms on a night like this one.

Then I went to Wales and found Caitlin's twin, Erin. She and I went to Ireland, crawled into the dark of a passage grave and found that darkness can have a heart. When we came through to the other side of the grave, I came home to Duxsowlas and put a healing question to the person I had once walked out on in anger. I could have asked the question then, but didn't.

Alex: Who was the person?

Solomon: My uncle.

Pause, as what Solomon has just said comes home to them.

Juliet: *(Quietly.)* And you were living with that unasked question during all your high school years and during our Parzival main lesson?

Solomon: Yes.

Jason: I had a feeling there was a hidden life going on inside of you, pulling us along in its undertow.

Izzy: We all had hidden lives, Jason.

Sandra: And hidden loves.

Jason: Hidden loves? What was your hidden love, Sandra?

Pause.

Sandra: (*Deciding.*) Her name was Gillian.

Jason: Gillian?

Sandra: Yes, Gillian.

Juliet: And how long have you been . . .?

Sandra: A lesbian? All my life long.

Sigune: And you never told us.

Sandra: I never felt I could.

Alex: When did she come into your life?

Sandra: Grade twelve. I almost told you, Solomon, when we were waiting out that storm in Prince Rupert. But you had Haida Gwaii on your mind and that seemed to be all you could handle.

Solomon: I was full of my own stuff, wasn't I? I asked a lot of you on that trip, all of you, all through those three years. Maybe I asked too much—

Jason: You did ask a lot of us, but you didn't just take. (*Pauses.*) You gave something back, to each of us. There were times I couldn't figure you out, but you made me think. You were right when you said I often didn't get it. Now I'm starting to get it.

Izzy: Tell us more, Jason.

Jason: I work at a bar, called the Matrix. Yesterday a guy came in for a drink—nothing new in a bar, but I knew he was an alcoholic. Something had rattled him and he was about to blow his sobriety. So I said, "Are you sure you want a drink?"

"You're damn right I'm sure," he answered.

"Any drink will do?"

"Any drink will do."

I poured a glass of tomato juice, set it before him and said, "Here's your drink. It's on the house."

Juliet: And if he had shoved the juice back across the bar and asked again?

Jason: I would have poured him whatever he wanted.

Silence.

Solomon: I wish there were more bartenders like you, Jason. I wish Hector, my friend, had met you yesterday. His life might be different today. I just hope *he* doesn't die on me.

Juliet: I'll remember him tomorrow, when we smudge the drum.

Izzy: Drum?

Juliet: I'm in a drumming group. We're singing in a pow wow this weekend. I'll pray for Hector, Solomon. We'll all pray for him.

Solomon: Thank you, Juliet.

Pause.

Sandra: You came to Vancouver to look for your friend?

Solomon: He's one of two people I came to find.

Sigune: And who is the other person?

Solomon: *(Deciding.)* Her name is Naomi, and she has been my hidden life, my hidden love.

Solomon looks up into the light and beyond it. His words are calm and clear.

I left her when I left my home and thought I would forget her, but I never did. I loved her the day I left Duxsowlas and all the time I was here. Even when I thought I wanted to love Anika, I still loved Naomi.

When I went home last fall after going everywhere but home, I hoped she would be there. But she had come to Vancouver with my dying grandmother and stayed to look for me.

So Naomi is somewhere in this city looking for me, and I don't know where to look for her.

Silence.

Juliet: What will you do now?

Solomon: Wait. And hope. There's nothing else I can do.

Another silence. The spotlights on Solomon and those sitting in the chairs begin to dim as the stage lights slowly brighten.

Sandra: I'm glad you came tonight, Solomon.

Solomon: I almost didn't come.

Sandra: I know. It was on your face when you walked through the door, as it was when you came for your interview in grade nine and I first met you. You didn't know if you wanted to join us, whoever we were, but you did. You became part of our class, and knowing you began to change us. I'm glad you came, then and tonight.

Solomon: *(Standing.)* Where's our grade twelve photo, Sigune?

Sigune: Here.

She goes to the coffee table, takes a photograph from the folder and hands it to Solomon. The class gathers around him.

Sandra: It's a good photo. We look as if we've finally gotten something together, all twelve of us, whatever our struggles may have been.

Alex: And here we are, seven years later.

Juliet: Not all of us, though.

Jason: But most of us have made it through. It's a mean and beautiful world out there and we've made it through for seven years.

Alex: I wonder where the world and we will be seven years from now.

Sigune: We'll find out when we get there. In the meantime, let's eat.

Izzy: Did someone say eat?

Sigune: Yes, someone did. That table full of food has waited long enough.

*She goes to the table. The rest of them follow her there, forming a
circle. They join hands.*

Juliet: Think of a grace, someone.

Sigune: Let's keep it simple. Blessings—

All: On the meal.

*The circle dissolves and the class of 1987 moves around the table,
plates in hand. Solomon talks with his classmates as he eats. Then
he sets his plate down on the table, goes out on the balcony and
stands for a long moment, looking up at the night sky. A light
brightens upon him as the light upon the table dims to a glow.*

Solomon: What are you
    looking for, Raven?

      For my name on the Grail,
      Raven.

    So, what do you see,
    Raven?

      Just a glimmer tonight,
      Raven.

    And tomorrow,
    Raven?

      We'll just have to see.
      (Pauses.) But not just my name, Raven—
      not just mine . . .

    Who else would there be,
    Raven?

      (Pause.) Naomi . . . Raven.

    Or Anika, maybe?
    You're still not sure,
    are you, Raven?

      I'm sure, Raven.

    Are you?
    But why would she be thinking of you?

Forget her, Raven. Lives move on.
You're on your own.

> I have friends, Raven,
> friends who love me.

So what, Raven?
Your friends are inside making merry
while you stare at the stars
looking for a glimmer of tomorrow.
Their love won't travel with you
into the dark light of tomorrow.
Tonight is the end of the line for them.
You're on your own.

Silence.

> You're wrong, Raven.
> I won't go to the Grail on my own.

Then who, Raven?
Who, for sure, is going to travel
that distance with you?

Pause.

> You, Raven heart.

Me, Raven?

> Yes, you. If no one else, you.
> Your name is on the Grail
> waiting for mine. Your name has always
> been waiting for mine, ever since
> that long night on Log Island when I first
> saw you glimmering in that dark circle
> cradled by the moon's sliver, caught fast
> and wanting to go through.
> So we'll go through, Raven—
>
> We'll go through that dark light together,
> you and I . . .

*Sigune appears on the balcony, as the light on Solomon dims down
and the light upon the table brightens.*

Sigune: Solomon?

Solomon: Yes?

Sigune: Would you come inside, please? I've prepared a surprise, and you need to be part of it.

Solomon: Then I'll come in.

He goes inside as Sigune calls the class together.

Sigune: Come, merry players, and gather around the table yet again, because we have a task to perform. Does anyone remember what day this is?

Jason: The more or less anniversary of our graduation.

Sigune: And?

She waits for a response then smiles.

I guess we need a reminder. Alex?

Alex enters, carrying a large birthday cake.

Alex: Happy birthday, Izzy.

A sudden recovery of class memory leads into cheers, as they push Izzy front and centre.

Izzy: You two have a scary memory.

Alex: There are things you don't forget.

Sandra: Twenty-five candles! You'd better light them and start blowing, Izzy.

Juliet: And forgive us for the absence of other gifts.

Izzy stops Sigune from lighting the candles and looks around at his classmates.

Izzy: There is a gift you can give me, here and now. You can start calling me by my real name.

Jason: And what is your real name?

Izzy: Isaiah.

Juliet: Isaiah?

Izzy: Yes, Isaiah. I lost it because a fond uncle christened me Izzy when I was four. I don't know how he came up with that name, but my family thought it was cute and so it's stuck with me until now. At twenty-five, however, I want my real name back and that's the gift you can give me.

Sandra: Isaiah. I like it, and yes, it's you. More you than Izzy.

Sigune: Well then, Isaiah, let's fire up this cake so you can make a wish to go with your renewed identity.

           Sigune and Alex light the candles.

Alex: There you go, Isaiah. Blow for all you are worth.

Isaiah: We'll all blow.

Juliet: What?

Isaiah: Make a wish, each of you, and then we'll blow together. That's my gift to all of you—a wish apiece on my cake.

           Silence, as each goes inward. Then Isaiah nods, and together they blow out all twenty-five candles.

Jason: *(Smiling.)* We've always been good for a blast of hot air.

Sigune: There's more than hot air here tonight. *(Handing a knife to Isaiah.)* The honour is yours, Sir, by kingly use.

Isaiah: This honour I will not refuse, and I will share it with my good friend, Solomon. *(To Solomon.)* Help me, please. This is one hefty cake.

Solomon: *(Stepping forward.)* Gladly, Isaiah, my good friend. Gladly.

           Taking hold of the knife, the two of them slice into the cake as everyone else claps and the lights fade out.

. . . I am dancing in the big house. The mask bears down upon my head. Its weight presses my feet into the earth beneath them. Yet I go on dancing, because the weight of the mask is no longer oppressive and my stepping feet know how to pass the weight on to the earth below.

I know now that the mask is a Raven mask, the half-mask my father never finished, the half-mask draped in black and waiting for an answer to the question of itself. The waiting weighs upon me, the waiting of the Raven for the moment of release from light to light. The waiting is now mine, as the mask is now mine to finish.

A singing voice reaches out to me. Whose voice? Yet the singing lifts my hands to the mask, as my feet on the big house floor counter the movement of the sun across the daylight sky.

My hands lift the mask from my head and into the light that comes from the smoke hole above me. The mask becomes one with the lifting of my hands and the singing that lifts my hands. Then its weight settles back onto my head because I choose to bear the weight of it. I can raise the mask and lower it as I choose . . .

And then the dream evaporates. The morning opens my eyes and I sit up on the couch.

The apartment shows few traces of last night's reunion, except for a wine glass that stands on the coffee table where someone had left it. Sigune and Alex and I washed up and cleaned up everything else before we went to bed.

I pull on my jeans and a T-shirt, and open the balcony door. The morning sun is sliding down the mountain slopes along the North Shore and the air is clean. At anchor out on the water, ships wait for tugs to come for them. All about them smooth water mirrors back the sky above.

Here and there, sounds of the city waking up to a Saturday morning reach me. Along Cornwall Street a man jogs as if jogging is more than just an iron discipline he has forced upon himself. A dog wanders after him, stops, sniffs at something left on the sidewalk, then wanders off somewhere else.

I glance down onto the street in front of the apartment. The car is gone, so I know that Alex has already left for work. Behind me I hear the sound of the shower in the bathroom.

I go to the kitchen and make a pot of coffee. A flash of sun from the southeast slips through the half-open window above the sink. A breeze brushes across the back of my hand as I pour a cup of coffee for Sigune and one for me.

Sigune comes into the kitchen, wiping at her hair with a towel.

"Good morning, Sigune."

"Good morning to you, Solomon. How did you sleep?"

"Well enough."

"Was the couch kind to you?"

"I've slept on mattresses far meaner than your couch. Here, for you."

"Thanks." She takes the coffee and sits at the small Formica-top table beside the sink. I set my cup beside the salt and pepper shakers that stand in the centre of the table, then sit across from her.

"And thank you, too, for helping us clean up last night," she says.

"You're welcome. It was a good party."

"Was it good, for you?"

"Why do you ask that, Sigune?"

"Because there were a couple of times when being together with the rest of us didn't look to be an entirely happy experience for you."

"A couple of times, maybe. But by the end, it was good."

"Sandra was right. Our class changed when you came."

I drink from my cup, then set it down again. "And I changed when I joined the class. Everyone helped me figure out where I was going, including you. I couldn't figure out what your name was all about when I came to the school, but I understand it now."

"Ah! And what do you understand about my name?" She gets up and refills her cup.

"It's about a woman who keeps knights from wandering astray. One knight in particular."

"You mean Parzival?"

"Yes, Parzival."

"And you, as well?" she asks, leaning against the stove as her eyes find and hold mine.

"Yes. Me, as well."

"Then you have the wrong woman in mind, Solomon. I wasn't your Sigune."

"Meaning?"

"Meaning I wasn't the woman in our class who was there for you. There was such a woman, but she wasn't me."

And now I understand. "You mean Anika?"

"Yes, Anika. She was your Sigune."

Her eyes continue to hold mine. It's over to you, they say.

"You're right. She was my Sigune, and I betrayed her. That's why she didn't come last night."

"Perhaps so, and perhaps not so," Sigune says. She scoops the cups and takes them to the sink.

"What other reasons would she have for not coming to a class reunion?"

"I can't say for sure, but don't be so arrogant as to assume that you alone would have kept Anika away if she had really wanted to come. But how would you have felt if she had come?"

She empties the coffee grounds into the compost bucket under the sink and begins washing the coffee pot and cups.

"I don't know how I would have felt, Sigune. Part of me dreaded meeting her, especially with other members of the class in the room. But my heart sank when I walked through the door and saw that she wasn't here—knew she wouldn't be here. And I knew I wanted to see her again, no matter what."

"And what would you do if you met Anika again?" Sigune folds the dishcloth and drapes it across the edge of the sink.

"Ask her to forgive me, if she would do that."

And then there is no more I can say. I place my elbows on the table and let my head come to rest in the cup of my hands.

Sigune's hands touch down lightly upon my shoulders. "I have to go to work. The place is yours for the day. Make your cousin at home when he comes. The shower is also there for you."

I look up at her. Her eyes tell me that her life has to go on and that my life will go on, too, whatever I am able to do about what I have just told her.

"Thanks. A shower sounds like a good idea."

"There's a towel for you on the rack behind the door."

Standing in the shower, I let the water run down my skin, and take my time washing my hair. When my shower is done, I stand before the mirror, rub myself dry and observe the face looking out at me.

I pull my shirt over my head and look again, as I once looked into the eye of a raven upriver from the beach at Duxsowlas. I was nine and the image mirrored in the raven's eye was mine. Myself gazing at myself.

A reflection? Or a revelation? Or both. A seeing of myself coming to meet myself from the far side of everything I would live through along the way.

I go back into the kitchen. Sigune has gone. The sun has climbed higher into the morning, and the pattern of light in the room has shifted from the sink to the table beside the sink.

My eyes go to the table. A breeze slips itself beneath a slip of paper tucked under the saltshaker and lifts the edge. Taking up the paper, I read the phone number written on it.

At the phone I dial the number, then wait.

"Hello?"

"Anika, it's Solomon. Please don't hang up on me."

I get off the bus and cross Commercial Drive to Joe's. Standing in the doorway, I look around the room. A couple of kids are playing pool at one of the back tables. A bearded man reads the latest edition of *The Georgia Strait* as he sits at one of the front tables and drinks his latte.

At first I don't see Anika, and then I do. She sits at one of the tables between the end of the counter and the front window, looking out at the street.

I sit, and she goes on looking out the window. From somewhere behind us a cue ball smacks into another ball.

"Forgive me, Anika. If you can."

She goes on looking at two children playing in the park kitty-corner to us. Then she turns toward me. Her eyes, as gray and clear as they have always been, are filled with pain and they are beautiful.

We sit a moment longer as her eyes take me in and pierce me through, the way they took me in that first day I sat in the grade nine classroom in a fire hall that had become a high school—and even the day before when I held the class photograph in my hand and gazed at that face looking into mine.

"Please, Anika. If you can."

Her hands reach for mine and our hands join together. Her eyes film over, but there is no flow of tears. My eyes also hold the tears in check. We both want to cry, but are beyond tears somehow.

The hands behind the counter make a cappuccino for a man who has just come through the doorway, while our hands stay joined together.

"We should order something," Anika says.

"I guess we should. What do you want?"

"A latte would be good."

"Me, too. I'll buy."

"No, Solomon. I'll buy." She places a bill upon the table.

"All right." I go to the counter, place our order and wait.

"I'll bring them to you," the man behind the counter says.

We wait in silence until our drinks come, then take our time as we stir the foam into the coffee and warm milk.

"How was the reunion?" Anika asks.

"It was good, but I missed you."

"I missed you."

"Was it because of me that you didn't go?"

"Yes, and no. More no than yes, I think."

"You mean you might not have gone even if I hadn't done to you what I did?"

"I might have gone to be with you, and Sigune and Alex. But not for anyone else." She smiles at the question in my eyes. "Did Sigune go through the class photographs?"

"Yes, from kindergarten on."

"Did you take a good look at me?"

"I couldn't take my eyes from you."

"Yes, but did you see me in relation to the class?"

Then I begin to understand. "Maybe. You were always front and centre, but also your own person."

"Self-possessed. Would that be a good word to describe me?"

"That could be the word, yes."

Our hands come together again.

"Would it surprise you if I said I never felt I was part of the class? Not really part of the class?"

"Even though you were there from kindergarten?"

"Even from kindergarten, I never felt part of the class, Solomon. I know I wasn't alone in feeling that. Some others who started with us or came later didn't feel part of the class, and left. Others stayed, like

Catherine, who never really knew if she belonged or not. But that was because several of our classmates were cool toward her at times. It was different with me. Everyone liked me, everyone accepted me, yet I still didn't feel that I really belonged."

"Why did you stay then?"

"Because I came to love the school and because I knew I had to stay, whatever I might feel. By grade nine, however, even my love for the school was wearing thin and I was thinking about leaving at the end of the year. Then one spring morning, you walked into the room and sat down beside Izzy. I looked at you as you talked about your grandfather, and I knew I had to stay."

"You stayed because of me?"

"Yes, Solomon, I stayed because of you. Then through you I became friends with Izzy in a new way, and with Alex, and then Sigune."

"I thought you and Sigune were already friends."

"Not so. We tolerated each other all through grade school and even into high school. It was only in grade eleven and through you that Sigune and I became friends."

Our hands stay together as I look out the window at the world walking past us along the Drive. I come back to the pane of glass and half-expect to see my reflection looking back at me, but the glass is clear.

"I don't know what to say, Anika."

"Then don't say anything, Solomon, until you know what you really want to say."

Another moment passes, and then I know. "I wanted to love you, Anika. God, how I wanted to love you. I spent nights asking myself what it would be like to have no one else in my life but you. And many times wanting there to be no one else."

Her hands tighten into mine. "And I didn't want to love you," she said, "but I did. I knew I wasn't the one you really loved or could love, yet I loved you and nothing could stop me from doing so, not even me."

Then we fall silent again, until she draws her hands away from mine. "Solomon, where did you go when you ran from me?"

"Several places, Anika."

"Tell me about it, Solomon. Tell me everything."

And so, after we order two lattes, I do. The words stream from me in a steady flow, and she listens until my telling is done.

"And she wasn't there when you went home?"

"No. She had stayed here to look for me, and now I'm looking for her."

Anika presses herself into the chair back and studies me.

"Are you sure about that, Solomon?"

"Sure about what?"

"That you're looking for her?"

"Why do you ask that?"

"Because you've been looking for her ever since I've known you. But do you really want to find her, Solomon?"

I look away, confused, yet I know she is onto something within me.

"Am I still in the way, Solomon? Have I always been in the way, somehow?"

I look back at her, into those clear eyes. "Maybe, once. For a long time, I wasn't sure which one of you I wanted to love."

"And now?"

"Now I'm sure, Anika."

"But you never tried to contact her for all those years. What was stopping you, really?"

What?

"I don't know. But I want to find her now."

Her eyes move to the window. "Then I hope you do, soon. No, I'll do better than that." She takes hold of my hands once again. "I want you to find her and I want her to find you. Whatever that takes."

Moved by her words, I drink her in. What did I ever do to deserve you in my life, Anika?

"And what about you?" I ask. "How has life been for you since I left?"

"It's been a life, my life. I have my degree now, my mother has moved elsewhere, and I'll be moving on soon. Perhaps I'll travel some and find out if the world is really round."

"It's round enough, Anika. What do you want to find as you travel?"

She smiles at me. "A life of my own, Solomon. Now that you and I have straightened things out."

And then her smile fades. "Solomon?"

"Yes?"

"There was a time when I not only wanted to make love with you but felt we would have to make love, at least once, to let each other go. Do we still need to do that?"

I look out the window once more. It would have been sweet then and it might be sweet now, but no—

"No, Anika. We don't need to do that."

I look right into her eyes so that she can see there is no doubt in mine.

And now I could love you, Anika. For the first time, I could truly love you.

Our hands tighten together, then come apart. She reaches for her handbag as we stand.

"Give my love to Sigune and Alex, and Izzy, if you see him again."

"Izzy has changed his name, to Isaiah. That's his real name."

She laughs. "Then tell Isaiah hello for me."

We walk outside into the clear air and light. She turns to me and we embrace.

"Goodbye, Anika. I hope you find that life of your own."

"I will, Solomon. Goodbye."

And our lives part.

He returned to the apartment to find Peter waiting for him in the living room, with Alex and Sigune and Isaiah.

"How did you make out?"

"I didn't," Peter said, "although I spent half the night trying to turn up something. Then I spent the other half in that park where we had gone with Hector, hoping he'd appear beside me. When the sun came up, I knew there was no point in sitting there, so I went to the food bank and helped Izzy, or Isaiah, I guess it is now, and then we came here. Alex and Sigune sang me a welcome song and here I am."

"And how was your day?" Alex asked Solomon.

"Good. I spent the afternoon with Anika. She likes your new name, Isaiah, and says hello, to it and to you."

"You saw Anika?" said Isaiah.

"Yes, I saw Anika." Solomon sat down in an armchair, stretched out his feet and rested his head against the chair back. It had been a good day.

"Who is Anika?" asked Peter.

"A special person who kept a certain warrior from riding into swamps. Now her part of that job is done."

The phone rang and Sigune went into the kitchen to answer it. A moment later she reappeared in the doorway. "It's Juliet. She's invited all of us to go to the pow wow she talked about last night. It's in North Vancouver. What about it?"

They looked at one another, and then Alex said, "Why not? Tell her we're on the way."

"Have you ever been to a pow wow, Peter?" Isaiah asked.

"No," said Peter. "We don't do pow wows where Nathan and I come from."

"Who is Nathan?" Sigune asked as she came back in the room and sat on the couch beside Alex.

"He's Nathan," said Peter, pointing to Solomon.

"Your name is Nathan?" said Alex.

"Yes. That was the name I grew up with and gave up when I left home, then came here. Solomon is my second name."

"But Nathan is your first name, and perhaps more your name than Solomon?" Sigune said.

"Maybe so, now."

"Well, then?" said Alex, looking at Isaiah.

"It would make things easier for you, wouldn't it?" Isaiah said to Peter.

"It would," Peter said. "But I'm not the person to decide."

"Well, what about it?" Alex asked. "Is it still Solomon, or Nathan, now?"

He straightened up in his chair and looked at each of them. "Nathan, please."

"Good," Peter said. "Well, let's hit that pow wow trail."

Nathan looked at Sigune and saw that she was crying. "Why the tears, Sigune?"

"Because you're crying, Nathan."

And he realized that he was.

They parked the car and followed the beating of a drum and chanting of voices to an open, grassy field.

Walking past tables filled with Native crafts—drums, dream catchers, T-shirts covered with Native art, bracelets, neckpieces, and long braids of sweetgrass—they found the area where the drums half-circled the field. And then they saw Juliet. As they approached the drum where she sat, the beating of a nearby drum lifted their feet into its rhythm.

Juliet smiled up at them from among the seven other faces that sat around the drum. Her eyebrows arched when she saw Peter.

"Hey, Solomon? Who's your handsome friend?"

"My cousin, Peter. And I'm now Nathan, Juliet."

"Since when are you Nathan?"

"Since always, and as of today."

"We all dunked him in the Inlet on the way over," said Isaiah, "so it's for real."

"Last night, Isaiah, and today, Nathan. Okay guys, are there any other name changes you want to tell me about?"

"That's it, for now," Sigune said.

"Then let me introduce you to the other members of the band," Juliet said and began to do that. At the last she came to an older man wearing a cowboy hat with a large eagle feather sticking out from the hatband. "This is Alfred, our leader. He calls the drum, Spirit Feather."

"With thanks to the eagle who let us have the feather," said Alfred, with a smile.

"Nathan's brother-in-law was the person I sent your way last fall, to the sweat lodge," said Juliet.

Alfred's eyes went inward. "Cameron. Yes, I remember him well."

"And Nathan's friend, Hector, is the person we prayed for when we smudged," Juliet continued.

Alfred's eyes went to Nathan and took him in. Then he nodded and smiled.

The drum that had been sounding brought their song to a close. The drummers stood and stretched amid a shaking of hands with one another and with others who had been listening as they played.

"They all look pretty happy," Peter observed.

"They should be," said Juliet. "They got a whistle on their drum two songs back."

"What does that mean?" Isaiah asked.

"Certain dancers carry eagle bone whistles," Juliet explained. "If a whistle carrier feels a drum is going at it in a good way, he dances up to that drum, blows on his whistle, and that drum gets to do its song again. It's an honour to have a whistle on your drum."

The drum next to Spirit Feather started to sound as the voices gathered around it rose into the last light of the sun.

"It'll be our turn next," Juliet said. She turned to Peter. "Do you drum?"

Peter smiled. "I've never sat around this kind of drum."

"But you do drum?" Juliet pressed.

"Yes. On a long log drum, in our big house."

"Then take that seat when the song comes to us, pick up a stick, and imagine you're in your big house. In the meantime, let's go dance."

Alex looked out at the dancers circling the field in the direction of the sun crossing the daylight sky. "How do you do this kind of dancing?"

"By following me out onto the field and letting your feet do whatever they do," said Juliet.

Sigune took Alex by the arm. "Come on. We'll figure it out as we go."

Nathan started to follow Juliet, when Alfred appeared at his elbow. "I'm sorry about your brother-in-law."

"How did you find out?"

"Juliet told us. We prayed for him, too, when we smudged."

Nathan's eyes followed his friends as they made their way into the circle of dancers. "Cameron was a good person. His life should have come to a different end."

"Yes, he was a good person but with an uncertain heart. I knew how his life would end as soon as he walked away from the sweat lodge, the last time he was with us. Maybe you and your cousin knew the same thing about your friend, Hector, even as you were trying to help him walk a different road."

"Yes, maybe we did."

"You have walked some long roads of your own," said Alfred, his hand now on Nathan's arm.

"I have. Not always very well."

"But you have good, strong feet, and a good heart. Trust your heart and the road you walk."

Alfred's hand lifted away, and Nathan walked out onto the grassy field.

"You dance in a funny direction," Peter was saying to Juliet as Nathan came alongside them.

"The same direction as the sun goes," said Juliet.

"We dance the other way, the way the sky goes around the North Star."

"Then you dance in a funny direction," Juliet said, laughing.

"How are your feet doing?" Alex asked Nathan.

"They're getting there," Nathan replied, "but they'll take their own time doing it. I used to drive my grandmother to despair whenever I tried to dance around the big house in preparation for a family potlatch."

But his feet did find the rhythm of the dance—a subtle two-step with each foot—and soon enough Alex and Isaiah were in step with him. Sigune danced alongside them, her feet having found the secret of the dance as soon as she walked onto the field.

All about them men, women and children danced. A jingle dancer moved gracefully, a fan of feathers in hand, her dress a rising and falling of many cone shaped lids from tobacco tins. A grass dancer moved past them, his feet beating firmly yet gently into the earth as if preparing it for some splendid ceremony. A young mother came abreast of them, absorbed in a rhythm from both another time and the moment in which she danced. A child lay upon her shoulder, fast asleep.

And then the song came to an end.

"Our turn," Juliet said, and they made their way back to the drum.

The drummers of Spirit Feather took their places as Alfred clued them into the intricacies of the song they were about to do. Peter sat beside Juliet and she handed him a drumming stick. Peter studied the stick as if waiting for it to tell him what to do. Then he tested it lightly upon the skin of the drum. "Okay, people," he said. "This will be a moment of truth."

Alfred looked around the circle and saw that the seat on the other side of Juliet was empty.

"Where's Andrew?" Alfred asked.

No one knew where Andrew was. The master of ceremonies called out Spirit Feather's name, and Alfred looked around again. Then he took up a stick, pointed it at Isaiah, then at the empty chair.

"Drum with us," Alfred said.

It was not a request but a summons. Isaiah blinked, swallowed, and then sat beside Juliet. "Stay with me," she whispered.

Isaiah nodded, and the drum erupted into life. All the sticks beat down upon its skin, and Alfred's strong, high voice led them into the opening words of the song.

Peter need not have worried. He was right there, and then Isaiah was there with Juliet and Peter. His look of anxiety gave way to astonishment, then broke into delight. Isaiah glanced up at Alfred and Alfred winked back, as Spirit Feather drummed its way into the second of four verses.

"Let's try that dance floor again," Sigune said to Alex and Nathan.

The sun had set by the time they rejoined the circle of dancers, and a soft red glow flooded the sky from the west.

"Isaiah may have found a second calling," Alex said, with a grin.

Nathan smiled back. "Maybe. We'll see."

The strong sounding that Juliet had called the honour beat took command of the drum, as the song soared into its final verse. And then the whistle sounded. Turning toward Spirit Feather, they saw the dancer before the drum. A bustle of long feathers rose and fell along his back as his feet stroked the earth beneath them. His feathered headdress caught the fading light and gave it back to a sky deepening toward its first stars.

A flash of amazement lit up the faces around Spirit Feather, and the drummers headed once more into the opening verse of the song. A delighted grin stayed on Juliet's face. Peter's eyes flashed as his stick rose and fell, and Isaiah's eyes widened with astonishment. One by one the dancers on the field moved toward the drum and gathered around it.

"Go and cheer on Isaiah and Peter," said Nathan.

"And what are you planning to do?" asked Alex.

"Keep on dancing out here and consider where my feet will go next. Go on. I'll come soon."

"All right," Alex said, "but don't go anywhere this time without saying goodbye. Understood?"

"Understood."

Alex started toward the drum and Sigune followed.

"Sigune," Nathan called.

She stopped and turned to him.

"It was a good day."

"I know."

"Did Anika phone you?"

"No, she didn't. That's why I know it was a good day."

Sigune lifted herself on her toes, kissed Nathan on the cheek, and then followed Alex back to the drum.

Now Nathan stood alone. A few other dancers had also stayed on the field, yet he stood alone.

He glanced up at the sky where the sun had been a short time ago. Well above the flood of red at the horizon, the first hint of a crescent moon gleamed back at him. Even though the darkness that would reveal it fully was still to come, the golden thread from the tips of the crescent around the dark circle cradled between them was already visible. Within the circle, the shimmer from the shining of the sun upon the earth was forming a name. His name.

Gwawinastoo—Raven's Eye, beholding Raven's Eye.

Somewhere, on her way to this coast and to Haida Gwaii, was another eye of the Raven: Súl an Fhiaich—Erin, his sister. But she was not here yet, so tonight there was only his seeing at hand to discern the name in the darkening circle.

But not my name only . . .

Go through.

Through what? And to where?

And then he saw it, hanging in the air before him, not visible to the eye, yet truly there: the Tlaamelas, the curtain of the big house through which he could pass from one reality into another.

It's a long road that has no turning.

The words were Erin's, spoken somewhere in Connemara on an evening like this one. But why these words now?

Then he remembered: Turn before passing through the Tlaamelas.

Making a full turn counter-clockwise, Nathan began to dance in the direction of the stars around the North Star, the direction of his people. As he made his way up the field, a few dancers passed him going the other way. Their eyes widened and then accepted his way of dancing.

He glanced up the field. A figure wearing a button blanket emerged from within a last spreading of light from the west. On the back of the blanket was the figure of a crescent moon.

His heart rising into his mouth, Nathan lifted his feet to move faster as the whistle carrier blew a fourth time upon Spirit Feather, and the beating of the drum took on fresh energy.

Go with the drum . . .

His feet steadied into the beat. Ahead of him, the figure in the blanket also moved with the beating of the drum. Then it stopped moving and stood still.

Now Nathan was only feet away from the figure draped in the crescent moon. The figure turned slowly and faced him.

Her eyes were as he had always remembered them but were no longer as young as they had once been. Yet they were still beautiful, the more so from the lines that radiated out into her skin from either side of them.

She looked back at him and into him and could not speak. Nor could he speak. Together they stood in the silence at the heart of the beating drum—the silence and the light shining from within her eyes.

Isaiah offers to drive us to where Naomi is staying, but we choose to take the bus. We need to be with each other and no one else, except for the others on the bus who have lives of their own to think about. Even the drunk who gets on at Hastings Street just before Main is content to entertain his fellow passengers without putting his face into ours.

We get off the bus on Commercial Drive, near Joe's, and walk one block east to Naomi's basement suite.

One block from Joe's . . . we had been so close the day I met Cyril, and even yesterday when I made peace with Anika.

Naomi makes tea. We drink it slowly and say little. Then I begin to tell her about Hector. She listens and goes on listening as I tell her about Margaret and Cameron. I want to go on and tell her more, tell her everything I have lived through since that day I walked out of her life, but suddenly my words fall apart.

She sets her cup down as she comes around the table to where I am sitting. Bending at the knees, she takes my face in her hands, lifts it level with hers and kisses me. My hands draw her to me, and hers close about the back of my head.

I had thought I would go back to Alex and Sigune's for the night, but I can't let her go. Not now. Not ever.

A long time later, when the night has become a silence waiting for that first movement toward a new day, our bodies come apart and we lie side by side. My breathing slows, then steadies into the darkness around us. For a long while the sound of our breathing is the only sound in the room.

"How long have you been here?" I ask at last.

"I moved in a week after Axilaogua went home. My friend, Janet, found it for me."

"And how did you meet her?"

"At the Friendship Centre. Looking for you."

I turn so that I can look at her. Naomi stays on her back, looking up at the ceiling. The space between us also turns, wanting something more now than the love we have just made.

"My old school isn't far from here," I say.

"And the friends you introduced me to, you went to school with them?"

"Yes."

"You made good friends. How long have you and Peter been down here?"

"Since the beginning of April, when my brother-in-law died."

"That's so sad." Now she turns toward me, her eyes wanting to find mine.

"Yes. I just hope Margaret can walk on from it."

"And Hector?"

I shake my head. "I don't know, Naomi. Peter and I tried. It's up to him now."

She looks away, a little smile on her face. "Funny, isn't it? You come home just when I've decided to stay here. You come to find Hector and almost don't find me. If you hadn't gone to that pow wow, where would that have left us?"

Yes, where would that have left us? I turn away and look out into the room I can barely see. Making love has opened a door and now we have to go through it.

"Nathan?"

"Yes?"

"What is it? What's going on inside that head of yours?"

I shrug. "I don't know. It's just that—"

"What?"

"I told myself just after we met, when we were standing at the drum and you were meeting everyone—I told myself that we shouldn't make love tonight. Not yet. Not until we had talked some things through. Then we came here, and you kissed me. Then I held you and couldn't leave you again . . ."

"Are you sorry we made love?"

"No. But maybe we should have waited."

"Waited? After all these years? For what?"

"Until we'd talked some more."

She brings her hand to my chin and turns me toward her. "Then let's talk. What do you want to talk about, Nathan?"

What? What do I want to tell you, Naomi?

She lies beside me, waiting, listening into my silence.

"Nathan?" she says after a time.

"Yes?"

"Was there someone else? Is that what you want to talk about?"

Is it? Maybe.

"Yes—and no," I say.

"That sounds interesting. Go on, please."

Is she smiling as she speaks? But she has turned onto her back again and I can't tell for sure.

"There was a girl in my class who fell in love with me, and for a long time I couldn't decide whether or not I wanted to love her. And then I hurt her, which made it even harder to figure out how I really felt."

"What made it hard in the first place for you to know whether you loved her?"

"Knowing that I still loved you, and knowing that she knew that, even though she had never met you."

"And when did this relationship come to an end?"

"Today."

She takes a deep breath, then lets it go. "My goodness! This has been quite a day for you. And you're sure it's over?"

"It's over, Naomi. And funny as it sounds, it never really started."

"You mean you never made love to her?"

"That's what I mean."

And then I want to ask her if there was anyone else in her life. But the question evaporates as soon as I remember the tears that had been in her eyes as we came together and the blood still drying on her thighs.

The silence between us shifts yet again and begins to deepen.

"Did Margaret tell you that she and I met, in Axilaogua's room at the hospital?"

"She told me, when I told her I was trying to find you."

"It was a horrid meeting. I wanted to kill her, Nathan."

"She was angry at me, Naomi. Not at you."

"Why was she so angry at you?"

"Because I walked out on her without saying goodbye."

Still on her back, she thinks about what I have said.

"Yes, you seem to be good at that—walking out on people, even people who care about you. Maybe especially people who care about you."

"Were you angry when I walked out on you?"

"Yes. Angry and hurt, and for a long time also wanting to find someone else I could love so I could get over being angry and hurt. But that someone else never came along and I had to find other ways to stop being hurt and angry."

"I guess I didn't make that easy for you."

"No, you didn't. Even though I knew in my heart why you had to leave Duxsowlas, it was hard for me to accept the way you left."

"I'm sorry, Naomi—"

And then my words stick together. I roll onto my back and look out into the darkness I have been going through, for the whole of my life.

"Why didn't you contact me, Nathan?"

Her words hang in the space between us. She turns to me and presses her question at me.

"You could have written or at least sent a message through Minnie, or phoned later on, once we got phones at Duxsowlas. But there was nothing, for all those years. Why not?"

Anika's question to me earlier in the day. Why not?

And then I hear myself say, "I didn't feel worthy of you."

Her breathing stops for a second as she takes in what I have said.

"You didn't feel worthy of me?"

"No, I didn't." I gather my words together, then go on while I still have the courage to go on. "Do you remember Hector's potlatch? After my uncle had shamed me for playing around with his Humsumth masks?"

"Yes."

"That shame was burning me up when Hector came into the big house as Hamatsa. Then the Humsumth masks came in and you sang to them. I watched you as you stood beside Adha and sang. You were strong and beautiful, and everything between us started to change and went on changing when I knew you weren't just my friend but a person I loved. But I didn't feel worthy of you. That feeling kept growing until the cat got my tongue and I couldn't even talk to you."

"But the cat let our tongues go, that night down by the river. Remember?"

"Yes. But even then I didn't really feel worthy of you."

"Not even then? After I had come to you as you were working on that damn pole in the hope that you would go down to the river with me? And after I had gone to all that trouble a few days earlier to empty my pencil case onto your desk, just so you'd know how I really felt about you? God, Nathan, what does a woman have to do to make you feel your worth?"

She rolls onto her side, as her hand draws me to her.

"And now, Nathan? After waiting for me all those years, then finding me and making love to me, do you feel worthy of me?"

My life opens out into the darkness about me as I turn to her and find her eyes.

"Well, Naomi, I guess I'd better feel worthy of you. And I do. If I'm not worthy, there's nothing I can do about it tonight."

Beyond the half-opened window, the wind rustles the leaves of a tree. Along the street a dog barks, then stops barking.

"Hold me, Nathan, please."

Her breath firm against my cheek, Naomi's arms close about me. Her face comes to rest within the hollow of my shoulder as the curves of our bodies find one another and bring our lives with them. Like the beating of a drum, her heart throbs against my skin.

Alive with stars that gleam like buttons on a blanket, the night breathes down upon us, then folds us within itself.

GLOSSARY

of Haida, Irish, Kwakwala and Welsh words in alphabetical order

Adha (Kwakwala) A revered grandmother

Axilaogua (Kwakwala) Woman who holds; used as woman who holds names

Bakbakwalanooksiwae (Kwakwala) Often interpreted as Cannibal at the North End of the World; called the Spirit of Being by Ernie Willie

Duxdzas (Kwakwala) Sees all things; clairvoyant

Duxsowlas (Kwakwala) See through

Eglwys Lleu (Welsh) Church of Lleu (cognate of the Irish "Lugh")

Ghe-la-kasla (Kwakwala) A greeting, "from the heart"

Gwawinastoo (Kwakwala) Raven's Eye

Haida Gwaii (Haida) Islands of the People, the Haida name for the Queen Charlotte Islands

Ha-la-kasla (Kwakwala) A goodbye, "from the heart"

Hamatsa (Kwakwala) The pivotal dance of the Kwakwaka'wakw (Kwakiutl) Red Cedar Bark Ceremony (T'seka); the focal figure in the dance

Humsumth (Kwakwala) The three mythical bird masks of the Hamatsa dance: Huxwhuxw, Crooked Beak, and Raven

Makwalaga (Kwakwala) Moon Woman

Sarn Mellteyrn (Welsh) Causeway of the lightning

Sinann (Irish) Shannon, as in the Shannon River

Sisiutl (Kwakwala) Double-headed Sea Serpent

Súl an Fhiaich (Irish) Raven's Eye

Tlaamelas (Kwakwala) The screen in the big house that separates the world of the big house floor from the world out of which the dancers come

Trwyn y Gwyddel (Welsh) Nose of the Irishman

Wanookqway (Kwakwala) People of the River

Weesa (Kwakwala) A name of endearment for any young boy

Xhaaidla (Haida) Skin, membrane, boundary, separating the visible, surface world from another world beyond the boundary

Xuuyaa Gut-ga-at-gaa (Haida) Raven Splitting-in-two

ACKNOWLEDGEMENTS

The journey continues.

My indebtedness to the people and printed sources acknowledged in *Raven's Eye* holds true for *Mirror of the Moon*. I am especially grateful to the families of Yah-Xath-anees (Ernie Willie) and Yataltanault (Carole Anne Newman) who came to the launch of *Raven's Eye* at the Vancouver Waldorf School on April 1, 2000. Their support of this story and of me contributed greatly to making that evening a memorable event in my life.

Doris Shadbolt's *Bill Reid* (Seattle/London: University of Washington Press, 1986), Ulli Steltzer and Robert Bringhurst's *The Black Canoe* (Vancouver/Toronto: Douglas & McIntyre, 1991), and E.N. Anderson's *Bird of Paradox: The Unpublished Writings of Wilson Duff* (Surrey, B.C.: Hancock House, 1996) were significant sources for the development of this volume.

Bill Reid's "The Spirit of Haida Gwaii" can be found in *All the Gallant Beasts and Monsters*, published by the Buschlen Mowatt Gallery in Vancouver, and in *Solitary Raven: Selected Writings of Bill Reid*, edited with an introduction by Robert Bringhurst (Vancouver/Toronto: Douglas & McIntyre, 2000).

The setting for Margaret's meeting with Bill Reid in Part Two was a benefit for the Rediscovery Movement held at the Buschlen Mowatt Gallery on December 8, 1992.

I am grateful to Marnie Duff for permission to use the lines from Wilson Duff's poem, "Death Is a Lie," as published in *The World Is as Sharp as a Knife: An Anthology in Honour of Wilson Duff*, edited by Donald N. Abbott (Victoria: British Columbia Provincial Museum, 1981).

The lines from "The Two Trees," by W.B. Yeats, are published in *Collected Poems*, edited by Augustine Martin (London: Arena, 1990), and are used by permission of A.P. Watt Ltd on behalf of Michael B. Yeats.

The lines by David Zieroth are from "This Side," as published in *When the Stones Fly Up* (Toronto: Anansi, 1985), and are used by permission of David Zieroth, with my thanks.

The lines by Kirsten Savitri Bergh are from her poem, "A Lake of Mirrors," and are used by permission of her mother, Linda Bergh. A student at the Hawthorne Valley Waldorf School, in New York, Kirsten died in an automobile accident on November 29, 1996. "A Lake of Mirrors" can be found in *She Would Draw Flowers*, published by Linda Bergh (4315 Xerxes Avenue S., Minneapolis, MN 55410) as a memorial to her daughter's life and work.

The story of Sinann in Part One can be found in both Lady Gregory's *Gods and Fighting Men* (Colin Smyth Ltd, 1970) and *The Celtic Poets*, translated and introduced by Patrick K. Ford (Belmont, Massachusetts: Ford & Bailie, 1999).

The story of Pliny's raven in Part One is quoted in *The Appian Way: A Journey*, by Dora Jane Hamblin and Mary Jane Grunsfeld (New York: Random House, 1974). The story of Floki's ravens in Part Two is from *Westviking*, by Farley Mowat (Toronto: McClelland and Stewart, 1965).

The Irish Proverb at the close of Part Three is from Padraic O'Farrell's *Irish Proverbs and Sayings* (Dublin: The Mercier Press, 1980)—a source I failed to acknowledge in *Raven's Eye*.

The lines from the Gospel of John in Part Three are from *The Jerusalem Bible*, 1985 edition.

The edition of Rudolf Steiner's *Philosophy of Spiritual Activity* referred to in the story is the translation by William Lindeman (Hudson, New York: Anthroposophic Press, 1986).

The writings of Georg Kühlewind, especially *From Normal to Healthy: Paths to the Liberation of Consciousness* (Hudson, New York: Lindisfarne Press, 1988), supported the writing of this story. I am also indebted to *Light Beyond the Darkness: The Healing of a Suicide Across the Threshold of Death* by Doré Deverell (London: Temple Lodge Publishing, 1996) for my work with that theme in Part Three.

I am indebted to Alec Nelson for permission to adapt an experience from his residential school years for use in the play portion of Part Two.

I continue to work from the translation of *Parzival* by Helen M. Mustard and Charles E. Passage (New York: Vintage Books, 1961). Linda Sussman's *Speech of the Grail: A Journey toward Speaking that Heals and Transforms* (Hudson, New York: Lindisfarne Books, 1995) strengthened my understanding of Parzival themes relevant to *Mirror of the Moon*.

I am grateful to Linda Bergh, Bert Chase, Anne Davidson, Sophie Perndl, Pat Reid, Linda Sussman, Eitel Timm, Ivan Walsh, Sally Williams and David Zieroth for reading the manuscript of this volume as it progressed and making valuable comments and suggestions. Owen Lange provided me with information about the weather patterns in the Vancouver area from the fall of 1993 to the spring of 1994.

Robert Adams edited the manuscript for publication. His comments and critique enabled me to deepen and strengthen the story in many respects. My thanks go to him for his efforts on my behalf.

A word about those to whom this book is dedicated: Stephen Edelglas, a friend and colleague in the Waldorf School movement, died on November 17, 2000. He was an appreciative reader of *Raven's Eye* during the last weeks of his life and would have understood from the heart Cameron's struggle in Part One of this volume.

Seis^^lom, my longtime friend and mentor in the path of the sweat lodge, has supported me personally over many years and has also extended himself to my colleagues and students at the Vancouver Waldorf School. It is with gratitude that I dedicate *Mirror of the Moon* to Seis^^lom and to the memory of Stephen Edelglas.

Philip Thatcher
North Vancouver, British Columbia
November 2002